International Acclaim for *Helpless*

"With razor-sharp emotional acuity, stoic detachment and incisive prose, Gowdy, one of Canada's boldest writers, looks beyond preconceptions in pursuit of underlying truths."

—*Ottawa Citizen*

"Brilliant.... Gowdy's prose is, as usual, clean and precise. There is not a single word here that doesn't further her story."

—*Edmonton Journal*

"An assured, perceptive, deftly delivered story."

—*Kirkus Reviews* (Starred Review)

"Absorbing reading.... [Gowdy's] true feat is the sympathetic portrayal of Ron himself, a man who seems painfully unaware of his own dark impulses."

—*Booklist*

"Gowdy consistently zeros in on strange minds, on propositions of difference in consciousness, and then resolves them through a kind of sympathetic intervention."

—*The Globe and Mail*

"Through Gowdy's fictional exploration we may exorcise our deepest fears."
—*The Independent*

"Gowdy's seventh novel, a nail-biting tale of suspense, spells extra work for manicurists everywhere. Highly recommended."

—*Library Journal* (Starred Review)

"Astonishing. We realize that it has been love, and nothing but love— Gowdy's enduring subject—that has been driving this time bomb of a novel all along."

—*The Vancouver Sun*

"Gowdy writes as if she's on a sinking boat and needs to throw out all the dead weight."

—*The New York Times Book Review*

"No one shades the darkness quite like Gowdy."

—*Eye Weekly*

Helpless

Helpless

A NOVEL

Barbara Gowdy

HARPER
PERENNIAL

Published by Harper Perennial, an imprint of HarperCollins Publishers Ltd.

Originally published by HarperCollins Publishers Ltd: 2007
This trade paperback edition: 2008

HARPER PERENNIL ®

is a registered trademark of HarperCollins Publishers Ltd.

HarperCollins books may be purchased for educational, business, or
sales promotional use through our Special Markets Department.

HarperCollins Publishers Ltd
2 Bloor Street East, 20th Floor
Toronto, Ontario, Canada
M4W 1A8

www.harpercollins.ca

Library and Archives Canada Cataloguing in Publication

Gowdy, Barbara
Helpless : a novel / Barbara Gowdy.
ISBN 978-0-00-200892-1

I. Title.

PS8563.0883H44 2008   C813'.54   C2007-907028-0

Printed and bound in the United States 9 8 7 6 5 4

Designed by Meryl Sussman Levavi

Helpless

Chapter One

Chapter One

O~N~ A SWELTERING afternoon in early June, Celia Fox stands at the railing of her deck and smokes the second-to-last cigarette she'll allow herself before going to work.

The apartment is small and stuffy (one of the drawbacks to living on the third floor of a Victorian house) but at least she and Rachel have this deck with its overhanging horse-chestnut tree whose glovelike leaves are already big enough to shade the entire front yard. From the railing of the deck you can see both the street out front and the lane that runs along the back of the stores on Parliament Street. Usually there's something going on in the lane, although right now, because it's so hot, not many people are out: only a legless man, dozing in his wheelchair behind the Shoppers Drug Mart dumpster, and the muscle-bound dog walker who holds all his leashes in one fist like a charioteer. An appliance-repair van drives by, and Celia wonders if repair places sell used air conditioners. Except she can't afford even a used one. And anyway, she has to finish filling in the modelling-school application if she wants to make the deadline.

Does she want to make it? She hasn't decided. Nine

strikes her as a little young to start trading in on your looks, although, if she chooses to believe the guy from the modelling agency, nine verges on decrepitude. When she told him Rachel's age he said he'd have put her at seven and a half, eight at the outside. "But that's okay," he said, eyeing Rachel as if she were a used car, "she can pass."

By this time Celia was regretting having let him buy her and Rachel iced teas in Java Ville, but he'd chased them up Parliament Street and he'd seemed, in those first few minutes, so boyish and pleasant.

"Little girls are a big deal right now," he told her. "For certain high-end ads they're pulling in close to a thousand, plus residuals."

Rachel's head snapped up from her book. "A thousand dollars?"

"That's right."

"I could be paid *a thousand dollars*?"

"Once we get that face of yours out there." He assured Celia that for girls with Rachel's potential the modelling school waived its fee.

"What does 'potential' mean?" Rachel asked.

"Beauty," he said. "You know you're beautiful, right?"

Rachel shrugged.

"Take it from me." He looked back and forth from her to Celia, clearly wondering the same thing everybody who met them for the first time wondered.

At which point Celia picked up the pamphlets and application form. "We'll have to read all this over," she said. She had no intention of satisfying his curiosity but she wasn't offended, either. Didn't she herself live in perpetual amazement that she could be her daughter's biological mother? She pushed back her chair, then saw by the inclination of Rachel's head that he was going to be set straight after all.

And here it came: "Some people ask if I'm adopted. Well, I'm not."

"Okay," the guy said.

"My father's black. Which is probably obvious."

"It would have been my guess."

With a new inflection of pride or challenge, as if she'd only recently figured out that this information *wasn't* so predictable, Rachel said, "He's an architect in New York City. His name's Robert Smith."

"Cool," the guy said. "An architect in New York City."

Or a veterinarian in Hoboken . . . Celia has no idea. She isn't even sure that his last name is Smith.

She goes inside and reads a depressing fiction piece in *Harper's* about a husband indulging his wife's bizarre mental breakdown. Then she shoves the cat off the piano and practises "Besame Mucho" for about half an hour, after which she forces herself to take another stab at the modelling-school application. She's still on the first page ("Would you describe your child as overly sensitive to criticism?" "Is your child afraid of dogs?") when Rachel arrives home, calling that Leonard wants to be a model, too. In exchange for free piano lessons, Leonard Wong accompanies Rachel to and from school. He's twelve years old but acts forty, a terrifyingly high-minded boy who sends his allowance to an orphanage in Shanghai.

"He's not really model material," Celia says tactfully.

"I know," Rachel says. "He needs braces. I didn't tell him, though." She comes over and presses a palm along Celia's bare, sweat-sticky shoulders. "Hey!" She has seen the application. "What's this still doing here?" She snatches it up.

"I've been having second thoughts," Celia admits. "Would you like some lemonade?"

"Not right now," Rachel says stonily.

Celia reaches for her cigarettes. "Let's go outside."

"It's like you don't even care if we're poor," Rachel says, following Celia onto the deck. She drops on the sofa and starts tugging foam from a hole in the cushion.

Celia has gone over to the railing. "Stop that—" nodding at the cushion. "We're not poor."

"Whatever."

"We're thrifty." Celia lights her cigarette. "Do you want to be a model? Forget the money. Do you want to spend all your time after school and on weekends rushing around to auditions and sitting for hours under hot lights and hardly ever having any fun?"

"The guy said a thousand dollars."

"It's not your job to worry about money."

"When you die from smoking, it'll be my job."

"I'm cutting down."

"Liar." She jumps up and comes over to Celia and hugs her arm. "Liar, liar!" she cries theatrically. "You smoke more than Mika, even."

Mika, their landlord and closest friend. "He's a social smoker," Celia says. "He doesn't count."

Rachel releases Celia and starts spinning around the deck.

"So," Celia says, "can I rip up the application?"

"You're the one who brought it home." She throws herself against the railing and slumps there.

"Good. That's settled then."

Rachel straightens. Something in the lane has caught her attention.

"What?" Celia says, turning to see. The guy in the wheelchair is gone. Across the street two pigeons peck at a dropped ice cream cone. "What are you looking at?"

"You don't have enough clothes on."

"Nobody could tell from there."

Rachel scoops up Felix, who has just strolled out onto the deck. "I think I'll go with you tonight," she says.

Chapter Two

CELIA WORKS TWO jobs. Mondays to Thursdays, from ten to six, she works at Tom's Video, a small, independent store owned by an easygoing ex–boxing champion named Jerry. (Tom was the dog, dead ten years ago now.) It can be dull sometimes, but it's close to the apartment and Jerry has no problem with her changing her hours if Rachel is home sick or has a day off school.

Until last September she worked Fridays as well, and then, on a tip from a customer, she landed a job performing jazz and blues standards at the Casa Hernandez Motel on Lakeshore Boulevard. She does this Friday and Saturday evenings from five thirty until nine thirty, after which Bernie Silver, who has been playing there since the early seventies, takes over.

It's the first time in her life she has played for money, or even tips. Always before, she was the person who accompanied Christmas carollers and drunken singers at parties. People used to tell her that if she ever made a record they'd run right out and buy it, so after slogging through two years at York University, she gave up on her declared (though never burning) ambition to be a sociologist and decided to concentrate on her music instead. But she hadn't even settled into a practice regime when she found out she was pregnant. She was only twenty-one. She was working part-time as a checkout clerk at Valu-Mart and living in a tiny two-bedroom apartment with her mother, whose knees had gotten so bad she'd been forced to cut back her hours selling lingerie at Eaton's. Worse, her mother had seen this coming. Every time Celia had arrived home late after a night out with friends, her mother had lectured her about birth control and abstinence and how raising a child on your own was no picnic, take it from her. Once, when all Celia was doing was lying on the sofa smoking a cigarette, she said, "You've inherited my sex drive." It was out of the question to let her think she'd been proven right, not that this topped the list of Celia's reasons for wanting an abortion. Still, she vacillated, secretly making and cancelling appointments at a clinic in Parkdale. Then one Friday night toward the end of her first trimester she dreamed she'd given birth to something inhuman and furry, and that settled it: she made an appointment for the following Tuesday. "This time," she promised the nurse, "I'm showing up." And she would have, she's certain, except on Sunday night, while she and her mother were doing the dishes, her mother suffered a massive stroke.

Celia never actually believed that the stroke was punishment for her lethal decision of two days earlier. It only felt that way. Her mother held on for six and a half months. Three times a day Celia went to the hospital to feed her. With an expression of infantile astonishment her mother watched the cutting of the food, the approach of the fork. She knew enough to open and chew, but that was about it.

She wore diapers, which Celia changed, saying, "This is good for me, Mom, this is teaching me the skills I'm going to need." Her mother looked on, interested, drooling, giving a start when Celia's tears hit her bare skin.

Death came the day before the birth, which meant that the funeral had to be delayed until Celia was up and around again. There weren't many mourners. Aside from an older brother who lived in Australia and sent a telegram, Celia's mother had had no living family. Celia's father certainly didn't count. He left when Celia was eight, took off for Florida with a woman named Hazel Beals. For almost three years he phoned every Sunday night, and gifts arrived for both her and her mother at Christmas and on birthdays, good gifts—cashmere scarves, jade bracelets, a white leather cinch belt—all chosen by Hazel Beals, no doubt, but her mother could live with that. "It's *his* money," she pointed out. And then he lost his job as a paint salesman and disappeared from their lives so completely that although Celia knew he now lived in Fort Lauderdale and her mother had always believed he'd come crawling back, she herself dreaded the thought of talking to him and even for her mother's sake couldn't bring herself to track down his phone number and deliver news she suspected he'd welcome. In any event, the little chapel was only half full: thirty people, some of whom tried to console Celia with the idea that, considering the timing, the baby might be her mother, in spirit anyway. Celia said she didn't think so. She refrained from admitting that the prospect of her mother and baby colliding in the ether had, actually, occurred to her as she was going into labour and then again—but only for about two seconds—when she saw the blue eyes.

* * *

THEIR CAR is a twelve-year-old two-door Toyota Tercel with ripped plastic seats, no CD player, and a stuck passenger door. To get in or out, Rachel has to climb through the driver's side, over the gearshift. But at least it has air conditioning. Mika, who could afford air conditioning, says that Happy and Osmo prefer outdoor air, meaning *he* prefers outdoor air. Ever since her mother told her that Mika sometimes speaks through the dogs as a way of letting himself off the hook, Rachel has noticed how this seems to be the case. Yesterday, when her mother returned from the hairdresser with her hair short and spiked and asked Mika what he thought, he looked at the dogs before saying, "Very smart," and, of course, that turned it into their opinion, not his, as her mother later pointed out. "*He* hates it," she said, laughing.

Rachel doesn't exactly hate it, but her mother's head now seems weirdly small and more of her scalp shows. Is she going bald? Rachel leans over the armrest to give her a closer look.

"What?" her mother says.

"Your earrings," Rachel lies. Her earrings are tiny pianos. "They're so cute."

Her mother shoots her a nervous smile. Driving makes her mother nervous. Everything makes her nervous, which is why Rachel didn't tell her about the fat man in the baseball cap. She wonders what he was doing, looking up at their deck . . . or maybe he was looking at the whole house— it's one of the original Cabbagetown houses and has a historical plaque. But then why did he duck behind the dumpster when her mother turned around? Well, maybe he just didn't want to be caught staring. If her mother had seen him she'd have called the police. George, the cook at the motel, is always saying that her mother needs a boyfriend to calm her down. Is her mother beautiful? Rachel thinks so, but nobody ever says she is. Her feathery little head makes Rachel sad. "Would you go out with Mika?" she asks. "I mean if he wasn't gay."

Her mother shifts gears. "I've never thought about it."

"You love him, don't you?"

"Of course, I do. Just not in that way."

"I love him in that way."

Her mother glances over. "You do?"

"If I was like, twenty, and he asked me to marry him, I'd probably say yes."

Her mother keeps glancing over. "Really?"

"Then we wouldn't have to pay any rent."

"We don't pay much as it is, let me tell you."

"But then we could all live together in the whole house. You and me and Felix and Mika and Happy and Osmo."

"Oh, I get it. This is about the animals."

Slightly offended, Rachel looks out her window. Mika teaches science at a private boys' school and is home by five o'clock on Fridays. So sometimes, instead of going to the motel, she goes downstairs to his place and they have supper together. Afterwards he likes to listen to her practise the piano, and then they watch *The Simpsons* on his flat-screen TV. Mika laughs at parts she doesn't find funny. She thinks it's because he's from Finland.

Yesterday, when she thought she was going to earn a thousand dollars, she told him she'd be staying home tonight. Now she feels she had better go to the motel and help her mother earn tips. Children aren't allowed in the Starlight Room, but nobody minds if Rachel looks in from the hallway and once or twice a night sings along. There's a Polish man named Tom who walks around slapping people on the back and shouting, "How are you, my friend!" and one time, after she and her mother had sung "Unforgettable," he stuffed a fifty-dollar bill into the tip vase. That made her mother happy but no matter how much money they get she still says she's a bad mother for bringing her daughter to a bar. "I don't go *into* the bar," Rachel reminds her. Mostly she plays video games or watches TV in the motel office or she sits in the kitchen with George and works on her drawings while he tells her about growing up in a Greek village and being so poor and hungry that one time he ate the raw garlic his mother had sewed into his underpants to ward off the evil eye.

Her mother's pay includes supper, anything on the menu, which George hasn't changed since 1973. They eat in the kitchen between the first and second sets. Tonight they both have French onion soup and mushroom quiche, while George stands at the counter and slices strips from a big hunk of meat. "Yuck," Rachel says. She's a vegetarian.

"Listen to her," George says. "The little girl who has never known hunger."

After her mother has finished her coffee and gone back up to the bar, Rachel takes her pad and markers out of her backpack and draws George as a boy in Greece. She gives him a wishing well and a stone house with red curtains in the window. When she shows him, he says, "There were no curtains."

"Not even rags?" she says.

"The rags were on our backs."

Her mother is playing "You Are the Sunshine of My Life." It comes down to them in bursts every time the bar door opens. George, as he always does when he hears this song, starts singing along: "You are the apple in my eye."

"*Of* my eye," Rachel says. "You are the apple *of* my eye." How many times does she have to tell him? He has a terrible voice. "Okay," she says, "I'm going up."

From the doorway she can't see all the customers, but she counts eleven, eight of them men and one a black man, sitting by himself at a table. There isn't any money in the vase yet, only the five dollars her mother puts in to get the ball rolling.

At the end of the song, with just the waitress and the black man clapping, her mother goes straight into the opening chords of "Besame Mucho."

"Rache, do you want to help me out?" she says, aiming the microphone toward the doorway.

Everybody looks around. Rachel lets her mother start, then comes in at "Each time I cling to your kiss . . ." The whole room has gone quiet. An old lady with frizzy pink hair like cotton candy conducts with a stir stick, but when the song is over and her mother brings the microphone to her mouth and says, "My daughter, Rachel, ladies and gentlemen," the lady swivels back to the bar.

Rachel smiles at the other customers, all of them clapping, and a woman scoots across to the vase and tucks in a blue bill. Five dollars. The black man gets up and puts a ten in the vase, then comes over to Rachel.

"I just want to tell you I think you have a beautiful voice," he says. His own voice is deep and important sounding.

"Thanks," she says.

"I'd like to shake your hand," he says, "if that's all right with you."

They shake. Her hand in his is almost white. She gets a delicate feeling, as though she were made of thin glass. "You wouldn't happen to be from New York City," she says, "would you?"

"Afraid not. Why do you ask?"

"Just wondered." She looks at her mother, who has started in on "Sophisticated Lady" and is watching her and the man.

"Rachel has to leave us now," her mother says. "Perhaps she'll join us later, before we both have to say good-bye at nine thirty."

"Thanks for the song," the man says. "You take care of yourself now."

He returns to his seat.

Rachel rubs her hand on her skirt. The hand he shook. One day she'll run into a black person who *is* from New York City and who will know her father. For a reason she can't explain, she's certain this is going to happen.

Chapter Three

*R*ON COMES OUT of the Casa Hernandez Motel so agitated that he can't remember having parked his van up the street at a closed gas station. He looks around the motel's lot, then goes to the neighbouring motel and looks there. It must have been towed, he thinks. Or stolen. "That's just great," he mutters. He starts walking toward the intersection, where he's more likely to find a cab. The sun is low but the heat of the day still swarms up from the pavement, and after a minute he's raining sweat. It occurs to him that if he were to drop dead from a heart attack, Rachel would hear about it. *A man died yesterday, right outside.*

Halfway to the intersection he remembers about the gas station and has to walk all the way back. The van is stifling; he should have left the windows opened an inch. He turns on the engine and gets the air conditioning going. How many drinks has he had? He isn't sure. Two, maybe. Two doubles. He gropes around in the glove compartment for the flask he has taken to stashing there. It used to be that after a couple of drinks he thought everybody could see right through him. A waitress saying "Do you want your check?" was really saying

"Get lost, pervert." At his father's funeral a woman told him he had always been different, and in the second before she added, "Taking apart your mother's toasters and things," her smile seemed pinched with disgust.

That kind of paranoia isn't the problem now, though. He almost wishes it was: anything but this tension, this anguish. He couldn't believe it when Rachel appeared in the doorway of the bar and started to sing, and it wasn't the performance of an innocent little girl, either, the way she smiled and swayed her hips. What sort of mother encourages her daughter to behave like that? Doesn't it amount to child abuse, forcing a girl Rachel's age to sing in a bar? When Rachel left, he quickly paid up and followed her. He wasn't even thinking beyond the fact that she'd probably be returning to the kitchen, where he'd glimpsed her earlier through the open door. And yes, there she was, hopping on one foot in front of the chef, who waved at her with a cleaver. An odd sight, and Ron knows that after another few drinks he might have taken it the wrong way and rushed in. Instead, he kept walking, right out of the motel. She's fine, he told himself. But he wasn't convinced. There were still all those guys in the bar . . . the black guy who had pretended to want to shake her hand so that he could touch her.

The flask, he now remembers, is on his kitchen counter. He considers going back into the motel and ordering a drink from the restaurant. Except that the place is almost empty; he'd just be drawing attention to himself. He wonders if the mother has noticed him hanging around her house. Not that she seems to be the vigilant type—far from it. But that doesn't make her a complete fool. He was careful, following her here, to stay a car length behind, and in the motel bar he sat in a corner, behind a stack of chairs. All the same, it would be pushing his luck to show himself again. He guesses he should go home.

Not yet. Leaving Rachel in that bar with those men goes against all his instincts.

HE SAW her for the first time a week ago Tuesday. He was returning from Tindle's Electrical Supply when he decided to head over to Spruce Court Public School. He knows all the elementary schools within a fifteen-minute drive of his shop and about once a week, if it's coming around to three thirty and he happens to be out on an errand anyway, he visits one he hasn't been to in a while. Sometimes it's just a slow drive-by. Other times he pulls over and pretends to consult his *Perly's Street Guide*.

That day the only parking spot was behind the school bus. He took it, although he usually parks farther down the street, where he's less likely to draw attention to himself. He switched off the engine, grabbed the *Perly's* guide, and rolled down his window.

Almost immediately the bell rang. A minute later the kids began pouring through the doors, the youngest ones first. He waited. Really young girls have never interested him. Neither have girls whose faces and bodies are starting to show their adult contours. His type is skinny, with olive to light brown skin and features that through some fineness of bone structure promise to remain delicate.

A pair of identical twins—Chinese or Korean, about eight years old—caught his eye. They had Dutch-boy haircuts and wore matching brown dresses with long full skirts. He imagined that they'd just arrived in the country and was touched to think how self-conscious they must feel in their unstylish outfits. One of them waved to somebody behind him. He shifted his gaze to the rearview mirror. An elderly, bowlegged woman was approaching from down the street.

When he looked up again, his view was being blocked by a tall Asian boy who was standing next to the van's front fender. Move, Ron silently ordered. As if he heard, the boy glanced around. He squinted at Ron, then read the side of the van . . . he actually mouthed the words: *Ron's Appliance Repair*. Ron bent over his *Perly's* guide.

"Rachel!" the boy called. "I'm going!"

Ron looked up. A thin blond girl was running across the lawn. A mixed girl, Caucasian and black. He'd never seen her before.

"I forgot to tell Luca something," she said when she reached the sidewalk.

She had enormous pale blue eyes.

"Where is he?" the boy said.

"I don't know." She scratched her neck, displaying the lovely line of her jaw. "I thought he was right behind me."

Her skin was light . . . tawny. Her hair, a miraculous chromium yellow, was pulled into a ponytail of tiny spiral curls, like the springs in old ballpoint pens. She had on purple jeans and a mauve T-shirt with "Super Star" across the front in silver letters. She searched up and down the street, and for a moment her gaze landed on Ron. A murky, underwater feeling enveloped him.

"I guess he's not coming," she told the boy.

And then they were walking away.

Ron jerked out of his reverie. He got the van going but waited until they had reached the end of the block before starting to follow. He stayed well back, slowing more than he needed to for the speed bumps. At Parliament Street he made the turn just in time to see them disappear into a video store. Should he pull over? No, too risky . . . the boy might recognize the van. He kept driving.

That evening, as planned, Nancy came around and cooked supper: baked ribs, potato fritters, and brown-sugar squash. The Number 5 Special she called it, because that's what it is on the menu at Frank's Homestyle Restaurant, where she waitresses. Ron filled his plate twice, then started in on a quart of chocolate ice cream. Nothing ever interferes with his appetite, but keeping his mouth full was also keeping him from having to talk, which, of course, Nancy picked up on.

"Something happen today?" she asked finally.

Yes, he said to himself, something happened. I fell in love.

Only as he thought it did he realize it was true. A ripple of terror went through him. He held up the ice cream container to see if there was anything left. No. Carefully, he set his spoon inside. "That guy I told you about," he said. "From Kentucky? He put in an offer on the Westinghouse." This happened to be the truth. As soon as he got back to the store, the call came in.

Her shoulders relaxed. "Really? A high offer?"

"Very high."

"Which Westinghouse is that again?"

"I only have one."

"Right, right." She tapped ash onto her plate. "Oh, the *I Love Lucy* vacuum!"

"Tank Cleaner, 1952," he said. It irks him when she gives the vacuums nicknames.

"I forgot to tell you. I saw that episode just last week at Angie's. Poor Lucy, she's lugging the vacuum all over the place, she's got the hose part hanging around her neck, and nobody wants to buy it and I'm like, if only she knew how much that thing would be worth in fifty years' time."

"I hope you didn't tell Angie," he said.

"Tell her what?"

"How much the thing is worth." Angie operates a nail salon that caters to hookers and welfare mothers whose boyfriends all seem to have spent time in Kingston Penitentiary.

"No, no," Nancy said, her forehead creasing. "I wouldn't do that. So, are you going to sell it to the guy?"

"I haven't decided."

He watched her clear the table. When he first met her she could stack six plates along her left arm. That stopped about a year ago, after her right leg started to spasm. All her sisters (a slew of them up in Timmins) get leg spasms apparently, but Nancy used to do hard drugs, and an old boyfriend kicked her unconscious once, so Ron suspects there's some neurological damage going on. Luckily, her boss has no complaints, provided she remains her friendly, perky self. Being cute doesn't hurt, either. She's Ron's age—thirty-seven—but from a distance you'd put her at seventeen.

"I told you Frank's revamping the menu," she said. "Right? Making it more kid friendly?"

Ron's thoughts were back with the girl. Rachel. His heart knocked painfully against his ribs. "I'm going to go down and check out the Westinghouse," he said, coming to his feet.

"I'll run a bath then," she said with a coy smile that seemed nearly incomprehensible to him, nearly lewd, for being so far from the pure and tender vision he was trying to hold on to.

It's a two-storey house. There's his shop on the ground floor at the front, kitchen at the back, living room, bedrooms, and bathroom on the second floor, and in the basement, under the garage, the locked apartment where he stores his vintage vacuum collection. As he passed through the shop he was hit by a tremendous urge to jump in his van and cruise the streets near Rachel's school on the thousand-to-one chance he'd see her out playing. His head swam, a film of sweat coated his body. Close to panic he opened the door to the basement and thumped down the stairs, fumbling in his pocket for the key.

Once inside the apartment, he moved around, gripping handles. He went over to the Westinghouse and felt a stab of grief to think of it gone. All his vacuums are in mint condition: chrome polished, motors and brushes refurbished, original unused bags. It's the Westinghouse, though, with its zeppelin-shaped housing, that gives him the most pleasure.

No, he thought, he couldn't sell it. Business was slow, especially on the home entertainment side, what with the cost of parts and labour almost equalling the replacement cost of TVs, VCRs, and CD players. But he'd survive. You don't sell a Westinghouse Tank Cleaner unless you're a lot more emotionally prepared than he was right now to deal with the loss.

Back upstairs he took down the bottle of Seagram's, half full and untouched for five years, and poured himself a double. Something had to give, he reasoned, and better this. Above him in the bathroom Nancy sang "Yellow Bird." He'd heard her play it on the banjo (she had an old banjo that used to belong to her mother) but when he was right there in front of her she sang so softly the strumming drowned her out.

He went still for a minute, listening. She sounded good. He thought what a nice person she was . . . not overly bright, but then he could do without bright. All she wanted was for the two of them to get married and live together in this house. Him, a fat appliance repairman, and this house, a redbrick dump in the middle of an industrial strip of auto body shops and burger joints. If he didn't appreciate how little he had to offer—so much less than she imagined— he'd be flattered. He isn't proud of the fact that he lets her think he balks at marriage because of her hysterectomy. It's an excuse she can accept, though. Every so often, as if she wishes she were selfless enough to release him to a fertile woman, she says, "You'd make such a great father."

Would he? He once read somewhere that the incest taboo is a powerful deterrent, but people don't go around admitting to desires like his, so who really knows? And yet look what happened with Rachel.

His heart started drumming again. What exactly *had* happened with Rachel? Were his feelings those of a father, a protector, or was he romanticizing his lust? He topped up his glass and tried to think about this honestly. Both feelings were there, he decided, one shielding the other. Like lighting a match and cupping your hand around it against the wind.

HE WOKE up the next morning believing that whatever had come over him was out of his system. The thought of Rachel gave him the expected pleasure, but nothing beyond that. Nothing he couldn't handle.

So he felt at breakfast. By nine thirty he was standing at the window and thinking about her mouth. An hour later, haunted by the image of her playing at recess, he closed his shop and drove to her school.

He parked two blocks away. The recess bell rang as he was getting out of the van and he had to force himself to keep an inconspicuous pace. At the bank of newspaper kiosks near the northeast corner of the playground, he bought a *Star* and pretended to read as he searched the playground.

She was over by the swings, playing a clapping game with another, bigger girl. Her T-shirt was pink today, the same pink as her lips. She had on the purple jeans again. White sneakers. "Okay, like this!" he heard her yell, and she demonstrated a series of quick, complicated claps. He watched until the bell rang, then he folded the paper under his arm and returned to the van, where he sat in a stupor of happiness.

Back at the shop he tackled a job—replacing the voltage control on a finicky model of microwave—he'd been putting off for two days. His happiness inspired him. But a customer phoning to complain about his repair of her humidifier broke the spell, and he began to see himself for what he was: a man gearing up for suffering. His meaty hands, as he sorted through a box of sockets, seemed to belong to somebody who would never rise above the small gratifications of his craft.

Around noon he made himself a couple of peanut butter sandwiches and ate them sitting on a kitchen chair out in the yard. His mind turned to Nancy's plans to grow tomatoes along the fence if he ever invited her to move in. He has always pitied her for loving him, but now that he loved somebody just as hopelessly he found himself in awe of her faculty for self-denial and acceptance. He decided to phone her, see how she was.

He caught her just as she was leaving for work. She told him she was feeling guilty about Tasha, her dog. "This place boils with the air conditioning off," she said, "but if I leave it running I'll get evicted."

"Bring her here," he said. It wasn't an offer he'd ever thought to make before.

She arrived almost weeping her thanks. She kissed his hands. He smelled marijuana smoke in her hair but decided to let that ride.

At two thirty a woman came by with a Black & Decker lawn mower he could see right away needed an overhaul, likely a new flywheel. The woman hoped he'd be able to fix it before tomorrow afternoon. "I'll do my best," he said, but by closing the shop earlier he'd put himself behind schedule and the prospect of working long hours made him anxious. What if he felt an urge to drive to Rachel's neighbourhood? Already the craving to see her again was leaking back. As soon as the woman left, he poured himself a rye and water, took it down to the basement, and drank in the company of his vacuums. That helped. Not enough.

He went back up to the shop and stood looking at his computer. Thousands of little girls were in there, but how did you get to them? If you wanted to open a site you had to click on a word or image, which he had a terror of doing in case he found himself confronted by something violent or sick. Beyond that he was fairly certain that downloading made you vulnerable to surveillance.

He told himself not to risk it. He finished off his drink

and considered Tasha, trembling in her basket. "What's going on?" he asked with a stirring of sympathy. She cast her bug eyes from him to the door, and after a moment his real reason for taking her in was, it seemed, revealed. He glanced at his watch. "Okay," he said. "Let's find your leash."

He parked, as before, a couple of blocks from the school. This time, however, he thought to put on sunglasses and a baseball cap. He paced himself to arrive just as the bell rang, then he let Tasha slow down and sniff telephone poles until he spotted Rachel coming out the double doors.

She lingered on the stairs. She was waiting for somebody—the tall Asian boy, it turned out. They took off toward Parliament. Feeling next to invisible in this neighbourhood of dog walkers, Ron followed close behind. Everything about her thrilled him: her thin brown arms, the insectlike hinge of her elbows, her prancing step, the shapely bulb of her head, her small square shoulders bearing the burden of her backpack, and even the backpack itself, which was mauve with a pattern of pink daisies.

Once again, she and the boy went north on Parliament and disappeared into the video store. This time, though, the boy reemerged almost immediately and continued up the street. Ron waited a minute, then remembered that Nancy's friend Angie had her salon in this neighbourhood, so he walked a little farther along to a bus stop, where he merged in with the crowd. Five minutes passed, ten. The bus pulled up. Ron wondered if Rachel had left by a rear exit, but why would she do that? He tied Tasha to a bicycle stand. He had to know what was keeping her.

She was behind the counter, sitting on a stool and drawing on a pad with a marker. She didn't look up, and neither did the woman at the cash register. A small blond woman with a hard, lean face. Ron strolled along the wall of new releases. He took down a DVD and pretended to consider it. "Oh, good, you gave me eyebrows!" the woman said.

"Mom, you *have* eyebrows," Rachel said. "And see! I drew your shadow behind you."

Ron replaced the DVD. A moment later a group of kids came in and he was able to slip around them and make his escape.

He went across the road to a restaurant and got a table out on the patio, tying Tasha to the railing. The video store closed at midnight, but he figured that the mother, or somebody, would be taking Rachel home long before then. If she lived in this neighbourhood, and she most likely did, he'd find out where.

IN HIS van down the road from the Casa Hernandez Motel, he watches the lights of the CN Tower come on. He has always considered the CN Tower a reassuring structure: hopeful and nostalgically futuristic, like a hand from one of those starburst wall clocks people had in the 1950s. It used to cheer him up. He finds this hard to believe. He finds it hard to believe that only ten days have passed since he had the self-possession to sit out on a public patio and drink nothing but coffee.

Now it's alcohol and never in the company of other people. He gets going after breakfast, a couple of beers. By the time he's closing shop to drive to Spruce Court for the three-twenty bell, he's put away another four or five and a double shot of rye. He parks in a different location every day, which might fool the neighbours but not Tasha: she knows where they're headed. She even seems to know that it's Rachel they're following, because when the boy drops her off (at Tom's Video or, as he has done two Fridays in a row now, at her house) she wants to keep going after her, right through the door.

So does Ron. He feels better, though, less on edge, and when he returns to the shop he usually gets in some good work while the feeling lasts. At sunset he makes another trip, this time to satisfy himself that she's not in danger. On weekends it's his only trip, a restraint achieved, just barely, by a steady, measured increase in his alcohol intake. He always half expects to find her house up in flames or to hear her screaming. This afternoon the fear seized him the minute he got home, and he drove straight back and kept vigil behind the Shoppers Drug Mart dumpster until she left with her mother in their car, and then he followed.

He realizes he'll have to make up some story for Nancy about where he's been all evening. She'll have phoned, for sure . . . she knows something's going on. A couple of nights ago she came right out and asked if he was seeing someone else.

"I'm a little stressed," he said. "That's all. The work isn't coming in."

It's coming in. He just isn't keeping on top of it.

What's eating away at him, aside from the craving to see Rachel, is his conviction that she's being mistreated. She sleeps in an unfinished basement, for one thing, as he discovered last night when he turned onto the lane that runs along one side of the house and saw her through the security bars of a cellar window. She was lying on a cot and staring up at the ceiling. There was a cardboard box with a lamp on it, but no carpet, just the bare concrete floor. He walked past again, and then again, and only dragged himself away when Tasha, objecting to being yanked back and forth, began to whine.

The cot isn't even the most disturbing part. The landlord is. He's not the mother's boyfriend or husband; Ron worked that out the day he followed her and Rachel home from the video store, and a guy sitting on the porch called, "Enjoy your supper!" when they went inside. It took a few more days for Ron to peg the guy as the landlord, but right off the bat he worried about Rachel's living in a house with a man who wasn't her father. His fears were realized last Tuesday night when he saw the two of them together on a porch chair, Rachel sitting in the guy's lap and the guy's right hand (Ron couldn't swear to this, but the more he goes over it in his head, the surer he gets) moving around beneath her pyjama top.

Where was the mother? It is unfathomable to Ron that the mother of a girl as beautiful as Rachel would leave her alone with a man under the age of eighty. But then this is a mother who makes her daughter sing for drunks and sleep in a cot on a concrete floor.

"If she were mine," he thinks.

If she were his, what wouldn't he give her? Wall-to-wall carpeting, a canopy bed, a top-of-the-line dollhouse.

Almost without realizing, stunned by his train of thought, he puts the van in gear and heads off.

Chapter Four

MIKA HAS HUNG venetian blinds on the basement windows and laid pieces of carpeting on the floor. The lumpy pullout bed Celia slept on last night now has a piece of plywood between the mattress and springs. When they came back from the motel, Mika was out on the porch but he didn't tell them what he'd done, and only now, as Rachel is going to bed, do they find out.

"He's so good," Rachel moans. "He's so good to people."

"I really should break down and buy an air conditioner," Celia says. She is sitting on the bed, testing the firmness. "If it's this hot in June, what's it going to be like in August?"

"Mika will buy us one."

"Well, we're not going to let him. He's already paying the whole shot for music camp."

Rachel curls up beside Celia. "If we do get an air conditioner, can we still sleep down here?"

"We won't need to, will we? Our apartment will be nice and lovely and cool."

"What if we were like Anne Frank? What if we had to hide down here or we'd be shot by the Nazis?"

"That would put things in a different light."

"Mika would have to sneak us down potatoes and, like, bread crusts. Right? Right, Mom?"

"I think he'd do better than that. Come on, let's go thank him."

The porch light is off. Mika says that the bulb burned out and then just seconds later the streetlight began to flicker. "Unseen forces at work," he says. About the venetian blinds, he says, "Osmo and Happy didn't want people peering in at you."

Celia bends to scratch Happy's ears. "Always looking out for us, eh?" The two dogs pant like bellows. "I'm going to have a long, cool bath," she announces. "You"—to Rachel, who is climbing onto Mika's lap—"five minutes, then off to bed."

When she's gone, Rachel touches Mika's hair. "Is your hair flaxen?" she asks, having recently come across the word in a book. "Is this what flaxen is?"

Mika's mouth moves as if he's talking, but he isn't yet. Rachel waits. Her mother has told her that he used to have a stutter and sometimes needs a few seconds to get the first words out.

"Flaxen is the fibre of the flax plant," he says finally. "It's blond and threadlike, yes." He holds up a finger. "Listen."

"What?"

"Do you hear that?"

"The siren?"

"No, listen. Wait, it stopped. No, there it is. Up in the sky."

Above the shush of a sprinkler and a woman yelling in a foreign language and the clatter of a truck barrelling down

Parliament Street, there's a scraping sound, like two stones being rubbed together. "Is it a bat?" Rachel asks.

"A nighthawk. Calling to another nighthawk. You can hear the second one now, farther off."

"What are they saying?"

"Oh, they're saying . . ." Another short pause. "They're saying, 'A lot of people are out tonight.'"

"They're saying, 'That man and that girl down there should take those dogs for a walk.'"

Mika slides her off his lap. "On the contrary, they're saying, 'Why isn't that girl in bed yet?'"

UPSTAIRS, CELIA uses her foot to turn off the taps. How is it, she wonders, that you can soak in water and not drown, or at least become saturated? We've got pores, she reasons. We're porous. It surprises her that she has never wondered about this before.

She closes her eyes and calculates how much money she made tonight: forty-two dollars in tips, and then her wages on top of that, minus deductions. Seventy dollars, give or take—enough to pay the minimum on her Visa card. Or should she get the car door fixed? Mika knows somebody at an auto body shop who will give her a deal.

She didn't consult Mika about the modelling school because even though he never directly confronts her or second-guesses her decisions, the question of how Rachel could be too young to pose in front of a camera and not too young to sing in a bar would almost surely have come up. The answer is, she's too young to do either, but at least when you're singing it's your voice you're showing off. So Celia argues with herself. Maybe she's jealous. Maybe she's balking at the possibility of Rachel's earning more in a few hours than she can earn in a week. No, it isn't jealousy. It's not wanting Rachel to turn into one of those clothes-obsessed, narcissistic child sexpots. For another couple of years, anyway, she'd like to keep her under wraps.

Keep her under wraps. She hears how that sounds. Her impulse is to be overprotective but she fights it. She dreads burdening Rachel the way she was burdened, not that her mother actively interfered with her life. Her mother watched her. She followed her around the apartment with her eyes, and when she was at work she had her friend Mrs. Craig listen outside the apartment door. There were no rules laid down—that wasn't her style. Whenever Celia did something to upset her, she'd start in about the harmful effects of that kind of behaviour on girls *in general* or on herself specifically, twenty-five years ago, how she had suffered from the very same mistakes and misjudgments. It was never, "*You* shouldn't . . ." It was, "Nice girls don't . . ." or "I wish I hadn't . . ." And then she'd sigh and leave the room or get back to what she'd been doing, as if she didn't really expect to be listened to. It was confusing. It left Celia feeling like a lost cause but also mysteriously entitled, possessed of an unreasonable power. Plainly, she was the centre of her mother's existence, and yet she can't imagine that her mother ever looked at her and thought, "Aren't I lucky?" or that she had nightmares about people coming to the door and saying, "A mistake was made, we have to take back your child." Celia remembers, after Rachel was born, leaving the hospital with this utterly dependent creature in her arms and wondering, "Why doesn't somebody stop me?"

None of which is to say that she'll be changing her mind

about the modelling school. The fact that Rachel gave in so quickly must mean she herself doesn't feel ready, and by the time she does, her body might not even be the right shape, although that's unlikely. If long fingers and toes are any indication, she's going to end up tall and lean like her father. In whose armpit Celia nestled as they walked from the Lava Lounge, where they'd discovered a mutual interest in Sarah Vaughan, over to Spadina Avenue, where he had a room you rented by the day. He was a destitute architectural student. He'd hitchhiked up from New York City to see the train stations of southwestern Ontario and Quebec. She hadn't had sex in over a year and he was agonizingly handsome, so when he couldn't find a condom she went ahead anyway. Afterwards he confessed to being engaged to a girl who wanted to save herself for marriage. "I betrayed you both," he said and looked so miserable that Celia patted his shaved head and made him instant coffee in a CN Tower mug. How strange, she reflects now, that Rachel should be the outcome of those few, not unpleasant, but hardly earth-shattering hours in a squalid room where the radiator banged and a woman out in the hall kept yelling, "That's *your* opinion!"

She's had this thought before, of course; she's just never been so impressed by it as she is now. But over the past few days a lot of things—known things—are striking her as remarkable. "Can you imagine?" she said yesterday to someone who was renting the new *Gone with the Wind* DVD. "There was slavery only a hundred and fifty years ago! Mammy was Scarlett's slave!"

It's as if the heat is slowing down her normally racing mind and urging her to see details and hidden implications. In her dreams, oddly enough, just the opposite is going on:

she glances over things, she misses the obvious. A couple of nights ago she dreamed that she and Rachel were driving along a highway littered with what she thought were pieces of tire, but when she said, "Look at all those pieces of tire," Rachel said, outraged, "They're armadillos! What if you hit one?" In a dream a few nights before that, she bumped into her mother on the street, and when she said, "But you died!" her mother told her, irritably, that the dead come back all the time, they're all around "if anyone cared to look."

RACHEL LIES on her cot and wonders if the black lamb is sleeping. It was so cute. Mrs. Dunlop took the class to visit it this afternoon at the Riverdale farm, and everybody tried to pat it through the fence but only Sindra, who has really long arms, could reach. "The coat isn't called fur," Mrs. Dunlop said, "it's called fleece." Rachel already knew this. The mother sheep was white, so the father must have been black, but then why wasn't the lamb brown? Or gray? Rachel didn't ask in case it was a stupid question. An old, scruffy man Mrs. Dunlop thought worked there (he turned out to be just a man walking by) told the class that when the farm was the Toronto Zoo back in the fifties, there was a chimpanzee who used to beg for cigarettes. "He'd go—" the man said, and he bent down right in front of Rachel and started huffing and tapping his fingers on his mouth. His pushed-out lips disgusted her but she didn't want to hurt his feelings so she stood there until Mrs. Dunlop tugged her away.

She thinks about lips. Fish have lips. Cats don't. Felix only has two lines, the same pink as his nose and the pads on his feet. His pads are like beans. For some reason he's scared of the basement. He sleeps out on their deck at night and eats moths. He's getting fat.

She wonders if the fat man in the baseball cap was looking at her mother. If he is in love with her mother from afar.

OUTSIDE THE rear service doors of the restaurant, Nancy lights a joint. Frank doesn't care. Whatever keeps her smiling is how he looks at it. She hears him through the open window, banging pots, whistling. He's through for the night. Not her, she has to wait for the family at table 3. They've settled their bill, but they're taking their time over dessert. Nancy's guess is they don't have air conditioning and want to stay cool for as long as possible. That's fine with her. They're nice people. Their little girl gave her the picture she crayoned of a woman with blue, droopy eyes, a crooked red smile, and a red-checkered apron. "Is that me?" Nancy asked because the resemblance seemed obvious.

The girl shrugged. "Okay," she said.

Okay. Nancy got a kick out of that.

As soon as they leave, she can mop the floor. She supposes she'll drive straight home and let Tasha spend the night at Ron's. Ever since those two fell for each other, she's been a third wheel anyway. "Stabbed in the back by my own dog," she jokes.

She slips her hand into the pocket of her apron and squeezes her psychic pouch, a plastic baggie containing clippings of Ron's hair from the last time she gave him a trim. You're supposed to squeeze the pouch and chant, "Red is your blood, red is my heart, deep is our love, never to part," and think of your boyfriend or husband smiling at you lovingly.

The more often you do this, the less likely he'll be ever to leave. Nancy can't imagine how she'd survive if he left.

"You set your bar too low," Angie tells her. "You can do better than hostile and chubby."

"Ron isn't hostile," Nancy says, although he is, sometimes, to Angie. And, okay, he could stand to lose some weight, but there's a lot of muscle there, too. Nancy has seen him lift a refrigerator and haul it across a room. Not that she expects this to impress Angie. "When it's just him and me," she says, "he's really sweet." She means in bed, where he's shy and careful of her and kisses her appendix scar. Before he came along, she thought men needed to hurt you to have a good time. She reminds Angie that she'd still be using crystal meth if he hadn't made her stop, and Angie imagines the typical drawn-out, ugly fight and says, "You've got me there."

Except that there was no fight. When Ron caught her smoking in his bathroom he didn't throw a fit. More than anything he was sympathetic. He told her about his drinking problem and how he'd beat it by going into a treatment program.

"Oh, I'm cutting down," she lied. In those days she thought that smoking, as opposed to shooting or snorting, was no big deal.

"It's hard to cut down by yourself," Ron said, and he wrote the name and number of a counsellor from the place where he'd gone for help.

She promised to make the call but never did. Then one night when they were sitting out on his back stoop and she was gnawing on her nails and shivering and talking too fast,

he said, "You know, I don't think I want to be with a junkie."
It wasn't a threat; it was information, as plain and unemo-
tional as somebody saying, "You know, I don't think I want
the pasta special." A week later she was in rehab. Nothing
other than the terror of losing him could have kept her
there. She still smokes dope but he's under the impression
it's only when her leg acts up. Too bad her drug of choice
isn't a prescription one. *That* he'd understand. He's the
most law-abiding person she has ever met. He's honest,
a man of honour. At least she used to think so.

She isn't buying his story that he's worried about business. After the hell you go through in rehab, a few slow
months aren't going to make you backslide. There has to be
another woman, and his feelings for her must be pretty
strong. What is she like? A cute little brunette probably. All
his old girlfriends, the ones Nancy knows about anyway,
were dark. Of course, none of them lasted very long. But if
a sexy woman like that sauntered into the shop and made
the first move . . . Nancy pictures a bored housewife. Or
one of those pushy real estate agents who keep coming
around and trying to get him to sell the house.

Or maybe she's just someone he met in a bar. A nice,
fun-loving type who already has a few kids and is dying to
have more. Her, Nancy can almost forgive.

HE DOESN'T think too hard about what it will all amount to
or why he has chosen the basement apartment instead of
one of the spare bedrooms. He concentrates on the job at
hand. First he clears out the storage space behind the shop.
Most of that stuff he moves up to the attic, the rest into the
furnace room. Then it's lugging up the vacuums. The storage

space is half the size of the apartment, and he has to shove the machines together. Where the housing of one machine touches another he buffers the connection with a rag.

He talks to them. "You'll be fine," he says. "This is only temporary." They seem to know better. They're dead weights.

Chapter Five

*H*E SELLS THE Westinghouse the next morning. The fact that it's only a verbal deal doesn't worry him, the buyer being a well-known collector who won't change his mind. With the five thousand dollars as good as in his wallet, he takes all the necessary measurements and drives to Home Depot, where he buys plaster patch, paint, crown moulding, baseboards, quarter round, finishing nails, wood glue, caulking, new faucets, a white shower curtain, and a toilet seat as soft as a cushion. The carpeting—white wall-to-wall, 100 percent pure virgin wool—has to be ordered, but the salesman promises it will be delivered by the end of the week.

He's driving home when it dawns on him that he hasn't had a drink since the night before, and he opens the glove compartment to take out the flask, then changes his mind. He doesn't need it. He's feeling purposeful and yet pulled along, as you do sometimes in dreams where there's no clear reason for your urgency. He has a sense of the minutes scrolling out just far enough ahead to allow him to see what needs doing next.

A woman is waiting for him at the shop. Apparently he

told her that her lawn mower would be ready this morning, and to his wonderment it is. On her way out the door she says, "You've got your work cut out for you."

"How do you mean?" he says with a quiver of apprehension. He is thinking of his work downstairs.

She gestures at the rows of lawn mowers still waiting for repair. "All those."

"Oh." he says. "Right. Well, it's the season."

He locks the door and drives the van around to the back and unloads from there, out of sight of any other customers who might show up. He wants to get a few hours under his belt.

He starts by tearing off the old baseboards. As he works he finds himself paying attention to the room, what it feels like to be in it. No musty basement smell, thanks to the de-humidifier. He should close off the air conditioning vents, though; it's too cold. He pauses to look at the windows, triple-paned for weatherproofing and coated with Mylar, which makes them virtually unbreakable. The security bars are bleak but if he paints them white and frosts the glass, they won't be so noticeable. He looks up at the acoustic-tiled ceiling and wonders about the soundproofing between here and the ground floor. He puts down the crowbar and goes back upstairs.

A couple of days ago a CD player arrived with a complaint about static. He carries down the components, scrapes the corroded wires and sets everything up. There's a CD inside, ready to go. He presses PLAY.

On comes the music, static-free. (So it *was* only the wires.) He is about to turn up the volume when he realizes that he knows this piece: "O mio babbino caro." Puccini.

His mother used to listen to it all the time. In fact, it's the one piece he can remember her ever having *sat down* to listen to.

He stays bent over with his hands on his thighs. Grief isn't what he's feeling; he's familiar with grief. This is nothingness. He has an impression of his bones hanging in black space, surrounded by the thick wet walls of his flesh. He goes to straighten, and a nauseating dread wallows through him and he has to lean on one of the speakers. He punches the next selection. It's another aria but not one he recognizes. He turns up the volume and lets the voices roar around inside him until the dread recedes.

Upstairs the singing is faint . . . and every few seconds is drowned out completely by a truck rumbling by outside.

"What do you think?" he asks Tasha, who watches him from her basket. "If we left a radio on in here," he says, "nobody would hear a thing."

He is sobered by how calculating he sounds. He tells himself that the room is a distraction, an idea, that there's nothing sinister about renovating a basement.

But it isn't until he picks up the crowbar again that the sensation of moving through a dream returns. When the baseboards are off, he rips up the old carpet, then cuts and bundles the pieces and carries them out behind the house, where the noonday heat seems to be baking all this—the watery, wavering light, his tranced mind, the intermittent, boxing-ring clang of an air hose from Vince's garage—into permanence.

At one o'clock he breaks for lunch. He wonders about that sickening dread, which seems to have struck him another lifetime ago, when he still had a choice between surrender and resistance. Whatever he does now, just standing here at the back door chewing his food, feels directed.

It's a quarter to five before he can bring himself to stop work again. There's an extension phone in the furnace room, but if it rang he didn't hear. He looks at the patched walls and painted moulding and allows himself to settle into thankfulness. Wasn't this what he was hoping for? To be consumed by something other than his craving to see Rachel? He thinks of the risk he's been taking, following her from school day after day. Teachers are supposed to watch out for men like him; how does he know that he hasn't already been spotted? Ideally, he should cut back to every other day or to a couple of days off and a couple on. Well, with the basement to occupy him, maybe he'll be able to.

He eats his supper up the street at Flame Burgers, then works in the shop until sunset. By now his pulse is galloping at the prospect of seeing her lying on her cot.

It is a shock, therefore, to walk past her house and find the basement windows covered with blinds. He pulls Tasha around to the back and looks through the rails of the wrought-iron fence. No basement windows at all along that side. His anxiety, which he has kept at bay for almost twenty-four hours now, rears up—he has a few moments of panic, picturing her down there with the landlord. To steady himself he pictures *his* basement room. A safe place, a sanctuary, that's how he sees it. He wonders if he should hang blinds. No, he thinks: curtains. Curtains are more cheerful. Just because the windows will be frosted doesn't mean there can't be curtains.

The idea absorbs him. He returns to his van, drives home, and starts searching through the boxes where the drapes from his parents' house have been tucked away all these years. It's the green-and-white-striped curtains that he's looking for, and when he finds them he takes them downstairs for dropping off at the dry cleaners. Then he pours himself a drink and goes and sits in the living room. On the coffee table is the book he was finding so riveting only a few weeks ago: *Tank Combat in North Africa*. He picks it up and leafs unseeing through the pages. The basement apartment is directly beneath this part of the house, and before he can stop himself he is fantasizing about Rachel down there, asleep. He begins to shake. Rye splashes out of the glass. He tosses the book on the floor and fixes his mind on what he plans to do tomorrow—sand and paint the walls, caulk around the bathtub—and after a few minutes he succeeds in bringing himself to that near-stupefied state of calm. He falls asleep.

When he wakes up, Nancy is standing in front of him.

"What time is it?" he says. He forgot that she was coming over.

She takes his hands and tugs. "Come on," she says. "Come on."

"What?"

"Let's go upstairs."

Afterwards, she turns her face into the pillow and cries.

"Hey," he says. "We're doing all right."

He rubs her back until she goes still. He hopes that's the end of it, but she says, "I thought you didn't want me anymore. I thought . . . you know . . . because we weren't having sex, you must be seeing someone else."

"Well," he says, reaching for his glass of rye. "I'm not."

"I had her"—a hopeless laugh—"I had her pregnant."

"I've no intention of getting anyone pregnant."

"You want kids, though, right?"

He empties his drink. His thoughts drift. And then he hears himself say, "There's always adoption."

She twists around. "What?"

Her astonishment triggers his own. "I'm just pointing out," he says, "that you don't have to get anyone pregnant to have a kid."

"But . . ." She comes up on her elbow. "Would *you* adopt?"

"I might," he says cautiously.

"By yourself?"

"I wouldn't do it by myself." Wouldn't he? Why is he saying this? The effect he is having on her, the shifting of emotion across her face, holds his interest.

"Would you do it with me?"

"Why not?"

"Really?"

"You're the woman in my life."

"I can't believe you're saying this." She sinks onto his chest. "We'd have to get married, wouldn't we?"

"Maybe not."

Silence. He can feel her deciding to let that go for now.

"A boy or a girl?" she asks.

"A girl, I think."

"A newborn?"

"They don't have any problems finding homes."

"So, how old?"

"Seven," he says. "Eight."

"That old?"

"It's just a thought."

A thought about bringing a woman into the picture. A

mother figure, who will provide a type of comfort he can't. It's a surprising turn of events, but here it is, and it must attest to the fact that all along he has been motivated by the better part of his love.

For a moment he sees himself in this virtuous light. And then he begins to grasp what it is he'll be sacrificing and he's resentful and confused and he gets out of bed, saying he forgot to lock the basement door.

Down in the apartment he paces himself into a more composed frame of mind. He doesn't want to do harm. He wants to rescue, to protect. Nancy will help him. He's not above admitting to himself that he needs her help. Should he let her see what he has done so far? He looks around. Why not? But she can't tell anyone. He goes tense with fear. What if right now she's on the phone to one of her sisters or to that evil-minded Angie? He leaves the apartment and blunders back up the stairs.

Chapter Six

SATURDAY MORNING IS when Celia gives piano lessons, first to Rachel, then, in exchange for discounted cigarettes, to Leonard Wong's mother, and then to Leonard. Today, however, the Wongs are attending some family function, and Celia has decided that rather than suffer in the stifling apartment she and Rachel will finally get pedicures at Angie's Nails, something Celia's friend Laura has been urging them to do for a couple of years now.

According to Laura, Angie used to be a plus-size model before being set up in business by her mafioso boyfriend, who, Laura likes to imagine, supplied the real-looking hands and feet featured in the window display. She says that the beauticians are Cambodian girls with hardly any English and so you have to figure that they're working for slave wages and you should give them big tips. The customers are everybody: single mothers, prostitutes, rich housewives, business women, gay men, Middle Eastern men. "Typical Cabbagetown," Laura says.

By which she means that in Cabbagetown nothing is typical. Dandelion seeds from the derelict yard of a rooming house sail over a hedge to land on the perfect grass of a mansion. Dollar stores share a wall with four-star restaurants. Along the section of Gerrard Street where Angie's Nails is, there's a drug-dealer hangout posing as a donut shop, a West Indian grocery store, a Tamil restaurant, a Chinese herbalist, a cosmetic surgeon's office advertising Botox injections, and a mysterious, always closed store called Belinda's, whose grimy window display of dolls, wigs, majorette batons, and stiff, frilly dresses for little girls never changes.

Angie's window is empty, the hands and feet gone. As soon as Rachel is through the door she asks the large, glamorous woman at the front desk—Angie, presumably—what happened to them.

"I had to take them down," Angie says. "It's so hot there, they were all melting."

"Are they wax?" Celia asks.

"Nope, real." She laughs at the look on Rachel's face. "I don't know what they are. Wax . . . plastic. So what'll it be today, ladies?"

"Just pedicures," Celia says.

"We play the piano so we cut our own nails," Rachel says.

"Gotcha."

They pick their colours (Celia goes for plum, Rachel for pale pink), then follow Angie's clicking high-heeled sandals and big, swaying rear end past the manicure tables to the back of the store. It's not so busy here. Only two of the many leather recliners are occupied: one by a black woman who looks to be in her late forties, the other by a dark, bearded man wearing a turban. Angie indicates where Celia and Rachel should sit, then says to the man, "She taking good care of you, Feroze, honey?"

He pulls his eyes away from the muted TV, which is mounted in a corner up near the ceiling, and gives Angie his full and serious attention. "No complaints," he says.

Celia and Rachel remove their shoes and stick their feet in the footbaths. "Long toes," Rachel's pedicurist says to her. She's smiling. She intends it as a compliment. "And pretty—" She touches her own hair.

"Thank you," Rachel murmurs. She accepts compliments graciously but a little sadly, as another child might accept a gift she already has.

"Women pay a lot of money to get that colour," the black woman volunteers. She's sitting directly across from Celia and Rachel. "That honey blond."

"She wants purple streaks," Celia says.

"Oh, no, no!" the woman cries.

"Not anymore I don't," Rachel says, flashing Celia an incensed look.

"No, you leave it just as it is," the woman says.

The woman's hair is a youthful mass of shiny reddish brown spirals like mahogany wood shavings. She's wearing a purple-and-yellow-striped shift and lots of gold bands on her wrists. If she hadn't spoken, Celia would have said she was from the West Indies—almost all of the older black people you meet are, originally—but her accent is American: New York or New Jersey. By the attentive tilt of Rachel's head, Celia can tell that she, too, has placed the woman as American. Oh, God, Celia thinks. She's going to ask her if she's from New York City and knows a black architect named Robert Smith.

And so she does, though not that directly. "Are you American?" she starts out.

The woman laughs. "Is it obvious?"

"Not *obvious*," Rachel says.

"Well, as a matter of fact, I am." Her smile shifts to Celia. "My daughter had to have surgery, a hip replacement. I came up to help with the kids." She nods toward the reception area, where a child around ten years old shakes a rag doll at a baby in a stroller. "They're staying close to the bowl of free mints," the woman says.

Rachel has dutifully craned to look. Now it's back to the interrogation. "You don't happen to be from New York City, do you?"

"How'd you know that?"

Rachel clutches her armrests. Since there's no stopping her, Celia decides to help her along. "Her father lives in New York," she says but feels unexpectedly ashamed, as if the woman must know it's a fabrication. "At least we think he does," she amends.

"He *does*," Rachel says.

"Okay," Celia says.

"He *does*. You don't *know*."

The implications of this exchange float out over the salon, over the bent heads of the pedicurists.

"Once a New Yorker, always a New Yorker," the black woman says genially.

The man in the turban is finished, his still rather longish toenails having been painted a clear gloss. The pedicurist slips a pair of rubber sandals on his feet and walks him to the drying table up at the front.

"He doesn't know about me," Rachel says, "that's why." That's why her father lives in New York, she means.

"I see," the woman says, evidently following.

"He's black," Rachel says.

The woman pretends surprise. "Is he?"

"He's Robert Smith. The architect."

"He's an architect!"

"Yes."

"Well," the woman says, "that's an interesting job." She looks down at her toes, which are being painted the same purple as the stripes in her dress.

Rachel keeps staring at her and then she shrugs and says, "I suppose so," and leans over to investigate her own toes. Just like that, she shakes off her disappointment that the woman hasn't heard of him.

I shouldn't get so worked up, Celia thinks. But it's distressing how Rachel persists in believing that she's going to run into a black person from New York City who, simply because he or she is black, will know her father. The odds, as Celia has told her, are a million to one (more like a billion to one considering that his last name might not be Smith and it's anybody's guess where he lives, let alone what he does). The odds of their meeting a black New Yorker *at all* are high enough. Why does the intermediary have to be black, anyway? And why won't Rachel entertain the possibility that after all these years her father might be living someplace else? "I have a *feeling*," is all Rachel will say. And yet between encounters with black New Yorkers her interest in his whereabouts seems to dwindle to nothing. She never asks about him, and the one time Celia sounded her out as to whether or not she missed having a father, she reflected for a moment and then said, "How should I know?"

"They must have run out of mints," the woman chuckles as her grandchild approaches, pushing the stroller.

"The lady said we could come back," the child says shyly.

"I'm done here, I think," the woman says. "Hi, honey," she says to the baby, who is clapping. "Say hi to the lady. See? Over there."

The baby stops clapping and gazes at Celia with large, gentle eyes.

"Hi, darling," Celia says to the baby. "Aren't you lucky to have your big sister to look after you."

"Big brother," the woman says.

"Oh, I'm sorry," Celia says.

The child—the boy—studies the rag doll in his hands. The woman slips on a pair of sandals and comes to her feet. "Nice to meet you," she says cheerfully.

"Yes!" Celia says too loudly. "Nice to meet you, too!"

The moment they're out of earshot Rachel hisses, "That was so embarrassing."

"I know," Celia says.

Rachel frowns up at the television. Celia takes a magazine from the table beside her and flips through the pages. This was supposed to be a treat, their first professional pedicures, which Rachel will now remember as the day her mother more or less announced that, when it comes to black children, she can't tell the boys from the girls. It wasn't his blackness, though. It was his red shorts and sweet, round face and his attentiveness to the baby. She wonders how Rachel knew. Or maybe she didn't know and simply had the sense to keep her mouth shut. Rachel has a social canniness far beyond her years. That this should be so strikes Celia with fresh pleasure and amazement. "I'm sorry," she says. Rachel sighs. Celia leaves her alone until they're both putting on the rubber sandals, and then she says, "That pink is perfect for you."

More sighing.

"Seashell pink," Rachel's pedicurist offers.

"Yes, my favourite pink," Rachel says in an unnaturally friendly voice intended to ostracize Celia further. "I have a lot of clothes this colour."

The black woman has left. Celia and Rachel are placed on the same side of the drying table, the side facing the reception area. As soon as their feet are under the light panel Rachel picks up a tabloid and pretends to be immersed.

Celia watches the action. It has gotten quite busy. The customers coming in all exclaim at how hot it is out there. A woman arrives with a box of chocolates she worries might be melted. They're for Angie, a belated birthday gift, but Angie says, "I need those like a hole in the head," and tells the woman to offer them around. The woman seems unoffended. She's freckled and small, with a face that's both childlike and weathered. She opens the box, declares the contents "kind of squished, not bad," and extends it to a couple of teenaged girls who are choosing their nail colours. "Get them while they're hot," she says. The girls each take one. The woman turns to Celia and Rachel. "Pot of Gold," she says, and then lets out a cry as her leg buckles. The box drops to the floor. The woman teeters. Celia, jumping to her feet, catches her by the wrist.

"Oh, jeez," the woman gasps. "I'm sorry."

"Are you all right?" Celia says.

"Yeah, I'm good. Thanks a lot."

Angie has come over. She puts an arm around the woman's waist and leads her to a bench. "Honey, why aren't you using that cane I bought you?"

"I left it somewhere," the woman mutters.

"Yeah, sure you did."

"Only one fell out," Rachel says. She has retrieved the box and is offering it to the woman.

"Oh, thanks, sweetie. Leave it there." She waves at the table. "Help yourself to as many as you want."

"You can have one," Celia says.

"Two?" Rachel says in a small, pleading voice, holding up two fingers.

So Celia is back in her good graces. "Okay," she says.

"Three?" Rachel tries.

"Three. That's it."

"I get these leg spasms," the woman informs Celia. "It's like somebody stuck a knife in you. Seriously. I've never had one this bad, though."

"That sounds awful," Celia says. She watches Rachel wiggle her fingers above the box. I'm a bad mother, she thinks. I'm a pushover.

Angie crouches in front of Celia and presses her big toe. "You're done," she says. "Unless you want to hang around and save more lives."

Chapter Seven

NANCY SETS DOWN her banjo and lights a joint. Something's bothering her. What? Is it Tasha? Whether Ron remembered to walk her?

Oh, now she remembers: it's the girl Ron told her about. Nancy can understand why he's worried, just not why he's *so* worried—following her around everywhere and watching her house. She keeps forgetting what she has figured out about this. He was abused as a child, that's it. She lets the smoke out of her lungs in a long, reassured breath. She would never ask (he would never say), but if he *was* abused, some things would make a lot more sense.

Usually when the weather's nice she practises out on the fire escape. But she's got the electric heating pad wrapped around her right knee and the cord doesn't reach that far. So she's sitting at her kitchen table, which is really only a shelf hinged to the wall. Anything bigger wouldn't fit. It's an attic apartment: one room, a window at either end. In the front window her ancient air conditioner rattles. The kitchen window looks out onto a blue spruce tree and the robin's nest she watched all spring. No two creatures ever worked harder than those robins, building their nest, guarding it, driving off constant attacks from crows. Then one afternoon it was empty. What happened? Did a gust of wind knock the eggs out? Did the crows eat them? This morning Nancy found a piece of blue eggshell stuck to her windshield and she could have cried.

From that point on, the day went downhill. First, her car wouldn't start. Then the bus never came, so she accepted a lift from a harmless-looking old man in a pickup. He kept glancing back and forth from the road to her lap, interested, she thought, in the box of chocolates she was holding. Finally at a stoplight he said, "Ya got something for me there?"

"Pot of Gold," she told him. "Not for you though, I'm afraid."

"Spreading it around, are ya?" he said.

"Pardon me?" she said.

He shoved his hand between her thighs.

She jumped out and walked the rest of the way, half running to get to Angie's before the chocolates melted. And after all that, Angie didn't even want them. And then, from running, her leg cramped and she had to borrow money from Angie for a taxi home. Frank was good about it when she said she wouldn't be able to work her shift, but she still felt guilty. She phoned Ron for some sympathy. "We don't have to talk long," she said to his machine.

That was eight hours ago. He must still be down in the basement.

She'd like to phone her sister Brenda and hear about the new baby, except if Brenda asks about her and Ron, she's liable to start blurting things, and Ron made her swear on her mother's life that she'd keep her mouth shut. He won't even let her call adoption agencies, not yet. "The minute you start broadcasting your plans," he says, "they fall through." And she thought *she* was the superstitious one. He says he intends to take it one step at a time, and the first step is fixing up a bedroom. Which, if you ask her, should be the third or fourth step, but try telling him that. He used to be sensible and easygoing; almost overnight he's become superstitious and stubborn. Don't get her wrong, she'll take the new Ron over the old, the new Ron being the one who wants the two of them to settle down together. She just needs time to get used to him, that's all.

Another thing about the old Ron . . . he was a person who minded his own business. Now he's obsessed with a little girl he's never even met. He thinks she's being molested, so it's sweet how upset he is, but Nancy feels—and she told him as much—that it's time he phoned Children's Aid. "You wouldn't have to give your name," she pointed out.

He frowned. He seemed to be considering it.

"A lot of children are in bad situations," she went on. "So that's why it's good we're adopting, right? Because then at least one little girl will have love and a safe place. Right?"

This perked him up. "You think she'll like the room?"

"Oh, yeah. Of course."

She held back from saying, yet again, that one of the upstairs bedrooms would have been a better idea. The adoption agency people will set him straight. And if they don't, the little girl will.

The little girl. If the agency people find out about their stints in rehab, Nancy has a feeling that the girl they get will be a leftover, somebody no one else wanted. She'll be hard to handle or stuck in a wheelchair. Nancy hasn't brought this up with Ron in case it puts him off. It doesn't put *her* off. The more unlovable the girl is, the more love she'll need poured into her, and Nancy is jam-packed with love. If the girl is in a wheelchair, she'll decorate it with pretty decals and push her around the neighbourhood. She'll massage her legs with essential oils.

She unwraps the heating pad from her own leg. The pain is a soft ache, not too bad. She tries phoning Ron again. "I guess you're still working," she says to the machine.

At least he's not with another woman, she can stop torturing herself about that. She can put away the psychic pouch.

She picks up the banjo again. "Yellow bird," she sings, "up high in banana tree . . ."

Chapter Eight

*H*IS MORNING IS spent painting the bookcase. After lunch, he cleans the brushes and carries the paint cans out to the garbage shed.

It comes to him, with the sound of the shed door banging shut, that except for buying a few posters and picking up the dollhouse from J. R. Miniatures, he's almost finished. The fact takes him by surprise, as if he heard it from someone else. He returns to the basement and looks around at what he's done. He starts touching things: the desk and chair, the dresser, the toy chest, the sofa. All the furniture is white. Yellow was what Nancy recommended—something warm and sunny—but white is purer, cleaner, the colour of nurses and angels, and against the mauve walls it turns out to be unexpectedly vibrant.

He touches the TV: a thirty-two-inch Samsung high-definition plasma. He runs a finger down the stack of Walt Disney DVDs. In the middle of the night, lying on the canopy bed among the stuffed animals, he has watched every one of them. If he had to choose a favourite it would be *Cinderella*, for obvious reasons, he supposes: the flight from the evil stepmother, the tiny feet. He straightens the stack and aligns it with the edge of the screen. He wanders into the bathroom and touches the unused bar of Ivory soap. The container of Johnson's baby powder.

It has been a form of worship, putting the apartment together. Not even when he was refurbishing the Westinghouse did he feel this kind of dedication to making a thing perfect. He strokes the chrome faucet and tries to recapture the sensation of being in a dream. He can't do it. The work was the lullaby, and with the work virtually over he finds himself wide awake. He's here, in the moment. In the middle of . . . what? What would you call this? Not an apartment really, not in the normal sense. Showroom, he thinks.

He climbs up to the kitchen and pours himself a drink. Then he goes into the shop, unlocks the front door, and checks his phone messages. One is from Vince, telling him that his car is ready. He finds his insurance forms and heads across the street.

A couple of days ago, while he was at the garage checking to see if Vince had installed Nancy's alternator, he noticed a 1994 silver Civic for sale at eight hundred dollars. He bargained it down to six hundred cash. "It'll do the job," Vince said, and for a quaking moment Ron thought Vince knew that the job was to cruise around Rachel's neighbourhood in something more anonymous than a van with Ron's Appliance Repair written on the side.

How will he explain the car to Nancy? As he's driving out of the garage, the thought of accounting for himself makes him feel claustrophobic. Nancy has been acting like a wife lately, ever since he mentioned adoption. Why did he do that? Thank God he refrained from saying he didn't want just *any* girl, but he showed her the basement room. The next morning, what horrified him even more than the heartless way he'd misled her was the glimpse he'd gotten of his fantasy—how it seemed to have a will and inevitability of its own. And yet his devotion to it held. As soon as he picked up a paintbrush, the dreamlike state returned.

A small car is easier on gas—there's his explanation, and it's not a lie. He drives on, relieved, and only now becomes conscious of where he's headed. A few minutes later, at twenty-five past three, he pulls up in front of the parched front lawn of Spruce Court School.

Four days have passed since he was here. Such has been the basement's compulsive hold on his mind. He massages his wet palm on the gearshift and tells himself that without the smokescreen of Tasha he'd better not get out of the car. He glances in the rearview mirror and is startled by his manic-eyed reflection.

What's happening to him? Three weeks ago he was a man in charge of his life. He worked in his shop, paid his bills, returned his phone calls. Maybe once or twice a week he drove by a school, but there was a line in his head and he never once came close to crossing it.

He's close now. Unless he finds another overpowering distraction, he's in trouble.

Chapter Nine

*H*IS MOTHER DIED on the morning of his eleventh birthday. She was on her way home from the Dominion Store with his chocolate ice cream cake when she stepped into the intersection against a red light and a car ran her down. At first she seemed unhurt. Several witnesses described how she got right back up and said to the driver, "You'll be paying for that," referring, it was presumed, to the smashed cake. Then she fell again.

He still can't believe it, not so much that she died but that only seconds away from death she mustered the nerve and presence of mind to lecture the driver. She'd been a shy woman and by her own frustrated admission a scatterbrain. The reason she'd called him Constantine, she'd said, was because it meant "firm and unwavering," unlike her.

Only *she* ever called him by his full name. Outside of the house he was Con, and from a very early instinct not to draw attention to himself he told people it was short for the more normal-sounding Conrad. He started going by the name Ron in his midtwenties, after buying Ron's Appliance Repair. For the sake of a single letter he couldn't see changing all the sales receipts and invoices, let alone the neon sign. His father, who was still alive and had always called him Buddy anyway, said, "Your mother would have understood." (Would she? In his dreams, the ones where she came back from the dead to finish the ironing or to wash the kitchen floor, she seemed sad and disappointed. "I'm no different," he'd tell her, and yet the truth was—and he had the experience of it every morning when he woke up—he *felt* different. He felt more himself: disguised by ordinariness . . . Ron of Ron's Appliance Repair.)

She was buried in a church cemetery in the tiny southwestern Ontario town where she'd been born. A few days later a group of women showed up at the house to ask his father if he'd like to donate any of her clothes to the Crippled Civilians. His father told them to take whatever they could find. "There isn't much," he apologized. Except for her winter boots and some boxes in the spare bedroom, he and Ron had already cleared out nearly everything: her clothes and toiletries, her metal hair curlers that reminded Ron of a bunch of tiny carburetors, her scarves and gloves, and all her old purses with their residue of pennies and lint-coated Chiclets. An antique toy dealer had bought the collection of stuffed monkeys, and a bookseller had carted off the books, though most of them were rippled and stained from her habit of reading in the bath.

And now the churchwomen. Once they were gone the only thing left that had been hers alone was the black-and-white framed photograph, which Ron's father said Ron could keep in his bedroom.

It was a photograph of a girl standing with her hands on her hips and her legs planted apart. Somebody had written

"Yvonne 6 years" on the cardboard backing, but Ron's mother had always doubted it could be her. "I never stood like that in my life," she said. She thought that the girl was her sister, Doreen, who'd been the strong-willed, confident one. Whatever the case, it made no difference to Ron. For him, the keepsake was the Y-shaped crack in the glass from the time his mother accidentally knocked the photograph off the mantelpiece. Being forked, the crack represented not only her first initial but also the warring emotions of protectiveness and exasperation that brought her most vividly to his mind. Not that he welcomed these emotions or was even able to name them. The thought of her was a barely lit fire that nobody, including his father, could be bothered to keep going.

So it was up to Ron. Alone, after school, he lay on the couch and visualized everything she would have done that particular day if she were still alive. He was faithful to her habit of starting one chore and then, a few minutes later, abandoning it for another. Sometimes he drew a chart to illustrate where the chores took her: from the kitchen to the backyard to the basement, and so on. The tangled circuit he ended up with seemed eerily significant, as if he had copied down a message from an alien. He gave the charts names— "Commander," "Junior," "Rochester"—after his favourite vacuum cleaner models, and then he put them in an envelope labelled, simply, MOTHER. Meanwhile, as he was doing all this, he yelled out replies to questions he imagined her calling from another room. "What?" he'd yell. "I'll be right there!" He set a place for her at the table but always whisked it away again before his father got home.

His father had given up his position as an Alcan aluminum sales rep and accepted a desk job at the head office. Sometimes on his way home he picked up takeout Chinese or Kentucky Fried Chicken. The rest of the time it was Swanson frozen suppers or canned spaghetti. Barbecued steaks on Sundays. After supper, instead of disappearing into the third-floor office as he'd always done before, he poured himself a rum and Coke and sat with Ron in front of the television.

Here, a complicated undercurrent of decorum came into play, based on his strict and, to Ron, still largely mysterious views on life. Jokes at the expense of drunks and confused old people weren't funny, but it was all right to laugh at overweight people getting stuck in doorways and blind people knocking over priceless vases. When *Mutual of Omaha's Wild Kingdom* was on, you rooted for the lion, not the gazelle, the wolf, not the deer. During commercials his father sometimes came right out and declared his positions in the form of warnings and words of advice along the lines of "Never do business with a man who wears jewellery" and "Bad poker players blink a lot"—flat, open-and-shut statements not necessarily connected to what they'd just been watching and often hinting at an acquaintance with the seamier side of life. One of his favourites was, "Nobody wants to hear the unvarnished truth," which Ron took to mean that there were things that he, Ron, wouldn't want to hear. What could they be? Was he adopted? Had his father killed somebody? Was his aunt Doreen, who said, "Holy shit" and "Kiss my ass," a sex maniac?

In the hour or so before his bedtime Ron liked to take apart and reassemble one of their small appliances. He had discovered that even without the expectation of his mother's praise to spur him on, he could still tap into pleasure, only of a different kind, hypnotic and private, which his father's casual interest hardly grazed. "Everything under control?" his father would ask. "You sure you can get that all back together?"

One night, as Ron began to dismantle the vacuum cleaner, the question was, "How many times did your mother break that thing?"

He sounded good-humoured, but Ron's instinct to shield her prevailed and he said, untruthfully, "She never really broke it."

"Pretty quiet around here," his father then said. "With just the two of us."

That his father might also be missing her came as a surprise to Ron. "Sometimes," he admitted.

It must have been only a few days later that his father brought up the subject of Margaret and Jenny. He asked if Ron's mother had ever talked to him about her old friend from high school Margaret McGraw.

Ron wasn't sure.

"I thought she might have mentioned her," his father said. "Margaret's grandfather, Arthur McGraw, was the co-inventor of the pop-up toaster. Before then you had to open up the sides to get the toast out."

"I never heard of him," Ron said, struck that it had taken two grown men to invent a simple release mechanism.

Ron's father went on to say that a couple of months ago he had run into Margaret McGraw—now Margaret Lawson—and found out she'd buried her husband the same week they'd buried Ron's mother. Mr. Lawson had been a rich chicken farmer but had died without a cent. It was possible, Ron's father said, that he and Ron had eaten Mr. Lawson's chickens, which were called Jenny's, after the daughter. "You'd like Jenny," he told Ron. "She's really smart."

Ron couldn't imagine liking a girl, no matter how smart she was. "Smart how?" he asked with a prick of jealousy.

"Well, she's only eight and she's in grade five. They've got her in a school for gifted children. On a scholarship, fortunately, because there's no money."

Ron wondered why, if his father knew so much about these people, he'd never mentioned them before. It wasn't the kind of question he felt comfortable asking, though. He asked how Mr. Lawson had died.

"Choked to death," his father said.

"How?"

"On a chicken bone."

"A *Jenny's* chicken?"

"I guess the man ate his own chickens."

"Holy smokes."

His father didn't seem to find this particularly remarkable. He wanted to get back to Mrs. Lawson's money troubles. He said that Mr. Lawson had been a compulsive gambler, a poker player. Eventually he'd lost everything—the chicken farm, their savings, everything.

"He must have blinked a lot," Ron noted.

It took his father a minute. "Right. He probably did." What it all boiled down to, he said, was that Mrs. Lawson could no longer make ends meet. The salary she earned as a receptionist for a foot doctor hardly covered the interest on her debts. Just last week, after holding off as long as she could, she sold Jenny's horse to the people who'd been boarding it. Ron's father didn't learn about the horse until too late.

"If I'd known," he told Ron, "I'd have tried to work something out. I said to Mrs. Lawson, I said, 'Listen, before things get any worse, you and Jenny had better come and live with my son and me.'"

Ron was still back with the husband. "What?"

"I told them they should live with us. Until they can get on their feet again."

"How long will that be?"

"We'll have to play it by ear."

HIS FATHER drove to get Jenny and Mrs. Lawson late Sunday morning, returning a few hours later with a U-Haul trailer in tow. Ron, who'd been waiting on the front porch, thought that they'd picked up the horse; somehow they'd managed to get Jenny's horse back. The truth was more incredible. They'd brought the furniture, and not just odds and ends but beds, dressers, chairs, tables, a gigantic dollhouse, plus boxes of dishes and towels and then all their clothes, in garbage bags and falling off hangers.

Under Mrs. Lawson's direction, Ron and his father unloaded the trailer and placed the furniture around the house. Their furniture, if Mrs. Lawson felt it didn't match or was in the way, got banished to the basement. Far from being the sad, rundown lady Ron had been expecting, Mrs. Lawson was high-spirited and young looking, a lot younger looking than his mother, though they would have been the same age. Where his mother had been on the heavy side, Mrs. Lawson was thin, with no hips or chest. She had wispy light brown hair, slanted eyes, and a small, flat nose, like a baby's. In a few weeks Ron would learn that she was part Chinese.

She called his father Clarkson, their last name. Ron she

called Constantine, though his father had introduced him as Con. Ron never went by his full name, and hearing it said, especially in front of Jenny, was torture. For most of the afternoon Jenny sat on the porch bench holding a pen and notebook and watching him as if this were *her* house and she resented the intrusion. Never once did she smile; she hardly said a word. When Ron's father told one of his blind-man jokes she narrowed her eyes. She wore yellow shorts and a puffy white blouse that looked too big and a yellow plastic watch, also too big, which slid around her wrist and which she kept checking. Off and on she jotted something on her pad, giving Ron the idea she was making a list of their belongings, but then he passed near enough to see entire sentences. He saw her chewed nails and the ladybug clips in her hair. Her hair was as fine as her mother's, only reddish blond. Otherwise, except for a birthmark on her cheek, she and her mother looked alike: the eyes, the thinness.

It was evening by the time everything was moved in. Ron's father offered to pick up some Kentucky Fried Chicken, but Mrs. Lawson said, "Your fast food days are over," and in her own frying pan made a mushroom-and-cheese omelet, which she served on her own white china plates. Over supper his father told stories Ron had heard many times before about the characters he used to run into during his travelling salesman days: the woman outside of St. Mary's who swept the highway in front of her house; the trucker who travelled with a pet squirrel in his glove compartment. Mrs. Lawson laughed. Jenny, as before, remained stony, and in her cool, lidless eyes and the clink of the spoon against her teeth, Ron sensed danger, not necessarily to himself but as if she were a wild animal that, for the time being, accepted the company of humans. She had changed into an old-fashioned-looking dress, navy blue and cone shaped. It had a white frill at the neck and in the middle of the chest a large pocket, like a door, in which the outline of her notebook showed. As his father began clearing the plates she removed the notebook and turned to Mrs. Lawson and said, "Mother, should I read my new story to them?"

"Maybe they'd rather hear it after dessert," Mrs. Lawson said.

Ron's father waved a hand. "Let's hear it now. Fire away."

"Jenny reads and writes at a grade-six level," Mrs. Lawson informed Ron.

The story was called "Moving Day." It was about how their furniture had been in an aunt's basement but was now arriving at the Clarksons'. The way Jenny read, in a singsong voice and with hand gestures, was astonishing, as if she'd practised over and over. She said that the weather today was lovely, not a cloud in the sky (an upward gesture), and that at the sight of the house, her heart (she patted it) leapt with joy because the brick was the same yellow as her old place. At this point she trailed off. She squinted at the page.

"Can I start over?" she asked, not looking up. A blush began to climb her face.

"Sure you can," Ron's father said. "You can tell it any way you want."

The blush had Ron enthralled. It was like a natural calamity. It drowned out the birthmark, then seeped away, like water into sand.

"Constantine—" she said. His attention snapped back. She was talking about how he'd almost dropped her dollhouse. She said she'd trembled with fear (a shake of her shoulders) but luckily nothing fell out. "All and all," she finished, "it was an exciting day of work and fun." She closed the notebook. "There's more," she murmured, "but it's not ready yet."

Ron's father said, "Well, that was great." He looked at Ron. "Wasn't that great, Buddy?"

"Yeah," Ron said.

One corner of Jenny's mouth twitched. She slipped the notebook back into the pocket of her dress.

Ron went on looking at her. Her bent little head with its strands of pinkish hair.

Chapter Ten

*I*T'S FRIDAY NIGHT, nine thirty. Rachel is lying on the porch sofa, listening to Evanescence. The iPod is Mika's, as is the penlight she's waving around. She directs the beam at her feet. After almost an entire week her nail polish is still perfect, not a single chip.

Inside, at his dining room table, Mika marks exam papers. Rachel can see the top of his head and his white hair—his *flaxen* hair—flitting up in the breeze from the rotating fan. Her mother is at the motel and won't be back until late because Bernie Silver is on holiday, so she's playing his sets.

At ten o'clock, her mother is going to call. Rachel can't decide whether or not she'll talk to her. Felix was the one who knocked over the lemonade, but her mother blamed *her* for putting the glass on a pile of books. And then she wouldn't let her help clean up. "I'll do it!" she yelled, grabbing the paper towels Rachel had raced to get from the kitchen.

As she was leaving she said she was sorry for losing her temper, and Rachel said, "That's okay," but only to avoid more aggravation. When you don't have a father, it isn't fair to have a mother who gets so mad. Maybe Rachel will tell her. She pictures her at the motel, her spiky hair and nobody putting money in the vase, and she lets out a frustrated moan to feel her anger softening. She turns onto her side, facing the street.

This next song is her favourite, "My Immortal." She sings along: "And if you have to leave, I wish that you would just leave . . ." She switches the penlight off and on to the beat. In ten days she's going to music camp. She wonders if Mika will let her take the iPod.

"Go ahead and fire me," Nancy says. She sinks onto the stool next to the chopping block and lights a cigarette.

"Forget about it," Frank says. "Nobody got splashed. Only one glass broke."

"By some miracle," Nancy says.

"You provided the entertainment." He gives the grill a last swipe with the wire brush, then tosses the brush in the sink. "Did you see how Andria clapped?"

Andria, his one-year-old daughter. He has four kids under the age of seven, and every Friday night his wife, Bianca, brings them to the restaurant for supper. Their tray of drinks was what Nancy dropped.

"She's so cute," Nancy says about Andria. "You're so lucky."

"I thank God every day." He pulls off his chef's hat and rubs his head. He's a large, bald, pink-faced man with round blue eyes that widen when he's listening to you, as if he's never met anybody more interesting. Even with his wife he does this.

"Are you okay to drive?" he asks.

"Yeah, sure." She rubs her knee. "Anyways, when I'm sitting it never—"

"Never what?"

She waves her cigarette. She's crying.

"Hey. What's going on with you?" He comes over to her. "Is it Ron?"

She shrugs.

"You still think he's fooling around on you?"

"No." She dabs her eyes with the hem of her apron. "I don't know."

"He's not hitting you, is he?"

That makes her laugh. "Ron? Are you kidding? He'd have to *see* me to hit me."

"Okay, look. Take some time off. Go visit your sisters. Relax."

His eager pink face hangs in front of her like a party balloon, and she finds herself ashamed of her unhappiness, and of her bad leg, too. She comes to her feet. "I'm good now, Frank," she says. She tells him to run on home and tuck in the kids, she'll close up.

When he's gone, she starts lowering the blinds in the restaurant windows. The Korean variety store across the street is still open, and the old man, the grandfather, is out watering the flowers they have for sale on the sidewalk. Big crayon-coloured flowers in the shape of birds' heads and scorpions and feather dusters. They sell black flowers, too: black tulips and lilies. Who buys those? Devil worshippers?

Devil worshippers make her think of her psychic pouch, and she takes it out of her apron pocket (she's glad she never got around to throwing it away), presses it against her heart, and goes through the rigamarole of chanting, "Red is your blood, red is my heart . . ." and so on, while trying to imagine Ron smiling at her lovingly. When was the last time he smiled at her lovingly? She can't even remember. No, she can: it was the night he said he wanted to adopt. They were so happy, weren't they? *She* was. But then he got all wrapped up in renovating the basement apartment, which she understood . . . sort of. Well, now the renovation is done, it's perfect, there's even baby shampoo and Ivory soap in the bathroom, and instead of taking the next step he's drinking hard again, and every time she tries to talk to him about phoning adoption agencies, he puts her off. He's says he's too busy to think about it right now, he's behind in the shop.

If he has changed his mind about wanting to adopt, which she prays to God he hasn't, why did he buy the soap and shampoo? A couple of nights ago he wanted the two of them to watch a National Geographic DVD about cheetahs, and when she suggested that they watch it on the new big-screen TV, you should have seen the look he gave her!

"I don't mean have sex or anything," she said. But she thought, So what if we do? It's not like it's our little girl's bedroom or anything, not yet.

She puts the psychic pouch back in her pocket and lowers the last few blinds. Maybe Frank's right, she tells herself. Maybe she needs to go away and leave Ron alone to work through whatever it is he has to work through.

"You DON'T know what love is," Celia sings to the businessman across from her. On a red ribbon around his neck he wears the plastic identity badge from whatever convention he was at earlier. Things couldn't have gone all that well because here he is, getting plastered all by himself. He moans along to the songs, occasionally shouts a lyric or two.

Except for him and a pair of hectically smiling middle-aged women who glance at the door whenever Wanda, to-night's waitress, comes in (it would seem they've been mis-led about the Casa Hernandez's eligible-bachelor population), the place is empty. At night, as Celia is discovering, people show up for Bernie, and when they find out he's on holiday they go either to some other bar or outside to the patio for the breeze off the lake.

She finishes the song with a little riff she picked up from Diana Krall. The man claps twice, two whacks of his outstretched hands, as if he were summoning slaves. The women smile apologetically and stand to leave.

Celia starts in on "Love for Sale."

"For sale!" the man blares.

Wanda comes over to pick up Celia's empty wine glass. "Cheapsteaks," she hisses, referring to the two women and meaning, of course, "cheapskates." She's from Serbia; she's only been in the country a year. Since the time she was tipped a hundred dollars by a table of French-Canadian hockey players, her idea of a reasonable tip has skyrocketed. She wags Celia's glass: Refill?

Celia shakes her head. At the end of this set she'll have a beer down in the kitchen with George. Before that, though, she'll phone Rachel. She can't believe she jumped down her throat over spilled lemonade. She can only think that the heat in their apartment is getting to her.

RACHEL AIMS the flashlight in his direction and switches it off and on. Is she signalling somebody? Ron checks his rearview mirrors. Other than a woman climbing into her SUV, the lane's deserted.

He has parked next to the dumpster. People park here all

the time, and the streetlight up ahead is burned out, so even with all the windows down he feels invisible. For a change, the landlord isn't on the porch. Neither are the dogs. It's just Rachel, by herself.

"Shine it at your feet," he says.

He wishes he'd brought along a pair of binoculars. And then it occurs to him: maybe he has. In the trunk he keeps finding things—nylon cord, a blanket—he can't remember having put there. He opens the glove compartment and fumbles around. Nope, no flashlight. Only his *Perly's* guide and the roll of duct tape he bought to secure the broken rearview mirror.

He takes out the tape and sets it on the dashboard. "Come on, sweetheart," he says. Her light seems to intensify and it is from this, rather than from the sudden dimness of the world around him, that he becomes conscious of the power failure. He climbs out of the car.

Rachel descends the porch steps. "I just want to see!" she calls over her shoulder. Ron starts moving toward her. It's dark but not pitch black, because of the cars on Parliament: Rachel aims her light that way, then sweeps it past him and looks down her own street.

He reaches the curb.

Should he cross? No, he thinks. Yes.

He takes a step.

She turns and runs into the house.

Through the living room window he makes out her staggering beam.

CELIA IS wrapping up her set with "Ain't Misbehavin'," and Wanda is over by the window, gazing dreamily at the Scotia

Bank building, where her married boyfriend works as a security guard, when the lights go out.

"Oh, my God," Wanda says.

The businessman across from Celia jerks awake. In the stumpy flame from his candle his face is ancient.

"The whole city, it went poof!" Wanda says.

"What?" the businessman says.

"Looks like a power failure," Celia tells him.

"Maybe is the terrorists!" Wanda gasps.

"I think it's too many air conditioners," Celia says, although she's feeling a twist of unease.

The man slides a cell phone out of his jacket pocket. Celia picks up a candle from the nearest table and heads for the bar to use the phone there.

"Forgot to charge the damn thing," the man mutters.

Celia gets a speeded-up busy signal. She tries again, but now there's no dial tone.

"This calls for a Manhattan!" the man declares. He slaps the table and turns to Wanda.

Wanda remains at the window. "Not one single light," she says.

"I'm going home," Celia announces.

The man comes to his feet. "I'd wait if I were you," he says. By grasping the backs of chairs he's making his own way to the bar. "Driving'll be chaos. Hell on wheels."

NANCY POKES her head out her kitchen window. "Ah, jeez," she says. She thinks it's her fault. Just as she turned on her air conditioner the electricity went off . . . in the entire neighbourhood, from what she can see.

* * *

"I HAVE a battery-powered fluorescent lantern," Mika tells Rachel. "Also a windup radio. We'll be able to find out what the story is out there."

He is heading toward the stairwell, Rachel illuminating his path with her penlight.

"You better have it," she says about the light.

"I'm okay," he says. "You just keep guiding me."

He takes a step down. The dogs follow. He orders them back upstairs, but Osmo squeezes by on his right side. Then Happy tries to go through his legs, and he trips. His head hits the wall. He reels, makes a grab for the railing and misses. He tumbles to the floor.

"Mika!" Rachel cries.

No answer, not a sound.

She races down the stairs, calling his name. She drops to her knees. His eyes are closed. He isn't moving. She shakes his shoulder. The dogs lick his face. The penlight slips from her hand and rolls away.

In total darkness she scrambles up the stairs. She gets to the kitchen phone and presses what she thinks is 9–1–1. Nothing happens. She drops the phone and runs outside.

At the bottom of the porch steps she bumps into someone. A man.

"Hey," he says, catching her arm. "What's going on in there?"

"I need to phone nine-one-one!" she cries.

"Are you hurt?"

"No! Mika, he fell! I think he's dead!" She starts sobbing.

"It's okay," he says. "I have a phone in my car. Come on. We'll phone."

Chapter Eleven

*T*HE DRIVING ISN'T bad. It's the pedestrians you've got to watch out for. All the way up Yonge Street gangs of teenagers are strolling into traffic, slapping hoods. There's a lot of excited shouting and hooting. Not having a car radio, Celia still doesn't know what happened but it seems unlikely there's been a terrorist attack.

And yet she can't shake her anxiety. She has to keep telling herself that Rachel is with Mika, and nobody is better prepared for disaster than Mika with his gas generator and windup radio and his boxes of candles and batteries. Right now, he and Rachel will be out on the porch. It's a clear night . . . they'll be looking up at the stars.

She holds on to this picture until she turns off Parliament and sees the police cars. She pulls over, slamming her foot on the accelerator instead of the brake and mounting the curb. She gets out. Kicks off her high heels. People are in the lane, people with flashlights. A plank of light falls alongside her.

Two policemen stand in the middle of Mika's living room. They blind her, then lower their beams. Mika is on the sofa. He holds a towel to his head. Seeing her, he opens his mouth.

"Are you Celia Fox?" the nearest policeman asks.

"Where's my daughter?" she says. Everything pulses: the room, the men.

"I'M NOT going to hurt you," Ron tells her. "I'm taking you somewhere where nobody will ever hurt you again."

She's on the floor. He didn't put her there . . . she slid off the seat. It crossed his mind that he should put her in the trunk but he was afraid she'd suffocate. Anyway, without streetlights, you can't really see into other people's vehicles.

"How are you doing?" he asks. He glances over. Her face is turned away. He can make out only the tender curve of her neck and the earlobe with its pearl stud, like a drop of saliva. "Is the air conditioning too cold for you there?" He adjusts the direction of the vents.

She's able to breathe, he knows that. He was careful not to tape her nostrils. It was like taping a doll. He had her mouth covered before she even began to put up a struggle. Which was pathetically easy to contain. He quickly bound her hands and feet and that was the end of it.

He has seen the same thing happen on nature programs: animals giving up once they accept they've been overpowered. He tries to explain the phenomenon to her: "You're in a state of shock. It keeps you from feeling pain or getting too excited. It's like being injected with a tranquilizing dart. Have you seen those TV shows, you know— *Discovery* and *National Geographic*, where the scientists shoot tranquilizing darts at the animals so they can give them medicine or take their measurements?"

He wonders if he's speaking too technically. That he can speak at all astounds him. His heart is going like a pump drill. His hands, from touching her, feel irradiated. Not since he was a child himself has he touched a child. This time he only did what was necessary to get her into the car and subdued.

The trip isn't a long one: fifteen minutes. He turns into the delivery lane and parks next to his garage, switching on his high beams. All the neighbouring businesses are closed for the day. Still, when he's out of the car he waits, listening, before going around to her door. "Ups-a-daisy," he whispers. He drapes her over his shoulder. She's as weightless as a garment bag.

His high beams, though he stays out of them, guide him across the lawn to the back entrance and straight through the house to the shop. Here, it is completely dark. With his free hand he feels along the counter to the basement door. "Good girl," he says, descending the stairs. At the bottom he puts her down while he goes to get flashlights from the furnace room and to move the car around to the front. When he returns, she's twisting and making choking noises.

"Hold on," he says, alarmed. His hands shake. He has trouble inserting the key. "Bingo," he says, finally jamming it in. He enters the apartment and sets the flashlights on their ends, then comes back for her. She has gone still and quiet. He carries her to the bed and makes a place for her among the stuffed animals. For the first time he notices how fast she's breathing, the rapid throbbing of her chest.

"Okay, let's get that tape off," he says.

His hands won't stop shaking but he finds a corner of the tape and gently pulls. Her lovely mouth, revealed, unsteadies him. He staggers to one side. "I'm a little nervous about all this," he confesses. He has a harder time unwinding the twisted tape from her wrists and ankles. He picks up one of the flashlights and leaves the room to get a knife.

"This should do the trick," he says when he comes back. She hasn't budged. He positions one of the flashlights to shine on her wrists and starts sawing. If he cuts her . . . He doesn't. He gets the tape off, then moves the light again and does her ankles. Her bare feet squirm under the duvet.

"Are you cold?" he asks.

She curls onto her side and begins to whimper—a pathetic animal sound, like a dog left to die.

What should he do? What he *wants* to do is sit on the bed and stroke her quivering little form. If he has ever witnessed anything more heartwrenching, he can't remember. He lifts the duvet and drops it over her legs. She flinches.

"I'll leave you to get yourself settled," he says. "There's a bathroom behind you, a clean glass if you're thirsty." The whimpering doesn't let up. He's not even sure she hears him. He keeps talking anyway, just in case. It's important she understand he isn't some kind of pervert. "If you get hungry or anything, bang on the door. I'll hear you. There's a twenty-four-hour variety store at the corner, and I can run out and get you whatever you like. Ice cream. A chocolate bar. Or I can fix you a sandwich. Grilled cheese. Bacon and tomato. Whatever you like."

The canopy's net curtains are tied back, and for the sake of being able to see her from the doorway he decides to leave them that way. He goes out and double bolts the lock. Her cries seep through. "It's for her own good," he mutters. "For her own good." The apprehension of what he's done, and what it signifies, is striking him in short, stunning blasts: he has abducted her; there's no turning back; it's too late.

He heaves himself up the stairs.

In the shop he paws through drawers until he finds a pack of matches. He strikes one after another as he heads for the kitchen. Nancy brought over a big scented candle a couple of weeks ago, and once he has that lit, he takes a couple of gulps of rye, then carries the candle and his drink back to the shop. He picks up the phone to call Nancy, but the line's dead. He tries his cell. It works, but at Nancy's end there's a rapid busy signal. She has only the one phone. He'll have to wait.

He walks over to the stairwell and listens. She's still whimpering. He returns to the counter and forces out a few whimpers of his own. He can't keep it up, though. A little wick of elation has ignited inside him and is burning through the pity and astonishment, the fear.

He has her. She's his.

Chapter Twelve

"O KAY," CELIA SAYS, once the police fill her in. She releases her breath. They shouldn't have said *missing*. Rachel
isn't missing, she just isn't here; she isn't back yet. Obviously she'd have gone running for help. Maybe the person
she's with is waiting for the phone lines to come back on.

"Celia . . . ," Mika says, coming to stand beside her. All
she can see is the white towel he holds pressed to his head.

"Why did you go down there?" she asks.

He hesitates. She knows he's only forming his thoughts
but his silence goads her. "I don't understand," she says, her
voice rising. "Why would you go down to the basement?"

"To . . . to . . ."

"To *what*?"

"Get the lantern."

"But you have *candles*. Up here. All those candles in the
dining room."

"I . . . I know. Celia . . . I'm . . ." He moves back to the
sofa and sits. "I'm so . . . sorry."

"You went down there in the pitch *dark*?"

"Rachel had the penlight. She was behind me, in the kitchen, guiding the way. Then the damn dogs . . . they . . ."

She stares at him, uncomprehending.

One of the officers is speaking. "What?" she says, turning around.

It's the black officer. He has introduced himself as Constable Joe Bird. The name of the other officer—the young, lanky blond one—she has already forgotten.

"We're checking hospital emergency rooms. But with the phones dead, information is slow in coming in."

"Why are you checking emergency rooms?"

"There might have been an accident. She might have fallen, running around in near-zero visibility."

"Oh, okay." Celia can picture this: a fall, a broken arm or leg.

"At Mr. Ramstad's suggestion"—Bird nods at Mika— "we've had officers around to Tom's Video and the variety store."

"Wong's Variety," the younger officer chips in.

"She hasn't been to either place but we're continuing to canvass stores and homes in the vicinity. What about her friends? Any of them live nearby?"

Celia shakes her head. "Only Leonard Wong." Why didn't Rachel go there? she wonders.

"No others in the neighbourhood?"

"Not nearby. I mean, they're all in Cabbagetown. Her best friend, Lina, lives in Regent Park, but I think she's away—"

"Do you have an address?"

Celia gives it to him and he uses his radio to pass the information to an officer outside. "Anyone else?"—turning to Celia again.

"From around here?"

"Anywhere. Someone she might have gone to if this Lina friend wasn't home."

"She has lots of friends from school. I don't know where they all live, though."

"We'll get those names in a minute." He sets his flashlight on the bookcase, pulls out a notebook, and holds it up to the beam. "Just to verify what Mr. Ramstad told us. Rachel is nine years old, small, thin build, light brown complexion, blue eyes, blond curly hair in a ponytail. Wearing a short white skirt and a red tank top."

"And earrings. Pearl studs." Why is she telling them this? Who's going to notice her ears?

Bird, however, makes a note. "Any visible scars, medical conditions?"

"No. Just . . ."

He waits.

"She's really pretty."

"Okay." But he doesn't write it down, and Celia is aware of coming across as one of those mothers who enter their daughters in beauty pageants.

"I mean, that's what people notice."

"She's an usually beautiful girl," Mika offers quietly. Bird's gaze shifts to him.

"Just a couple of weeks ago," Celia says, "this guy from a modelling agency chased us up the street. He wanted her to take a course."

"What agency?" Bird says alertly.

Celia tells him. "The guy's name was Jason, I think. Yeah, Jason. He seemed all right."

"Anyone else bothering her?"

"Not that she's said."

"Any strange phone calls?"

"No."

Bird returns to his notes. "Father's whereabouts unknown," he reads.

"That's right."

"And there's no other family—no cousins, aunts, no boyfriends or ex-boyfriends she's close to."

"Just us." She glances at Mika, who is visible at the edge of Bird's light. He has let go of the towel, and the bump on his temple is stunningly large. "God, Mika," she says. "Shouldn't you go to the hospital?"

"I'm fine," he murmurs.

For a reason that isn't clear to her or doesn't seem worth pursuing, not right then, Mika has to wait out on the porch while she takes the officers through the house. They begin in her and Rachel's apartment. Bird has instructed her to speak up if anything is missing or appears to have been disturbed. The cracked and toppled ceramic planter out on the deck, the unlocked screen door, the piles of books and sheet music scattered all over the carpet . . . is this how things were left? Celia admits that it is. In the scouring wash of the flashlights she's seeing the handprints on her walls and the worn, shiny places on her upholstery. She opens her desk drawer and takes out the three photos of Rachel in her white lace dress. She hands them to the young officer. "This is her."

"Whoa," he says quietly. He passes them to Bird.

Bird studies each one.

"I keep meaning to get them framed," Celia says.

"She's a beautiful girl all right," Bird says.

It's a concession, an apology, and Celia feels free to press her earlier point: "People remember her."

"When were these taken?"

"Last Christmas. For her school concert. Mika took them."

"Is he a photographer?"

"Well, not a professional."

"Has he taken any other pictures of her?"

"A few." She wonders at his asking. "Over the years, you know."

"Can we borrow these?"

"Okay . . ."

"We might want to start getting her face out there."

"Really?"

"When the power's back."

But why doesn't he imagine that Rachel will be found by then? They've only been searching . . . Celia peers at her watch: a quarter to eleven. "You've been here, what, half an hour?"

"About forty minutes," the young officer says.

"Forty minutes," she repeats, unable to gauge whether that's a long time or no time at all.

A voice comes over Bird's radio. "Go ahead," he says and steps out of the room. Celia hears something about bringing in the canine unit.

"You guys sure are pulling out all the stops," she says to the young officer.

"Dogs can be a big help in the dark."

"Oh. Right." She hadn't thought of that. "So they'll need to get her scent, won't they?"

"If you could let us have some articles of clothing." He clears his throat. "Unwashed articles, that would be great."

She leads him back into her bedroom and rifles through the overflowing laundry basket. She gives him T-shirts and shorts, and he takes a large plastic bag out of one of his pockets and drops them in. "Lucky I'm not a clean freak," she says.

"Don't worry," he says. "I'm not either."

"It's so clean in here," she says as Bird rejoins them. A moment later she realizes she meant *hot*, it's so hot.

In Rachel's bedroom Bird sweeps his light over the dresser. "This is hers?" He's pointing at the brush.

She says it is. Both men, she only now notices, are wearing latex gloves.

"Can we borrow it as well?"

She shrugs, helpless. "Go ahead."

The young officer sets everything he's holding on the bed. From a pocket he extracts another, smaller bag and slips the brush in.

"My prints might be on it," Celia warns.

"That's okay."

Rachel's toothbrush gets put into yet another plastic bag, and it occurs to Celia that they're collecting DNA. "Is this routine?" she asks, indicating the bag. "Do you do this whenever you get a call about a . . ." She can't bring herself to say *missing*. "About a child?"

Bird takes a few seconds to respond. "If the child is supposed be at a certain place and isn't at that place, and there's been a preliminary search, then it's routine, yes, to start collecting evidence."

She nods, though his back is to her. He's a straightforward, careful man, and she appreciates that. She feels the kindness in him. Somebody calls again on his radio and she tenses, but it's only more news about the canine unit. She makes her way back to the living room, where the young officer is studying the snarl of computer wires behind her desk.

"I guess that's an electrical hazard," she says.

"We'll probably be needing your hard drive," he says. "Mr. Ramstad's, as well. So we can go over the chat logs, see who she's been talking to." He looks up. "You never know, right? With kids?"

He seems scarcely more than a kid himself. She wonders about his mother, if his mother worries about his having such a dangerous job, and what it is she herself could be facing suddenly catches up with her. She takes a step, bashing her knee against the coffee table. "Shit," she says. She hobbles toward the deck.

"Are you okay?" He guides her with his light.

"It's just . . . why haven't they found her?"

"Ninety-nine times out of a hundred, kids turn up safe and sound. Especially in cases like this, where there's no sign of forced entry."

The red flasher from a police car strobes the leaves of the horse chestnut. "God, maybe she got on a bus to get *me*."

"Is that a possibility?" asks Bird. He has come up behind the officer.

"No . . . no, she wouldn't . . ."

"Does she normally take buses on her own?"

"She doesn't go anywhere on her own." Her attention has been caught by the scream of approaching sirens. "I should be out there looking."

"No problem. We'll just do a check of downstairs then."

"Where are my shoes?" She glances around. The two

flashlights cross on the floor in front of her, and she stumbles sideways, hitting her leg again. "Shit," she says. "Shit, shit, shit." Horrible, nightmarish images are assaulting her: Rachel tied up, bleeding. Naked . . .

"Shit, shit." She lurches toward the stairwell. Bird is saying something. She grasps the banister and staggers down to the landing, where she falls. An unearthly, rattling cry heaves out of her throat.

Bird kneels next to her. "Are you all right?" He helps her to her feet. "We'll go in the squad car," he says. "I'll drive you, okay?"

"Okay," she whispers.

"We'll just do a quick check of downstairs—"

"No. Now."

Chapter Thirteen

*T*HE RINGING PHONE drags Nancy out of sleep.

"I need you to come over right now."

She sits up. "Is it Tasha?"

"Tasha's fine."

"What's going on?"

"I'll tell you when you get here."

"What's the time?"

"One thirty."

"Okay, well, I just have to get dressed, if I can find the flashlight—"

"The power's back."

She tries her bedside lamp. "Oh. Right."

"Hurry."

BECAUSE OF construction along Laird Avenue, Nancy is forced to backtrack down to Don Mills Road before heading north again. Never once in the three years that she and Ron have been together has he called her in the middle of the night, so she's more than a little nervous. Has a wife he never told her about shown up? Has he shot an intruder?

Maybe he killed somebody by accident, a car accident. It's no secret to her how much rye he puts away these days before getting behind the wheel. She turns on the radio for any reports of a hit and run, but the news is all about the generator failure and people spending hours stuck in elevators and subway cars.

The shop, when she arrives, is dark, the blinds closed. The door, though, is unlocked. She enters and pats along the wall for the light switch. Before she can reach it, a lamp comes on.

"What took you so long?"

He's sitting behind the counter.

"You scared me." She pushes a lawn mower out of her path. "Laird's a mess. I ended up driving around in circles. So what's going on?"

He just looks at her. His big shoulders heave with his breathing.

"Ron?"

"Do you love me?"

She swallows. It's not a question he asks. "Of course I love you."

"Would you do anything for me?"

"Of course I would." She reaches across the counter to hold his hand. "What are you asking me for?"

"Rachel's here."

"Who?"

"Rachel. The little girl."

"The one you've been following?"

"She's downstairs."

"What?"

"I was at her house. Parked across the street. I had this

feeling. She was out on the porch." He's muttering now, not meeting her eye. "The power goes off. She runs inside, then a minute later runs out again, hysterical, saying somebody fell or died. She's not making any sense. So I got her in the car and brought her here."

"What did you do that for?"

"I told you. She was hysterical."

"If somebody died, shouldn't the police—"

He pulls his hand free. "I don't care if somebody died. It's not my business. If the landlord died, good. I care about Rachel being safe."

Nancy nods, distracted by his use of the girl's name. "You haven't ever talked to her, have you? Before?"

"What has that got to do with anything?"

"You just sound like you know her."

"I know what she's been going through." His mouth twists. He grabs a ballpoint pen and begins to click the end.

"So—" Her leg is giving out. She upends the recycling box and sits. "So what are you going to do?"

He keeps on clicking. "I'm going to keep her."

"What? Here?"

"Yep."

"For how long?"

"As long as it takes."

"As long as what takes?"

"As long as it takes for her to adapt."

"Adapt?"

"To her new surroundings."

The clicking is like a stopwatch, urging her to hurry up and understand. She needs a cigarette. She slides her purse off her shoulder but before she even has the pack out he says,

"I don't want you smoking in the house anymore. It's bad for her lungs."

"Oh, sorry." Rattled, she lets her purse fall to the floor. "I don't know, Ron. I don't know, I don't know. This is, like, kidnapping."

He balances the pen across a jar of paperclips. "Only if we get caught."

"*We*? What do you mean, *we*?"

"If we stay cool and collected, everything will work out. After a while she'll start to feel safe. She'll want to stay because for the first time in her life she'll understand what it is to live in a real home. We'll be like parents to her. She'll have both a mother—a good mother—and a father."

. A crack of longing opens in Nancy. "But she'll *tell* people."

"We'll keep her down in the basement until we're sure she won't. That religious couple who took Elizabeth Smart." He glances up. "In California."

Nancy thinks she remembers something. "Yeah?"

"They talked her out of her parents in less than a week. Anyway, when we've gained her trust, even her love, and I'm hoping we can gain her love, we'll cut her hair, dye it, maybe straighten it—I'll let you look into all that—then we'll close the shop and the three of us will drive to Florida. I'll say to people here I've been offered a business opportunity. I'll sell this place. There are ways you can do that long distance."

Nancy comes to her feet, shakily, and goes around behind the counter. "Oh, Ron." She drops her forehead on his shoulder. "I know you're only trying to help her, keep her from abuse and all that, but you could go to jail for life. The police will be looking everywhere."

"Not here they won't."

"How do you know?"

"Grid searches for missing children have a three-kilometre range. Four, tops. We're outside of that. Anyway, nobody saw. It was dark, and she . . . she just came running up to me. It was like . . ."

"Like what?"

"Like it was ordained."

"How do you mean?"

"Fated. Written in the stars."

Nancy rubs her forehead on his shoulder. She had no idea he believed in that sort of thing. She wonders about the mother's horoscope, what it said for today, and feels a wrench of sympathy. "But the poor mother."

He scrapes back the stool. "The mother's a pimp." He goes to the basement door and quietly opens it.

Nancy grabs the stool and sits. "Do you hear anything?"

"No." He shuts the door.

"Have you been checking on her?"

"I thought—" He turns. "I thought you could do that."

"What? Are you kidding?"

"She's still scared of me."

Up until this moment Nancy has been imagining that the girl came with him willingly. "You didn't tie her up or anything, did you?"

"I restrained her in the car. I had to." He swipes an arm over his face. "Will you go down?"

"Ah, jeez. Then I'm an accessory."

"I'm not asking for my sake."

The girl will be hiding under the covers, hardly breathing. Nancy knows that kind of fear.

"Just see if she's asleep," Ron says. "If she isn't, ask her if there's anything she wants. You're good with kids. Tell her she's safe here."

Nancy sighs. "Ah, jeez."

"For *her*."

"Yeah, okay. Okay. But holy Christ, Ron. This is way too—"

"Hold on. She might be hungry."

While he goes to the kitchen, she bends and flexes her leg. Could she ever do with a cigarette or, even better, a joint. She searches under the counter for a bottle. The one she finds is empty. When he returns she asks if he wouldn't mind running back and pouring her a shot of rye.

"What for?" He has a glass of orange juice in one hand and in the other a banana and a can of Pringles.

"I need something for my nerves."

"You'll be fine. I don't think either of us should drink until this is over. I don't want you smoking your dope either. We have to stay clearheaded." He gives her the food and juice. "The basement door is never to be left unlocked," he says. "That's the cardinal rule. So I'll open it, then lock it behind you, then you knock when you want to come out. Turn the flashlights off. There are two of them. Turn the desk light on."

FROM THE door Nancy can tell that the bed is empty. "Sweetie," she says. "Where are you, sweetie? Are you in the bathroom?"

She's lying on the floor, huddled between the bed and wall.

Nancy sets the glass and food on the desk and crouches

down. The girl has blond curly hair and darkish skin. Funny . . . Nancy imagined stringy brown hair and pasty skin. She goes to stroke the hunched-up back but at her touch the girl lets out a petrified squeal.

"Okay," Nancy says. "It's okay. Did you fall out of bed?"

Silence.

A stuffed monkey is caught in the folds of the bed curtains. Nancy untangles it and lays it next to the girl's right hand. "You know what? We should turn on a light. It's so gloomy down here." Forgetting Ron's instructions, she leaves the flashlights going and switches on the light outside the bathroom. "That's better, eh?"

The girl starts to shiver. For a moment Nancy can't remember why this is happening. The mother, she tells herself. The mother drags her to bars and lets men molest her. The landlord molests her.

"I know you're scared, sweetie," she says, crouching again. "I'd be scared, too, eh? But nobody's going to hurt you here. I promise. I cross my heart"—she crosses her heart—"and hope to die. Okay? Okay, sweetie?"

The girl turns her head.

Right away Nancy recognizes her. To cover her surprise she looks over at the desk. "I brought you a glass of orange juice. And a banana and potato chips."

The girl murmurs something. Nancy twists back around. "What, sweetie? What did you say?"

"I want to go home. I want my mom."

"I know you do," Nancy says desperately. She can *see* the mother: that worried, friendly look she had. "But you can't right now, okay?"

"Why?"

"Because . . . because somebody fell and hurt them-selves, right? At your house?"

"Mika."

It sounds like the name of a dog, or a baby. "Right. Mika fell . . . and it's all crazy there, with the ambulances and everything."

"Did he die?"

"What? No, no, he didn't die. He'll be fine. But you won't be unless you get some sleep. Why don't you climb back into bed? Aren't you cold? The darned air conditioning's turned up way too high."

She touches the thin, bare arm. There's no reaction, so she begins to rub it. After a moment she slides her hands under the ribcage and tries lifting. This, too, is allowed. Only now does the smell of urine reach her. She runs a hand over the girl's bottom. "That's okay," she says. "We'll get you cleaned up."

In the bathroom she removes the damp skirt and un-derpants while confessing about wetting *her* pants once, in grade three. "Everybody in the whole school found out because the teacher made me change into my gym clothes."

The girl seems dazed. If she remembers Nancy, she's not letting on. She lets herself be wrapped in a towel and steered toward the bed. The bottom sheet is damp so Nancy keeps on nudging her, over to the sofa. "That a girl," she says, hoist-ing her up. "Would you like your juice now?"

The girl nods.

"How about a bite of banana. No?" She brings the glass over. As the girl starts to drink there's a noise outside—Ron knocking against something or dropping something. The girl's hands slide up the glass.

"Whoops," Nancy says, retrieving it. "That's just my dog, Tasha. You'll meet her. She's really cute. Part spaniel and part wiener dog."

"I want to go home now."

Nancy sets the glass on the side table. The noise outside has made her aware of Ron listening in the hall. "For Pete's sakes, I haven't even told you my name. I'm Nancy. What's your name?" Pretending not to know.

"Rachel."

"Rachel. That's so pretty. Okay, Rachel, I'm going to strip the sheets and bring you some fresh ones and then maybe you can finally get some sleep. How's that, eh?"

"And then can I go home?"

Nancy moves over to the bed. "We'll see."

The girl starts to cry. Nancy hurries back and kneels in front of her. She finds the cold feet. She kisses and rubs them while babbling she doesn't know what: nobody's going to hurt you here, we're your friends, we're going to help you, I promise, I promise.

At some point the sobs settle into whimpers and finally the girl drifts into sleep. Nancy goes on gazing at the beautiful tear-streaked face. What can Ron be thinking, she wonders. How in the world could anything so perfect ever belong to *them*?

"Is she all right?" Ron whispers.

Nancy brushes by him with her armload of laundry. Up in the shop she drops the bundle, sits on the recycling box, and covers her face with her hands.

"What happened?" he says.

"I met her before. I met her mother." She looks at him.

"Where?"

"At Angie's. Remember last week I told you about my leg giving out and this woman catching me?"

Something hard slides into his eyes.

"Well, that was *her*. That was Rachel's mother. And Ron, she was so *nice*."

"Is she awake?"

"Rachel? No, she's asleep on the sofa. She wet the bed."

"Hey!" he says suddenly.

It's Tasha. She has gotten hold of Rachel's skirt.

"Tasha, no!" Nancy cries. The dog is zigzagging around the lawn mowers. Nancy rushes over and snags her collar. She starts to yank the skirt away.

"Let me do it," Ron says sharply.

Down on one knee, he forces open Tasha's mouth.

"Bad girl," Nancy says, frightened.

The skirt is caught on a tooth. Gently, gently, Ron works the material free.

"Is it okay?" Nancy asks.

"What?" He's out of breath. He grabs the door frame to pull himself up.

"Did she rip it?"

"No." But he hasn't checked. He's frowning down at Tasha, who is wagging her tail and looking up at him. "Rachel likes dogs," he says. "Tasha could be good company for her."

Nancy was braced to hear the opposite: Tasha has got to go. She was already feeling relief at the thought of taking Tasha home, getting away from here. But this also is relief.

She straightens, then freezes at the sound of a police siren. Ron cocks his head. The whooping grows louder before it starts to fade.

Nancy's heart goes on hammering. She thinks of the terrorized little girl asleep on the sofa, and her eyes brim over. "We can't keep her, Ron. We *can't*. I'll drive her back, okay? I'll do it."

He seems to realize that he's still holding the skirt. He drops it on the counter.

"I'll say she was running around all hysterical, like you said. You were afraid she'd run into traffic so you brought her here because . . . because . . ." She can't remember why he brought her here.

"Nance." He takes her hands in his.

"Yeah?"

"We let her go and we're throwing her life in the garbage."

"Okay, so you tell the police what you saw. The landlord and everything."

"She's been here all night. I had to duct tape her. I locked her in a basement. Do you really think the police won't have a problem with that?"

"Then you shouldn't have . . ." Her voice crumples.

"It's going to be all right."

"How?"

"We're going to make it all right."

"How?"

"By eliminating risk. Following the plan."

"What plan?"

"The one I've been spending the last five hours figuring out. It's not hard, it's not complicated. I'll tell you what you have to do, step by step. Today—now—you go home, pack up your clothes and clean out your fridge."

She tugs her hands free. "I have to make her bed."

"Right. Right. First, you make her bed. Then you go home and pack your things. I've got boxes you can use. How much longer do you have on your lease?"

"What?"

"When's your lease up?"

"October. Why?"

"We'll pay your rent until then. Subletting is too much trouble. Don't bother with your furniture and dishes. We'll get them later."

She shakes her head. He's going too fast.

"The money's no problem. I'll sell another vacuum if I have to. So, you move in here. Then you phone Frank and say I've offered you a job doing the accounts, answering the phone, and you've decided to take it because the doctor ordered you to stay off your feet."

"You want me to work for you?"

"One of us has to always be here, right? As long as we keep the radio going and the doors are shut"—nodding toward the basement—"the door up here and the one downstairs, anyone who comes into the shop won't hear a thing. I've tested it out."

"Ron."

"What?"

"She wants to go home."

He blinks, then goes behind the counter. Without looking at her, he says, "There should be some clean sheets in the upstairs cupboard."

*　*　*

RACHEL DREAMS that she and her mother are swimming underwater in a dark, cold lake, and even though they aren't wearing snorkels they can breathe. "This is incredible," her mother says. "I had no idea human beings could do this." For some reason, Rachel isn't all that amazed.

When she opens her eyes the shining circles on the ceiling give her the impression she's still underwater. Then she sees that the circles are from the flashlights, and she knows where she is. She looks carefully back and forth, past the stuffed animals and through the sheer curtains that hang around the bed.

Nobody else is in the room. It's quiet, except for the sound of a truck rumbling by. It's light outside. The last thing she remembers is being in the chair and the lady kneeling in front of her and saying, "We're your friends."

She slips one hand under the duvet to feel the bed. Dry. She still has the towel around her waist, though. The lady said she would change the sheets, and she must have, but she didn't bring her any clean underpants.

She has seen the lady before. Where? At Tom's, maybe. "Nobody's going to hurt you," she kept saying, but the man had *already* hurt her, taking off the tape. She knows where she's seen *him* before: he's the man in the baseball cap, who was staring up at their deck that time. She thinks of how he looked at her when he put her on the bed, and it's as if he's suffocating her, crushing her bones, and she curls into a ball and tries to see the lady's face instead, her nice face. She remembers the lady saying that Mika didn't die. She holds onto this—*Mika didn't die, Mika didn't die*—and is soothed.

She has to go to the bathroom. Clutching the towel at her waist, she finds an opening in the curtains and slides her feet to the floor. This carpet is like fur. The toilet seat is like a pillow. While she's peeing she listens for sounds upstairs. She wonders if the man and lady are asleep or even still at home. She doesn't flush, in case. Back in the other room she goes to the door and tries the handle. Locked, but then she knew it would be. She looks around. A huge dollhouse in the corner. Posters of Cinderella and Pocahontas on the wall. This must be a little girl's bedroom, she thinks. But where is the girl? Is she dead?

She peers into the dollhouse. There's a switch next to the front door and she turns it on and the whole house lights up. A lady doll stands at the kitchen sink. A man doll sits at a desk, his hand resting on the phone.

Phone! A cry of hope escapes her. Do they have a phone down here? As soundlessly as she can she opens and shuts the desk and dresser drawers. She checks the shelves on either side of the TV. She lifts the lid of the toy chest and feels between stacks of Barbie dolls still in their packages.

She hears herself whimpering and clamps her hands over her mouth, then realizes that the towel has fallen off, and she gets it and wraps it around her waist. She lies on the floor again. If the man comes in, she'll crawl under the bed. If it's the lady, she'll ask when she can go home. The lady said she couldn't go last night because there were ambulances. There won't be any now. There might be a police car, though. She'd better not tell the lady. She'll tell her that sometimes she stays overnight at Lina's, so her mother is used to her not coming home and won't be worried.

But she *will* be worried. Rachel can just see her. She'll be crazy with worry.

Chapter Fourteen

CELIA LOOKS AT her watch. Seven forty-five. It must be later than that, she thinks. "What time do you have?" she asks Lynne, the plainclothes female officer sitting across from her on Mika's sofa.

"A quarter to eight," Lynne says.

"It feels like at least nine."

"I know," Lynne says. She dabs her forehead with a Kleenex. "It's already a scorcher out there."

Celia, who is shivering, who has been shivering off and on all night in brief spurts as if she were receiving electric shock treatments, says, "There's a fan in the dining room."

"Oh, I'm fine," Lynne says. She tucks the Kleenex up her sleeve. "A sedative won't knock you out, you know, hon. It'll calm your nerves is all."

"I don't want my nerves calmed."

"I can understand that." She comes to her feet. "Well, I'd better see about your coffee then."

A second plainclothes officer, also named Lynne, went to make a pot half an hour ago, but Celia's phone started ringing (her line has been extended down through a cold-air vent into

Mika's kitchen) and this other Lynne is answering. Given the
state of Celia's finances nobody expects anything like a ransom demand. It's more a case of taking messages and, of
course, there's a possibility that a person with information
will call here rather than the police. "She's doing all right, considering," the other Lynne tells people. "Holding her own."
She has a loud, sociable voice. Both Lynnes do. They remind
Celia of the farming wives you see in movies, the capable,
sturdy women who turn up in times of crisis. They've yet to
question her or even leave her alone for more than a few minutes so she suspects that their mission, aside from answering
the phone, is to try to keep her from falling apart.

She can't afford to fall apart. There's something she's not
remembering, some person or place Rachel would have gone
to. For at least four hours, from eleven o'clock last night until
well after the power and phone lines came back on, she and
Constable Bird drove around banging on doors and searching parks and laneways. Because they were in radio contact
with the other constables, Celia knew Rachel hadn't returned and she dreaded returning herself but by then there
were close to a hundred officers scouring the neighbourhood
and Bird said her time would be better spent compiling a list
of suspicious men, by which he meant not just the homeless
men in the ravine and a few of the scarier video store
regulars—she'd already told him about these—but any man
who had ever paid Rachel a little too much attention.

So they drove back to the house. Mika by then was at the
hospital; he'd apparently been talked into going as a precaution. "Nothing to worry about," Celia was told. She found a
pad and pen, lit a cigarette, and sat at his dining room table.
Suspicious men . . . she didn't even know where to start. With

the exception of Mika and a handful of others, all the men she could think of, if she imagined them looking at Rachel, seemed to betray some hungry, gnawing quality under the surface. She decided to get her address book and write down the name of every man she knew. She had finished this much when the two Lynnes arrived, along with a senior investigator who wanted to ask a few more questions.

He sat across from her. He had a pockmarked complexion and small, intelligent eyes. His questions were personal. Had Rachel been upset about anything? *No.* How had Rachel been getting along at school? *Great.* Good marks? *Not bad.* Nobody bullying her? *No, no.* Any teacher on her case, wanting her to stay after class? *No.* Did she ever talk about her father? *Rarely.* Did it bother her that she'd never met him? *Maybe, deep down.* How did she get along with Mika Ramstad? *Great.*

And just then Mika himself returned, and Celia went over to him and clutched his hands.

"How are you, dear?" he said.

"Oh . . ." She shrugged. "How are *you*?" He looked terrible, his head wrapped in a bandage, his eyes swollen and bloodshot.

"I'm fine," he said. "No lasting damage. Celia, listen . . ."

She waited.

"They've asked me to . . . stay at a friend's for a few days."

"What?"

"It seems I could get in the way here."

"Get in the way?" She turned to the investigator. "What's going on?"

"Unfortunately," the investigator said, "there's a risk of residents contaminating evidence."

"*I'm* the resident. He owns the place!"

"It's all right," Mika said.

"No, it isn't."

One of the Lynnes, coming in from the kitchen, said, "It's just procedure, hon."

"Let's do what they ask," Mika said. "They have their reasons."

She stared at him, wondering at his compliance, and then it struck her that maybe the police suspected him of something, of somehow driving Rachel out of the house, and she turned again on the investigator. "He's been looking after Rachel since she was three years old!"

"I appreciate that."

"I'll come back," Mika said. "As soon as I can."

She shook her head. "This is wrong."

"I'll phone you."

"Where will you go?"

"I'm not sure yet. I've got to drop in at the school."

"Oh, fuck, Mika."

"Celia, they're going . . . they're going to find . . ."

"I know."

"She's smart and she's brave."

He took the dogs. As soon as he was out the door she listed to the investigator what he had done for her and Rachel over the years. The gifts, the money, the ridiculously low rent, the babysitting, the school projects he'd worked on. With each fresh example she sliced her right hand against her left in a flailing gesture that made her feel as though the tendons in her arms had snapped. The investigator let her rant. He even seemed sorry for her. But he stood his ground about the need to "freeze the house."

She went into Mika's bedroom and collapsed on the bed. Back came the images of Rachel being raped and beaten, every possible horror. Celia writhed, a pillow pressed to her face. The pain was incredible. Only the thought of how useless she was being had her finally pulling herself together. She wiped her face on one of Mika's T-shirts and returned to the other room.

It was dawn. The forensic team had arrived and gone straight to the basement. Outside, television crews were setting up, and there was a police command post in a mobile home parked down the street. Everything was in high gear. Celia felt another band of anxiety squeeze her chest. At some level she still refused to believe that Rachel had really vanished. "What if she just walks through the door?" she asked the Lynnes, and they said it was entirely possible and had been known to happen. But then their job was to keep her hopeful. She smoked cigarettes and mulled over her list. Where she had phone numbers and addresses she wrote them in and she put check marks beside the men she had qualms about, however unjustified. Twitches started up in both of her eyes.

BIG LYNNE (Celia is now mentally referring to them as Big and Little) returns with the coffee. She says, "Jerry from the video store says he'll stick your paycheque straight into your bank account, and call him if there's anything he can do. And your friend Laura is dying to talk to you. Where's your cell?"

"I don't have one."

"Oh. Well, all right, then, you can use mine."

"Later, maybe. Has Mika called?"

"Not yet." She sips her coffee. After a moment she says, "You can't be too comfortable in that dress, hon."

Celia is still wearing her cocktail dress from the night before. Nylon stockings, slippers. "I haven't thought about it."

"If you like, I can scoot up to your apartment and bring something down. Shorts and a T-shirt or whatever."

"Aren't I allowed to go up there?"

"Oh, no. You can go up."

"Can I go outside?"

"You can go anywhere you like. Forensics will want to talk to you but they'll be here awhile."

"I was thinking if I just walked around, I might get a feel for where she was and which way she went." She is envisioning a kind of psychic jet trail, still intact.

"That sounds like a terrific idea. The only thing is, all the reporters and cameras."

"Oh, right."

"They're down the street a ways but we can't stop them from using their telephoto lenses."

"What if I went out the back door?"

She changes into grey track pants and an oversized grey T-shirt. Instead of her regular baseball cap she puts on an old Tilley hat, and she borrows a pair of Mika's sunglasses to hide more of her face. Little Lynne, who is going off shift and will return later to relieve Big Lynne, accompanies her past the two officers patrolling the lane, which is otherwise deserted, so Celia continues on by herself. She feels drawn to the front of the house and at the first intersecting alley she turns east to start circling around.

The sight of media trucks shakes her—there are so many. The street is closed off, and a policeman is directing pedestrians away from the trucks and cameras down a corridor of yellow tape. Heart pumping, expecting at any moment for somebody to shout, "That's the mother!" she allows herself to be herded along. Up ahead, on the sidewalk across from her house and behind more tape, a crowd has gathered. As she gets closer she recognizes people: neighbours, customers from the store. None of them even glances in her direction. They're looking at the house. What are they hoping to see? *Her* at a window? She hears a man, a stranger to her, say, "There *is* no father," and another man say, "So who's that guy who's always on the porch?" The voices, the murmurs, are like thick, muffling webs she has to break her way through. She edges around to the rear of the crowd and steps onto a low retaining wall.

Her house—she never noticed before—leans into its neighbour. Somehow she finds the sight unbearable. She steps back onto the pavement and walks into the lane, as far as the dumpster. Is this where Rachel ran to? Would she have crossed the street? Glancing around, Celia feels a growing conviction. She closes her eyes and imagines Rachel's face.

Involuntarily, she begins to sway. She is aware of herself, her half-crazed self who never believed in telepathy, swaying in the throes of belief. Which way did you go? she thinks. Which way, which way? And eventually it seems that Rachel hears: the eyes widen, the mouth opens and shuts like a baby's mouth in sleep. "Where are you?" Celia whispers. No answer, no gesture, but the face is alive and listening. "I'll find you," Celia says. "Hold on."

NANCY OPENS her eyes. She's on Ron's bed, wearing only her underwear and shoes. Light streaming in through the blinds lies like straps across her bare legs. "Holy Christ," she says, remembering the girl.

Her jeans and tank top are in the bathroom. She quickly pulls them on and hurries downstairs. Tasha is whining at the kitchen door so she lets her outside, then goes into the shop. "Ron?" she says before she hears him climbing up from the basement.

"Were you checking on her?" she whispers.

"Just listening." He glances at her leg. "How is it?"

"Better. What happened? Did I conk out in the bathroom?" Her memory of last night ends with sitting on the toilet and pressing a hot facecloth to her knee.

"On the bed. I came up to see how you were doing and you were asleep."

"Why didn't you wake me?"

"I did. You told me to leave you alone."

"Really?" She can't imagine that.

"I thought I'd give you until seven."

"Did she wake at all?"

"I haven't heard anything."

"Okay . . . well . . ." She looks around for her purse and notices that the pile of sheets is gone. "Did I do a laundry already?"

"I did."

"Huh." She shakes her head. "I had a dream . . ." A dream about doll-sized underpants hanging on a clothesline.

He shuffles some papers on the counter. "Were you stoned last night?"

Was she? No, she hasn't smoked since yesterday at lunch. "I was just really tired. That's all. Stress knocks me out, especially when my leg's acting up." She sees her purse hanging from a floor lamp and she gets it and feels around inside for her cigarettes.

"The boxes are in your car," he tells her. "How long do you think you'll be?"

"A couple of hours."

"She was okay, right? When you went down?"

When she went down to make the bed, he means.

"Well, yeah," Nancy answers, "but she didn't really wake up."

His big face puckers with worry.

"I can get my stuff later," she offers.

"No. Let's stick to the plan."

"If she starts crying, I don't think you should go in."

"I won't."

"She's too scared of you."

He nods.

"Jeez, Ron . . . I can't . . . this is so . . . unbelievable."

He takes her in his arms. "You're doing fine."

Outside, on the sidewalk, she pauses to light a cigarette. Her body buzzes, the electric feeling she used to get coming down from meth. Trying not to limp or shudder, she walks to her car. She drives at exactly the speed limit. None of the streets seems familiar and she wonders how she knows where to go. The red front door to her house is another mystery. Maybe this is the wrong place, she thinks, but the key works.

She brings in the boxes and drags them up to her apartment. In the coffee can where she stores her dope there's a joint already rolled and she sits at her kitchen table and smokes it, then she opens the fridge and drinks what's left of a bottle of orange juice.

Almost everything else, what little there is, has gone

bad. She pours a quart of sour milk down the drain and throws some withered tomatoes into a garbage bag. Already her leg is bothering her again.

She limps across to her living room area. There, on the coffee table, in shiny blue paper with a wide gold ribbon, is Ron's present. She had completely forgotten that today is his birthday. The present, which only yesterday she was so happy about, is a black T-shirt that says *Plug It In* on the front. For the life of her she can't remember why she thought that was funny. The card is even stupider. It says, *Another birthday?* over a picture of a bear with his pants down, and then inside it says, *Grin and bare it!*

Impatiently she shoves the present beneath the sofa. Even more repellent to her than the shirt and card is the prospect of celebrating. She goes over to her closet and lifts a load of blouses and skirts off the rod and dumps them in a box. She hasn't got much in the way of clothes, in the way of anything for that matter, so the packing takes only about fifteen minutes. The last few boxes she fills with her aromatherapy candles, her china upside-down clown, and, after some thought (will she ever again feel up for playing music?), her banjo and songbooks.

Hobbling badly now, she carries the boxes one at a time down to the car. Nobody she knows walks by. Nobody even glances at her.

There's more traffic, though. She's conscious of people in other cars. Without really thinking, she turns on the radio and punches in the all-news station.

". . . Described as nine years of age, small, thin build with blond curly hair, blue eyes, light brown skin . . ."

She swerves, braking just in time to avoid running down

a pair of teenage girls. They pound the hood of her car. "Fuckin' bitch!" one of them shouts.

She stares straight ahead.

"Police are canvassing the area on foot," the reporter is saying, "searching homes, stores, garages, and backyards. Seventy men and women from the province's Volunteer Emergency Response Team have been called in—"

She turns the radio off. She seems to be outside the car, watching herself: a woman in an orange tank top, gripping the steering wheel of a red Cavalier.

On almost every radio station they're talking about Rachel: ". . . Went missing from her Carlton Street home last night . . . ," ". . . Small, thin build, nine years old . . ."

Nine surprises Ron. He'd have said eight. Everything else coincides with his expectations: the grid search, the volunteers being called in, and the landlord (who has the peculiar name of Mika, Mika Ramstad) not dying after all, only suffering a few cuts and bruises. "We have a Rachel hotline set up," a police spokeswoman says. "We ask anybody who may have seen or heard anything to call it at—" Ron switches stations. ". . . No leads yet, but it's still very early in the investigation—"

He keeps switching stations until he finds music. No leads yet, he repeats to himself. And there won't be any, either. What could anybody have seen or heard? Shapes, shadows, the sound of a child crying and a man comforting her. Remembering how Rachel held his hand as he led her to the car, he feels a rush of love and he takes the underpants out of his pocket and holds them to his face.

He washed them along with the sheets and skirt; he had to in case Nancy asked where they were. But he can't bring himself to part with them. Not yet. They're mauve with a pattern of white coils. The leg holes are so small his fist won't fit through. He stretches the waistband along the ruler that's fastened to the edge of the counter. Seven and a half inches. Double that and you've got fifteen. A fifteen-inch waist, he says to himself, amazed, slipping the underpants back in his pocket.

He could use a drink.

Those days are over, however, so he goes to the kitchen and brews a pot of strong coffee, then fixes his regular breakfast of six slices of bacon, four scrambled eggs, and four pieces of toast. He has had only a few bites when it occurs to him that if he lost a few pounds Rachel might not find him so terrifying. He wasn't always this big. Until his midtwenties he looked pretty good, and he wouldn't mind looking that way again, for her. Say he lost five pounds a week . . .

He gets up and scrapes his meal into the garbage.

It's a quarter to eight; Nancy has been gone nearly an hour. He wonders whether he should be more worried about her than he is. Right now, at this moment, she could be talking to the police. Never trust a green-eyed woman, his father used to say. Well, his father never met Nancy. Sure, she feels sorry for the mother (Nancy's the type of woman who feels sorry for mass murderers) but her hunger to have a child of her own is at the bottom of who she is. No, he assures himself, Nancy's all right, Nancy won't betray him.

Without realizing, he has taken the underpants out of his pocket again. He folds them and puts them back. He should get down to work, he thinks, keep his mind occupied. He carries his cup of coffee into the shop and considers the Honda mower, which has been sitting around for almost a week. With these self-propelled models, it's usually the clutch, a simple matter of adjusting the gap between the bolts. He grabs his screwdriver and steps through the clutter, pausing to listen at the basement door and then going cold as it comes to him that maybe the reason for the silence is that she has stopped breathing. People die of fright. They choke on their own vomit.

A pulse beats in his throat as he opens the door and descends the stairs.

The bed is empty.

"Rachel?"

He looks in the bathroom. Not there. No way she could have gotten out. The dollhouse lights are on. Was that her doing? The toy chest isn't quite closed and he lifts the lid, prepared to find her crammed inside. He goes down on his knees and peers under the bed.

There she is.

"Hey," he says.

She's on her stomach, head tucked into the floor, arms straight at her sides.

"I just wanted to make sure you're all right," he says. Her left foot jerks. "Listen, Rachel," he says, his voice catching in his relief. "I'm not going to hurt you. I would never hurt you."

The foot jerks again. A long, graceful foot, dusky pink on the underside. To squeeze it in a gesture of comfort and reassurance, would that be wrong? Yes. *She's too scared of you.* It takes everything in him, all his strength of will, to grasp the bedpost and pull himself up.

"What do you think of the dollhouse?" he says. "It's what's called a Colonial style. The next time you're looking at it, turn on the switch next to the fireplace."

He is speaking too loudly. For a moment he seems to know her terror and he picks up a stuffed animal, a zebra, and presses its spongy body between his hands. "Everything here is for you, you know," he says. "The DVDs, the books, the Barbie dolls. If there's anything else you'd like, you only have to ask." He sees that she has drunk some of the orange juice but that the banana is untouched. He opens the can of Pringles. Full. "Nancy will be back soon. You can tell her what you want for breakfast."

He sets the zebra on the bed and pulls up the duvet, patting it into smoothness. Outside, right by one of the windows, the dog begins to bark. "Must be a squirrel," he observes.

Or a person. Not a customer, though . . . it's too early for customers. And they never pull into the lane. He wipes his wet palms on his shirt. Hearing no tread on the outside stairs, no pounding on the door, he relaxes and says, "Would you like to meet Tasha? How about I go get her?"

And so he does, returning a few minutes later with the dog under his arm. As soon as he puts her down she runs to the bed and pokes her head under.

"Tasha, meet Rachel," he says.

Tasha backs up, wagging her tail, whining for Rachel to come out.

Ron waits. After a minute he realizes that with him in the room, nothing's going to happen. "I'll leave you two to get acquainted," he says. He's about to shut the door when he takes another look and there's her arm reaching out to pat the dog on the head.

Chapter Fifteen

RACHEL WAS THREE weeks old when Celia learned at the reading of the will that her mother hadn't been as financially strapped as she'd always let on. There were Canada Savings Bonds, Bell Telephone Class A shares, and over thirty thousand dollars in Treasury bills. During her pregnancy Celia had dimly envisioned keeping the job at Valu-Mart while leaving her baby in the care of a Jamaican woman she'd heard about, a grandmother who loved children and charged next to nothing. She had reconciled herself to finding a cheaper place to live. Now, not only would she be able to look after Rachel full-time, she'd have enough money to stay in her mother's apartment and to buy some half-decent baby furniture. Rachel had been sleeping in an old red wicker basket next to Celia's bed, so a crib was the first priority, but Celia also bought a changing table, a monitor, a dresser, a rocking chair, and a rug.

The day before the furniture was to be delivered, she and a few of her friends cleared out and wallpapered her mother's bedroom. The wallpaper had a pattern of blocky, cockeyed letters from which monkeys hung by their hands and tails. The rug was pale pink. The handles on the dresser drawers were lime green and fish shaped. Once everything was set up, Celia walked Rachel around, saying, "This is yours and this is yours and this is yours . . . ," feeling for the first time a glow of worthiness. But that night, the first night she and Rachel spent apart, she lay awake in misery, as if the separation had been brought about by force. Eventually she lifted her baby out of the crib and carried her back to the basket, and not for another five years did they ever again sleep in separate rooms.

"I'll make a lot of mistakes," she had warned Rachel in the hospital. "I know how to change a diaper and that's about all."

That was enough, as it turned out. From the first day, Rachel nursed without any fuss and she slept four hours at a stretch. Celia could hardly believe her luck. None of the books she'd read had prepared her for things to go so smoothly. Given her situation, she was supposed to, she was *entitled* to, get so lonely and depressed she'd want to jump off a bridge. Yet here she was, doing fine. Nobody believed her. "Good for you!"—she heard that a lot. Everyone seemed to think she was putting on a show. "You're a brave young lady," the caretaker of the apartment building, a mournful old German named Klaus, told her almost every time she and Rachel passed him in the halls.

If he only knew. As far as she was concerned, a husband, even a wonderful husband, would have only gotten in the way. And her mother . . . Her mother had thought that breast-feeding was medieval and that babies should be left to cry. It was impossible to imagine how the three of them could have lived together, and yet just as impossible to imagine how she and Rachel could have abandoned her when she had already been abandoned by Celia's father. But then the problem of living together never arose. It was as if, in her bones, her mother had known about the pregnancy and in a fit of heroism deeper and truer than her conscious will had decided to take herself out of the picture. For Celia to think of the death in these terms was easier than to accept that there was nothing, no sense or virtue, behind its glaringly convenient timing.

Her oldest friend, Laura Colemen, was the only person who didn't just assume that her mother would have been a great comfort and support. But Laura was like everybody else in suspecting her of having a harder time of it than she let on. "Don't tell me you never get bored," she said. "I'll believe everything else, but not that you don't get bored."

Twice a month, on a Saturday afternoon, Laura insisted on babysitting so that Celia could go to a movie or read in a coffee shop, just be by herself for a few hours. Celia usually ended up walking around fretting, imagining Rachel's confusion and uneasiness. Who was this skinny woman with her jangly bracelets and loud voice? Where was the woman with the leaking breasts? Laura was clumsy. What if she dropped Rachel? In store windows Celia would catch her anxious reflection. Thoughts that at other times stayed buried would begin to assail her. She'd be ashamed, in a stingy, resentful way, about not having informed her father of her mother's death, let alone that he had a grandchild. And then she'd get sad about her mother, who had never allowed herself a moment's lightheartedness, whose one passion, music, had been discouraged by her own mother, and yet despite that and despite being so frugal she did things like separate two-ply Kleenexes so there'd be twice as many, she paid for Celia to take piano lessons.

At a certain point of wretchedness, she would return to her apartment building and stand in the hall outside her door, listening. Either she'd hear nothing or the TV or Laura on the phone. When she finally brought herself to go inside (and not even an hour would have passed since she'd left), Laura always looked at her as if she were an alcoholic caught with a drink in her hand.

Don't tell me you don't get bored. She didn't, though. There was too much to do. There was the feeding and bathing, the diaper changes, the laundry, all the usual chores. And unless it was pouring rain, she took Rachel out in the stroller for at least an hour every afternoon and let her be ogled by the neighbourhood women, some of whom came right out and asked, "Are you the mother?" It occurred to Celia to be offended but she could never muster the outrage. "Well, I gave *birth* to her," was the extent of her sarcasm, and even then a note of disbelief crept into her voice.

Her inheritance lasted three years. Before it was completely gone, she made up flyers that said "Piano Lessons in My Home" and taped them to telephone poles near her apartment. There was plenty of interest, but either she was charging too much or something about her phone manner put people off, because only one person made an appointment.

His name was John Paulsen. He looked to be in his late thirties, tall and gaunt with milky skin, a big sculpted head and short black hair combed forward like a monk's. He had an accent she couldn't place—Scandinavian? Dutch?—and a tentative, formal way of speaking. "I should like to play a little Bach before I die," he announced right away. She wondered if he was terminally ill, but then Rachel emerged from the bathroom, and after being introduced to her he said,

"Rachel is the name I plan to give to my first daughter." So there were a few years in him, anyway.

"Do you have sons?" Celia asked.

"No, no . . ." He tapped his hands together. His fingers were extraordinarily long. "I mean to say, if I am ever . . . *fortunate* enough to marry and *have* a daughter."

It was agreed that he would come two afternoons a week. He was self-employed, he explained; he could make his own hours. She asked him what he did.

"I take care of my investments," he said.

He had investments.

But no talent, no ear. Mondays and Thursdays from two until three thirty in the afternoon, Celia sat beside him on the bench and battled to get him through the most elementary of exercises. His utter lack of rhythm and coordination staggered her. Those wonderful fingers, which never fumbled unbuttoning his coat and which plucked an eyelash once, from Rachel's cheek, went sloppy and thick on the keyboard. At the end of the lesson everyone would be frazzled: him murmuring, "Forgive me," Celia babbling about not losing hope (he was, God help her, her only student), and Rachel actually wringing her hands.

Rachel adored him. He spoke respectfully to her; he seemed to arouse in her three-year-old heart a desire to rescue. As he did in Celia's, but for her there were also flickers of lust. His bony wrists, his noble profile, his whole starving-aristocrat elegance coupled with his hopeless musical ambitions had her wanting to lay him on her bed and tenderly peel off his clothes. She hadn't even looked at a man in almost four years and had never been attracted to anyone so delicate, but his delicacy was exactly why she could imagine him sliding into her life. Not a hulking intrusion but a tasteful ornament. Who had investments! Without any encouragement on his part, aside from his habitual gallantry, she began fantasizing marriage, a house with a yard, no more guilt about how much she spent on cigarettes, no more buying her bras at the Dollar Store.

It took two months before he finally played his first little ten-bar tune straight through. To celebrate, she asked if he would like to stay for tea, and somewhat to her surprise (he was always heading off to meetings with bankers and stockbrokers) he said, "I would like that very much indeed." She used the good china and served lettuce-and-tomato sandwiches on white bread with the crusts sliced off. He gobbled them down. He seemed happy and relaxed as he told them about growing up in Oslo and Frankfurt, the only child of a pediatrician mother and financier father.

"Our father lives in New York City," Rachel said when he paused.

"*Your* father does," Celia corrected.

"He's black," Rachel said.

"Is he indeed?" John said. He smiled at Celia—a complicit, amused smile. A *husbandly* smile.

The following Thursday he stayed right through supper and Rachel's bath and then, at Rachel's insistence, he read her her bedtime story.

"Do you want some Kahlua?" Celia asked when he came back into the living room. She was on her third glass. "Or would you rather go straight to sex?"

He fingered the knot of his tie. "I should like to have a quick cleanup first," he said.

A shower, he meant, and by himself. She found this

completely endearing. She waited for him in bed, wondering if he would come to her naked or wrapped in a towel. Wrapped in a towel, she decided correctly. In fact, he didn't discard it until he was under the covers.

They kissed, or at least she kissed him. His body was unexpectedly soft and unmuscled, like foam tubing. Nothing she did succeeded in giving him an erection, and finally he rolled over onto his back and pulled the sheet over himself. "Forgive me," he said. "With Rachel in the next room, I can't feel right."

"She's asleep."

"I find myself . . . feeling somehow responsible . . ."

What was he getting at? Celia came up on her elbow. "Responsible for what?"

"Of course, she's *your* daughter . . ."

"That's right."

"I keep seeing her little face."

Celia lay back down. She got the picture: the attraction in this household was Rachel, not *her*. Come to think of it, maybe Rachel was the only reason he'd been showing up at all, week after week. "You'll never play Bach, you know," she said, delivering a hard truth of her own.

"Yes, I'm a lost cause. I should—" He turned to face her, holding the sheet at his throat. "I should like to continue paying you, since you had every right to expect that—"

"Don't worry," she cut him off. "We'll be fine."

ON MONDAY afternoon, to distract Rachel from his absence, she took her to Riverdale farm in Cabbagetown. As he was leaving, John had asked if he might visit occasionally, but Celia told him she didn't think that would be a very good idea. It was Rachel he wanted to visit, not her, although that wasn't the reason. The fiasco in bed had begun to sink in. She was feeling ridiculous, and so entirely over her lust that his bony head and pole-thin wrists, his pale complexion, all the parts she had swooned over, were now striking her as unhealthy, maybe even catching.

She told Rachel he had to go away.

"Where?" Rachel asked.

"I don't know, honey. Far away."

"But he's our student."

"He *was*," Celia said, "but he's finished now."

"But he loves us."

"Yes, he does," Celia allowed.

"So he has to come see us."

"He can't anymore. He's gone away."

Rachel thought a minute. "Hey!" she said. "He's gone to New York City!"

"You know what?" Celia said. "I'll bet he has!"

Rachel's hands opened at the obviousness of her logic. Her face brightened. In her world so far, it was a plain and unwavering fact, something to be counted on, that the men who loved you ended up in New York City.

They left for Riverdale farm after her nap. The sky was clear when they set out but it clouded over while they were on the bus and darkened a few minutes after they got off. The thunder and rain started before they were halfway down Carlton Street. Celia raced the stroller under a tree and tried to pull up the hood. It was stuck.

A man materialized, asking if she needed help. He gave the hood a few tugs. "A screw fell out," he said. "If you would not . . . not mind waiting, you could wait"—he gestured at the house behind him—"on the porch here while I . . . I can fix it."

He sounded like John Paulsen, that northern European accent and the hesitancy. He brought them towels to dry themselves off with, and after he had fixed the stroller he invited them to stay for lemonade. Celia accepted. The rain was torrential now; they were going to have to wait it out.

She felt the oddness of the situation: a man with John's accent and beautiful manners turning up at the same time that she would have been giving John his lesson. Physically he resembled John not at all. He was a little over medium height, fit and compact with a round, ruddy face and straight, white-blond hair. She had a feeling she'd met him before, but his name—Mika Ramstad—was new to her, and they seemed to have no friends or history in common. And yet . . . This porch, the rain, the white wicker furniture, and the two of them smoking cigarettes and talking about their lives while Rachel sat with his little dogs and squished her hands into their fur—there was a homey familiarity to it, a relief.

By the time they left she had arranged to rent his upstairs apartment for one-third of what she was currently paying. He had been prepared to let her have it for nothing until she got herself a job, but she said that would be going too far. You would think that she would find his generosity to a complete stranger suspicious—Laura did—or that, in light of what had happened with John, she would mistrust her reading of the situation. At Laura's urging she tried: she thought, God, maybe he's a pervert, but she couldn't bring herself to believe it. As for her getting romantically involved, that wasn't going to happen; she was pretty sure he was gay.

"Why shouldn't he be what he seems?" she said to

Laura. "There are genuinely sweet people out there. And anyway, I'm lucky. I get these huge strokes of luck."

"Like what?"

"My mother's money. Rachel."

"Just don't let your guard down."

Six years later Celia remembers this: how Laura had looked at Rachel as though she were surrounded by a host of demons. She remembers John Paulsen and writes his name on her list of suspicious men.

Chapter Sixteen

*T*HERE'S A CUSTOMER picking up his Black & Decker hedge trimmer when Nancy returns. She shoulders her way through the door, already talking. "It's on the radio. They've got a—" Seeing the man, she stops. The box she's holding begins to slip from her grasp.

"Just put it over there," Ron says to her. He nods at the cleared space to her left. "So that'll be fourteen dollars and thirty-nine cents," he says to the man, who already knows this. He has repeated it for Nancy's sake, to impress upon her that the man isn't from the police.

Nancy sets the box down. Her face has broken out into red splotches. The man glances at her, then gives her another look. "Hey," he says. "Frank's Homestyle, right?"

Nancy shakes her head.

Ron says, "She used to work there but I lured her away."

"That's too bad," the man says. "For Frank, I mean. So it's . . . Annie, right?"

"Nancy," Nancy murmurs.

"Nancy. Sorry. Remember my daughter? She drew your picture on her placemat?"

"Oh, yeah," Nancy says. She does remember. She wipes her hands on her jeans.

"She really liked you, she thought you were great."

"Huh."

He seems finally to register her agitation. He quickly signs the Visa receipt and grabs his trimmer. "Well," he says, "good to see you again."

When he's gone, she sits on a humidifier. Ron goes to the door. Her car is parked at an angle, taking up two spaces. "You've got to pull yourself together," he says.

"I'm not used to this," she says.

"What happened?"

"What *happened*?"

"Are you all right?"

"It's on every radio station!"

"I know."

"I was like *this close* to phoning the number they gave and turning you in. This close!" She indicates with her thumb and forefinger. Her red nail polish is chipped down to the cuticles.

A calmness spreads through him, a calm thrill. What if she had turned him in? It would be all over with by now: the arrest, his confession. "What stopped you?" he asks.

"What do you think? I love you! How could I send you to jail? They murder guys like you in jail."

"Guys like what?"

"Child abductors!"

"We haven't abducted her, we've rescued her. All right? You're doing a brave thing. The bravest thing you'll ever do in your life." He believes this. She looks up at him with her big, hopeless eyes, and he wonders if what he feels for her is love or pity or gratitude. "Let's get those boxes in."

Walking to her car, he remembers Rachel's underpants, and when he comes in again, while her back is turned, he slips them out of his pocket and tucks them under the laundered skirt.

NANCY BOILS up a pot of oatmeal and stirs in butter and lots of brown sugar. If Rachel doesn't like oatmeal there's also a peanut-butter-and-jam sandwich and some ginger-snap cookies. The important thing is to get her to eat. "Even a chocolate bar would be better than nothing," she tells Ron.

"I could run out and get one," he says.

"Let's see how this goes."

With her leg still shaky she needs to hold on to the railing, so Ron carries the tray. Tasha is whining behind the basement door, and she thinks, alarmed, Now he's locked up my dog. But instead of running out into the hall, Tasha runs over to the far side of the bed, where Rachel must be lying.

"It's just me, sweetie," Nancy says. Behind her, Ron pulls the door shut and turns the key.

Nancy waits. After a moment Rachel comes to her feet. She holds the towel around her waist.

The sight of her, so dainty and afraid, gives Nancy a shock. In her mind she had made her bigger, calmed her down. She limps to the bed and sets the tray on it. "I brought your clothes and a bite of food," she says.

"Am I going home now?"

"No. Not now."

"But the ambulances won't be there."

Nancy pretends not to hear. "You'll want to put these on," she says, handing her the skirt and underpants. "I'm going out later to buy you some more stuff. You'll have to tell me what you'd like. Shoes and socks, right?"

"My mom . . ." Rachel says. She starts gasping. She presses the clothes to her stomach. "My mom . . ."

"Okay," Nancy says, "let me help you." She tugs the clothes and the towel out of Rachel's grip, then holds the underpants open for her to step into. When nothing happens she takes a leg and puts it in. She puts in the other and pulls the underpants up. Rachel continues to gasp but she steps into the skirt and pulls it up herself. "That a girl," Nancy says. "Okay, now I've brought you oatmeal with brown sugar. Or there's—"

"You told me . . . you . . ."

"Take deep breaths," Nancy says. She presses her hand to Rachel's quaking chest. The heartbeat flutters against her palm. "Deep breaths. That's it. There you go."

"You told me . . . I . . . I . . . could go home today."

"Did I?" She can't remember, but it's possible, the way she was babbling on last night. "Jeez, I'm sorry, I shouldn't have done that. Ron, he's the nice man who brought you here, he thinks you won't be safe at home. So this is where you're going to be staying for a while." She picks up the bowl and spoon. "Will you eat a bit?"

"Why won't I be safe?"

Nancy briskly stirs the oatmeal. How much is she supposed to tell? She wishes she hadn't got so stoned; she can't think. "Your mother . . ." No, better not bring the mother

into it. She starts again: "There's a man, and he wants to . . .
he might hurt you."

"What man?"

"The man in your house. I guess he isn't your father."

"My father lives in New York City."

"Okay."

"He doesn't even know about me."

"Is that right?"

"What man do you mean?"

"Well, isn't there a man who lives in your house?"

"Mika?"

"I guess that's him."

"Mika wouldn't hurt me. Are you crazy?"

"Well, sweetie . . ."

"You're crazy!"

Nancy puts down the bowl. "Sweetie, we're only trying—"

Rachel runs past her to the door. "Let me out!" she
screams, shaking the handle. At her feet Tasha jumps around
barking.

Don't come in, Nancy thinks to Ron. Her leg buckles and
she falls to her knees in the same instant that Rachel falls to
hers. She crawls over to the child and takes her in her arms. "I
know," she says. And she does. She knows this helpless fury.

"I want to go home," Rachel sobs. Tasha frantically licks
her face and hands, whatever bare skin she can get at.

"Quit that," Nancy scolds, pushing at the dog, who goes
still and then squats and pees.

"Oh," Rachel says.

"Tasha hates rejection," Nancy explains. "Well," she
says, "that'll leave a stain."

Rachel sits up. She has stopped crying. "Here, Tasha," she says, holding out her hand. The dog comes wagging over. "Poor Tasha," she coos. "Poor little puppy."

It's a tricky moment. If Nancy doesn't play her cards right, she can see the whole uproar starting again. She goes over to the food and brings back the plate of cookies. "Watch this," she says, breaking a piece of cookie off. "Tasha, sit." The dog sits. Nancy places the cookie on Tasha's nose. "Stay, stay, stay . . . Okay!" Tasha jerks her muzzle and catches the cookie in her mouth.

"Good girl," Rachel says. She pats Tasha's head.

"You try," Nancy suggests.

Rachel breaks off a piece and puts it on the dog's nose. Tasha does her trick. Meanwhile Nancy nibbles at the cookie in her hand. "These are delicious," she says. "You should try one."

Rachel looks at her. "If I eat, will you let me phone my mom?"

"Oh, Rachel." She feeds Tasha the rest of her cookie. She's tired of telling half-truths: she's no good at it, and this girl is too smart. "The police are looking for you, right? And they can trace phone calls and then Ron and me, we'll be arrested."

"But you can block the number."

"They can trace it no matter what you do."

"If somebody doesn't call her, she won't know I'm alive." Her eyes are filling again.

Nancy is aware of Ron listening out in the hall. "I'm sorry, sweetie," she says. But she nods and holds a finger to her lips. "It's too risky."

Rachel's face has gone blank.

"Do you want to brush your teeth?" Nancy says. "I think you should brush your teeth."

"Okay," Rachel says quietly.

When they're both inside the bathroom, Nancy shuts the door.

"So you'll phone?" Rachel whispers.

"Yeah, I will. From a phone booth, I guess." She sits on the toilet seat. What's the harm in letting the mother know her daughter isn't dead? Not that she intends to take this up with Ron.

"Promise?" Rachel whispers.

"I promise."

"When?"

"When I go out to buy the clothes. You'll have to give me the number."

"Four-one-six—"

"Not yet. Wait till I get a pen and paper from upstairs. But hold on—how will she know I'm not, like, some crank? Anybody could call and say they've got you."

"No, they couldn't," Rachel says excitedly, "because we have this secret word that if a stranger ever had to pick me up from school? Like in an emergency? They would have to say the word or I wouldn't go with them."

"What is it?"

"Pablito."

"Pablito?"

"It's the name of a mouse puppet I had when I was little."

"Okay. Pablito. That's good. And listen, sweetie." She tugs free the elastic band that is about to fall out of Rachel's hair. "Ron isn't a bad man. He's kind and gentle, he really is. There's no way he would ever hurt you. It's just, he has a plan for everybody's own good, and we have to make like we're following it."

"Did you have another girl before?"

"Before when?"

"Was there a girl down here? Was this her bedroom?"

"Oh. No, no, there wasn't anybody. We were thinking of adopting, and Ron did some renovating." Her misgivings about the room and her puzzlement—why is it again that Ron didn't renovate the spare bedroom?—come back, and she stands and turns off the tap. "We'd better get out there."

WITH THE tail of his shirt Ron wipes his forehead. He hates it that Rachel is still so distraught. He had hoped that the room and the dog would have had a soothing effect by now. Compared to what she's used to—a cot on a concrete cellar floor, the threat of that Mika guy coming down—she's in paradise. She just doesn't know it yet. He wouldn't be surprised if she was waiting for him to take up where Mika left off. Well, she'll find out that not all men are molesters. The promise he has made to himself is that any physical contact will be instigated by her. He won't invite her to climb onto his lap, but if she wants to, if she wants to kiss him good night, he isn't going to deny her the expression of her natural feelings.

Patience and self-control—these are his strengths as he sees them. Also a certain ruthlessness, which isn't inherently his but which he finds he is able to muster when the situation calls for a clear head. He thinks of how the zoologists and conservationists you see on TV are sometimes forced to finish off a wounded animal or airlift a rogue male to new territory. What good would these people be if they gave in to the screams of protest? Under pressure, a person of character resorts to what he has judged, in less traumatic moments, to be the most humane course of action.

Rachel crying for her mother, though . . . it's hard to take, hard to listen to. Little girls want their mothers. His father once told him (they were talking about Jenny and Mrs. Lawson) that the bond between daughters and mothers is the strongest there is. Provided the mother isn't abusive or neglectful, Ron took him to mean. He had expected Rachel to be frightened, at least for the first day or two, but he hadn't thought she'd be as desperate as she is to get back to that pathetic woman who calls herself her mother.

Thank God for Nancy. If she can get Rachel to eat, it'll be a big step. He's going to try to keep his distance until she's eating and feeling more at home. He should ask Nancy to find out if there's a particular book or author she likes. The books he got her were all recommended by a clerk at Indigo, a young girl who struck him as being unsure of herself, and also he made the mistake of saying the child he was buying for was eight. He has seen Rachel reading on her porch, he knows she's a reader. His hope is that she'll let him read to her sometimes, at night after her bath, the two of them lying on the bed together. Father and daughter. Interesting to hear her say her father doesn't even know she's alive. Mika must have been one happy man when he learned *that*.

What's going on in there? He gets up and presses his ear to the door. Silence. He sits back on the step.

He wonders if Rachel might like to read his pamphlets. They aren't complicated; he wrote them for the general public, and a lot of the information is entertaining. For instance, when you turn off the motor of the Electrolux LX the front cover pops open and a spring-loaded lever ejects the bag right across the floor, sometimes as far as six feet. He wishes he had an LX so he could give her a demonstration. He'll show her the machines he does have, in any case. They'll be hers eventually, the ones he isn't forced to sell. Everything will be hers.

Chapter Seventeen

*T*HE CLOUDS HAVE been building since eleven o'clock, and now there's thunder and the first smatterings of rain. "Another hour, hour and a half!" Big Lynne calls from the porch.

She's talking about the news conference, which was scheduled to be held out on the front lawn at two fifteen. As she predicted, it's being postponed until the storm passes. "Rain won't hamper the search one bit," she says, coming in and giving Celia's shoulders a squeeze. "Don't you worry about that. If anything, it'll spur it on."

Celia's dread amplifies. She doesn't really think that Rachel is out in the open, but she doesn't rule out the possibility, either. Not knowing where she is turns every place, every house and garage and abandoned store, every trunk of every car and now every ditch and field, into a place she might be.

The postponement, though . . . she needs it. Her statement, which is going to be a direct appeal to the abductor, doesn't feel right yet. She rereads what she has just written: *You don't have to go through police channels. A close family*

*friend has offered himself as a go-between. I have instructed him
to help arrange for Rachel's release under any terms you may set.*

Will he understand what she's getting at? She would
rather come right out and say she's open to blackmail but
the deputy police chief asked her not to. He said it would
put the message out there that money can be made from
abducting children.

"That's not my business," she said. "I can't care about
that." Except she does care about Mika's being allowed the
freedom to negotiate, and since he isn't in the clear yet and
could be detained at any time, she agreed to tone down her
language.

What she's counting on, of course, aside from the fact
that the abductor will be listening, is that Rachel is still in
the world. On TV a little while ago there was a guy saying
how, when it comes to stranger abductions, a child has to
be found within five or six hours to stand any real chance of
being found alive. But Big Lynne snorted and told Celia not
to listen.

"The time factor is only one element," she said heatedly.
"All sorts of variables come into play."

"Like what?" Celia asked.

"The particular individuals involved, for starters. The lo-
gistics of the search. Premeditation, whether or not it played
a part." She waved her arms around. Her face had gone pink.
Clearly the risk of Celia's hearing just this kind of statistic
was why she'd tried to dissuade her from turning on the TV in
the first place.

"It doesn't matter," Celia said. "I know she's alive."

"Well, then she is," Big Lynne declared, "I trust that,"

and whether or not she was being sincere was something else that didn't matter.

Celia knows what she knows. Rachel is alive, and now her, Celia's, job is to give the abductor reasons to want to keep Rachel alive. She writes: *You have in your care an amazing human being. She hopes to be a vet one day. She loves animals, especially dogs and cats, but she loves all animals, including snakes and lizards.*

She's thinking that he might own animals: guard dogs, rats. She imagines a paranoid loner who's either out of work or in a minimum-wage job. Constable Bird believes he acted on impulse—he saw a pretty little girl looking for help, and he grabbed her, just as someone else might grab a wallet left on a park bench.

"But then why is Mika a suspect?" Celia asked. This was a couple of hours ago; she'd given up searching on foot, and Bird was driving her around again.

"Mika's a person of interest," Bird explained. "From our point of view, it didn't look great, I have to tell you. We arrive on the scene, he's bleeding, there's blood at the bottom of the stairs. Is it only his blood? Also, the way he responded to questioning. Taking his time. Working out his answers."

"Oh, no! That's just how he talks! He's trying not to stutter! Oh, God, I should have said!"

"Okay. Well, we weren't aware of that."

"Tell the investigators."

"I will. You can tell them, too."

"But I still don't get why he's even a . . . what did you call it . . . person . . ."

"Person of interest."

"Why he's even a person of interest if you think some guy grabbed her."

"Listen, if forensics supports Mika's story and he passes the polygraph, he moves to the back of the line."

Celia's heart lifted a little. "Do you know where he is?"

Bird knew how to find out. He radioed someone to call Mika and give him the number of Big Lynne's cell, which Big Lynne had stuck in Celia's purse.

As soon as Celia heard his voice she started to cry. She thought she'd finished crying and moved on to a more solid kind of agony, but now she sobbed while Mika said soothing things she could barely hear over her own noise, and Bird left the car to search an alleyway. When she calmed down she asked Mika to repeat what he'd said about being sure Rachel was alive.

"I have a sense of her," he said. "It's strong."

"Do you see her face?" Celia asked. "Because I do, when I close my eyes. Not all the time. It comes and goes. I can't hear her voice for some reason. I mean, you'd think I would."

"But you see her."

"Just her face. I see her blinking and breathing. Breathing with her mouth open. And it doesn't feel like something I'm making happen. It did at first, but now it feels like something outside of me, something coming in."

"I don't see her," Mika said. "I'm aware of her. In that way that you are when someone is behind you, or in the next room. I can feel her fear. She's . . . frightened but she isn't hurt."

"That's what I'm getting. But, Mika, you don't even believe in this stuff."

"I do now."

She pressed her forehead against the passenger window. "The thing is," she said. "I felt it coming." Only now was she allowing herself to remember.

"Like a premonition?"

"More a feeling like I was supposed to be alert, you know? Everything was jumping out at me. Little things. And I was having these dreams where people, my mother, they were saying, 'Pay attention! Look around!' But I didn't . . ."

"You've done nothing wrong."

"Oh, I've done plenty wrong." Bird, who was back in the car, glanced over. "But, Mika, I street-proofed her. Right? I mean, she *knew* never to talk to strangers, no matter what. Right?"

"We don't know that she talked to anyone, Celia. We don't . . . know that."

She listened to him breathe. "Anyway," she said, "Constable Bird says you're not a suspect, you're a person of interest. And, oh! You have to tell them about your stutter. Why you sometimes don't speak right away. Bird said they thought you were working out your answers."

"I see."

"So tell them."

"I will."

"When will they let you come home?"

"Maybe tomorrow."

"Have you had the polygraph test?"

"Not yet. They've taken a DNA swab, though."

"They took one from me, too."

"They're being thorough. That's what we want. We should be grateful."

She watched Bird leaf through his notepad. When she'd

decided she wanted to be driven around some more, she'd asked for him especially. That he might have a wife and kids waiting at home never crossed her mind. Now, really looking at him for the first time, she saw the wedding band. She saw his thick wrists and arms and the creases at the edges of his eyes. A horizontal scar sliced through his mat of black hair just above his ear, like a mark of swiftness. She wondered if he'd been stabbed. To Mika she said, "I'm being treated like a diva. Everybody's tiptoeing around me. I ask for something and everybody snaps to."

Bird smiled over at her. "We should be heading back," he said.

He meant so that she'd have time to work on her statement for the news conference. She told Mika about her plan to appeal to the abductor. "Should I beg?" she asked him. "Will he give a shit?"

"No," Mika said after a pause. "I don't think begging will work. I think you have to put yourself in this person's shoes."

"How the fuck do I do that?" She felt herself crumbling again.

"He has kept her alive," Mika said. "We both feel it. To me it says he wants something in exchange for . . . letting her go. Probably money."

"What money?"

"I have money. Don't worry about that. He isn't likely to call the police . . . or Crime Stoppers. So first of all you have to tell him he can call you directly, on your cell. No, you don't have a cell. I'll give you mine."

"Okay." If he actually called, would she be able to talk to him? Would she stay coolheaded enough to hear what he had to say?

"Or maybe he should phone me," Mika said, picking up on her anxiety. "Yes, that's better. A family friend. He phones me. It's a new number, I don't think I gave it to you."

She repeated the number out loud while motioning for Bird to write it down.

"Tell him he can call at any time," Mika said, "day or night. Assure him that our dealings will be kept confidential."

"Will he believe that?"

"He might. He'll *want* to believe it. Tell him you have no interest in seeing him captured or punished, you only want your daughter back. And then I think . . ."

"Yes?"

"Tell him who she is. Make him know her."

RACHEL ALMOST blows the whole thing. As soon as Nancy comes into the room she runs over with the phone number and says, "I found some paper and Magic Markers!" and Nancy has to think fast.

"So now you can draw pictures!" she says.

"What?" Rachel says.

"He's right outside!" Nancy whispers, taking the phone number and sticking it in her back pocket, where she's hiding the pencil stub and the piece of paper she brought down. She sees that the cookies and sandwiches are gone, and she says, her gladness genuine now, "And you found your appetite, too, eh? What else can I get you? How about a cheeseburger?"

Rachel pulls her eyes from the door. "I'm a vegetarian," she says.

"Oh," Nancy says. "Well, it's healthier, I know that."

"It's not because it's healthy. It's because eating meat is cruel."

"You're right. I've got to stop." She's serious. She sits on the sofa.

Rachel sits beside her. "When are you going to phone?" she whispers. Her breath smells like peanut butter.

"Soon," Nancy whispers. At normal volume she says, "How about pancakes?"

"Why can't you go right now?" Rachel whispers.

"I'll go as soon as I can." She doesn't feel ready is the reason, she hasn't worked up her nerve. "With lots of butter," she exclaims, "and maple syrup!"

Rachel sighs. "I should have a salad or something."

"A salad! Sure. What kind? Caesar? Mixed greens?"

"Whatever."

The sound of Ron thumping up the stairs has Rachel sitting straighter.

"Okay, he's gone," Nancy says. "You've got to watch what you say."

"Why does he stay out there?"

"He doesn't want to scare you."

"But why does he stay there when you come in?"

"Oh. Well, he's got the key. He's the only one who can open and close the door."

"He's spying on us."

"No, no. He's just . . . he's worried about you."

"Why?"

"He cares about you a lot."

Rachel screws up her face. "He doesn't even know me."

Nancy can feel the conversation moving toward dangerous ground. She looks at the ceiling. "There must be a customer," she says.

"Is this a store?"

"Sort of. It's a house. Ron and me, we live in the upstairs part, and then on the first floor he has a shop. He fixes small appliances. You know, lawn mowers, vacuum cleaners."

"Can I see?"

"It's not safe."

"Not safe for who?"

"For any of us."

"You're kidnappers," Rachel says, getting off the sofa. "You think you're being so nice but you're nothing but kidnappers." Her voice is rising. "What do you want? Money?"

"No—"

"Well, for your information we don't have money! We're poor!"

"Nobody wants your money."

"What do you want? Why are there all those Barbie dolls?" She swipes at her tears.

"They're for you. Sweetie—"

"Quit calling me sweetie!"

Nancy closes her eyes. Don't cry, she commands herself. The throb of a car stereo bounds through the room. Out in the yard, Tasha barks once.

"What's the matter with your leg?"

Nancy opens her eyes. Her leg has gone into a small spasm. "It does that sometimes," she says. "Kind of creepy, eh?"

"Do you take a prescription drug?"

"When I remember. It gives me headaches."

Rachel covers her mouth with her hands. "You're that lady! From Angie's Nails!"

"That's right," Nancy says. She's incredibly tired. She lets herself sink back against the cushions.

"My mom caught you when you fell."

"I know."

"She saved you."

"She did. It was really nice of her."

"So how can you be so mean?"

"I'm going to phone. I promised and I will."

"Do you remember the secret word?"

Nancy has to think. "Palomino."

"No! *Pablito!*"

"Right. Pablito."

"You forgot it!"

"Pablito." Nancy sits up and tries to look more alert. "Rhymes with burrito."

Rachel stares at her.

"Sort of," Nancy says.

"You have to do it now," Rachel says. "Right *now*."

Upstairs, the customer left. "She ate all the cookies?" Ron says, noticing the empty plate. He lowers the volume on the radio.

"And the sandwich," Nancy says. She watches the customer—a short, wiry woman who from the back could have been her oldest sister, Libby—climb into an SUV. Libby has six kids under the age of ten. All Nancy's sisters have more kids than they can handle. "What time is it?" she asks.

"Ten to two."

Nancy seems to snap out of a dream. "Jeez, you're kidding! It's like night out there."

"We're in for a storm."

She turns to face him so that he won't see the pencil and piece of wadded-up paper in her back pocket. "What are they saying about the search?"

"It's the usual drill. Nothing to worry about. They haven't a clue. Literally."

"Okay, then, I was thinking of driving to Gerrard Square and buying her some clothes."

"Doesn't she want a salad?"

"I'll pick up something from Valu-Mart on the way back. She wants the clothes right away."

"That's good. See? She's already adapting." He rings open the cash register. "How much do you need?"

"A hundred, hundred and fifty."

He comes around and plants the money in her palm. "Are you all right?"

"Yep." She forces a smile. Those little brown eyes of his usually don't miss much.

"You're going to hear things," he says. "On the radio, in the checkout line, wherever. Don't let it get to you. In fact, don't even listen to the radio."

"Right." She's dying for a smoke.

"And lay off the dope. I can smell it in your hair."

IN THE farthest corner of the Gerrard Square parking lot Nancy opens the driver window a crack and lights a joint. The rain is pounding down so hard that the phone booth, only a few feet away, is almost invisible. If she wanted, she could take this for a sign that she and the phone booth aren't in tune right now, on a psychic level. She could drive off and forget the whole thing. Except she promised. And in her book you don't break a promise to a kid, especially a kid who can see right through you anyway.

She blows smoke through the crack. Just a few puffs, she tells herself. Got to stay clearheaded.

Now there's something Ron said that makes sense. When she's with him, everything makes a kind of sense, but when she's by herself, hardly any of it does. This whole business of driving to Florida and straightening Rachel's hair . . . what was that about again? And why does he hate the mother so much? Oh, yeah—she remembers—because the mother brings Rachel to bars and makes her sing. But is that so bad? Nancy's father used to bring her to bars and make her wait in the cold truck where drunks banged on the window and offered to keep her warm. She told this to Ron only a couple of months ago and what he said then was, "Someone should've turned that bastard in." Okay, so why didn't he turn the landlord in the first time he saw him feeling Rachel up under her pyjamas? He could have driven to a phone booth and called Social Services, used a made-up name, and he wouldn't have had to worry about the lines being tapped, either.

The phone at Rachel's house will be tapped, all right, Nancy can be sure of that. She digs the piece of paper out of her pocket, extinguishes the joint, grabs some coins from the change holder, climbs out of the car, and for about the tenth time in the past few hours seems to wake up. What is she thinking? She has to buy the clothes *before* she makes the call. The police will be all over the phone booth in five minutes, she can't come waltzing out of Zeller's with a bunch of new clothes that just happen to fit a nine-year-old girl and expect she'll be allowed to drive off.

She heads across the parking lot, not running, wanting the rain to slap some sense into her. A backing-up van forces her to jump out of the way, and she finds herself thinking about the time her father almost ran her over with his truck. She was seven maybe. She and her sisters were holding

hands and skipping down the middle of some deserted concession road that seemed raised to heaven because of the fog
lying on the fields and packed in the ditches. They had on
their good dresses (they must have been returning from
church or someone's birthday party) and were yelling, "We
don't stop for nobody! We don't stop for nobody!" Which
didn't mean much, since there was nobody to stop for. But
after a while a truck appeared . . . it was like a ghost truck,
breaking out of the fog. They slowed a bit. They didn't let go
of one another's hands, though, not until Libby said, "It's
Daddy!" and then they all ran to the ditches. All except for
her. She froze. A lot of time seemed to go by—blank, peace-
ful time—before the truck roared past, barely missing her,
the wind of it spinning her around so that she saw her father's
wild face hanging out the driver window, looking back. Her
sisters were in awe. "You nearly died!" they said. "He nearly
ran over you!" They kissed and patted her, and so did he,
later. He told his friends who came to play cards that she
had nerves of steel.

If only, she thinks, entering the mall.

Her hair is plastered to her head. She's shivering and
limping. How will she be able to shop without arousing the
suspicion of the security guard? But nobody seems to notice
her, and once she's digging around in the bargain bins, she
starts to feel better, almost like a real mother. Aside from underwear, socks, and T-shirts she gets a pair of sneakers in what
she hopes are the right size (she has noticed that her own
feet are only slightly bigger than Rachel's), a pair of fluffy
pink slippers, two pairs of shorts, a striped sailor jersey, a
pink pleated skirt, two pairs of jeans (one blue, one purple),
and a pink cotton nightgown. The checkout girl doesn't look

twice at her, and the security guard doesn't grab her arm as she's leaving. In fact, he holds the door open and says, "It's cleared right up."

It has. A good sign. She throws the bags into the trunk and walks toward the phone booth. And just stands there, feeling her nerve give way. She climbs back into the car and lights a cigarette. What she needs, she tells herself, is some relaxing music. She turns on the radio and punches around for the easy-listening station.

". . . She loves all animals," a woman says in a whispery, emotional voice, "including snakes and lizards."

Nancy's hand goes still.

"Even insects," the woman says. "We had hornets in our apartment once and she got stung, but she wouldn't let me kill them. Rachel has always forgiven any harm done to her, so I know she will forgive you, if—"

Nancy frantically changes stations.

". . . It's not too late for you—"

She hits the knob again. ". . . That it might be too late, but there's always—"

She switches off the ignition and sits, puffing on her cigarette. She can't believe it. Every time she turns on the radio . . .

She's being tested, she thinks. Her love for Ron is being tested. No, it's not even that anymore because who is going to believe she isn't his accomplice?

She will forgive you.

Will she? Nancy thinks dully. She opens the car door, then remembers about fingerprints and takes a couple of Kleenexes out of her purse.

Chapter Eighteen

*T*HE RAIN IS a loud spattering, like something frying in a pan. A few minutes after it starts, the man, Ron, comes pounding down. Rachel shunts to the far side of the bed. But he's only letting Tasha in. She waits until he's back upstairs before she'll even move.

"Here, girl," she whispers, patting the bed. The dog jumps up and lies next to her, and she nuzzles the soft black fur, which reminds her of Happy's fur. She bets that Happy and Osmo know she's in trouble. Last year when she was at science camp, they moped for the whole two weeks. She wonders how upset her friends are and if they're leaving flowers in front of her house. She cries a little to imagine her best friend, Lina, crying.

She wishes she knew what time it was. One thing this room doesn't have is a clock. Nancy left about fifteen minutes ago, it feels like. So maybe she has already made the phone call! "Maybe, maybe," Rachel whispers. She gets out of bed and eats a Pringle, her eyes on the television. There isn't cable—she checked—but what if there's a satellite dish? What if she's on the news!

She finds the remote and presses ON. A fuzzy screen comes up. She changes channels, all the way from 2 to 60. Nothing. She hits MENU, then INFO, then some other buttons, and then she hunts around unsuccessfully for a satellite remote.

Outside in the rain somebody is hammering. She carries the desk chair over to one of the windows and climbs on, grabbing hold of the ledge. She can't quite reach the curtains. She climbs down, piles the seat with books and tries again.

The security bars don't surprise her. The windows do, though, the frosted panes. Why are there curtains when you can't see in or out anyway? If this were *her* room and she were a kidnapper she would cover the windows with grilles, like the ones at her school.

A small hope seizes her. She gets down and starts searching for a pole, a broom handle, something hard and long. Except she has searched before, she knows what's here. Still, she opens drawers and cupboards. She opens the closet, which doesn't have hangers, then pushes up the lid of the toy chest and takes out the doll on top: African American Princess Barbie. "Loser," she says, to think of him buying it. Even when she played with Barbies she never had any of these princesses, who are only good for gliding around and giving orders.

Under African American Princess Barbie is Imperial Russian Barbie. She takes her out and considers the large, pointed crown. She tears open the packaging, removes the doll. The crown is hard, harder than she'd really expected, and the doll itself is just about long enough. She goes to the desk, rips a piece of paper off the pad and with the orange marker writes: *My name is Rachel Fox. I'm locked in the basement under the store that fixes lawn mowers. The man is Ron. The woman is Nancy. Don't believe them that I'm not there. They are liars.*

She folds the paper into a square. On the front and back she writes *HELP* and then tucks it into her pocket. She doesn't intend to put it outside right away (it'll only get soaked) but she wants to have it ready. All she needs to do now, while the hammering is going on, is to make a crack big enough that when the rain stops she can slide the paper through. She picks Barbie up by the feet and climbs back on the chair.

The hammering outside is fairly steady. "One, two . . . ," she whispers, establishing the rhythm. On "four" she hits Barbie crown-first against the glass and almost falls forward as the doll's head caves in. She adjusts her grip higher up the body, squeezes the doll between the bars, and tries a few short, sharp taps. The head still collapses but not as much as before. The crown stays firm. To make sure Ron can't hear, she continues keeping time with the hammering.

The glass doesn't break, though. She switches to gouging with the crown's peak and after a few minutes produces a scratch. Her heart begins to race. She gouges faster. She forgets about the hammering, about Ron coming down. She doesn't even register the books sliding out from under her. At the last second she grabs for the bar and misses, knocking over the chair and falling on top of it.

Tasha jumps around, yelping. "Quiet," Rachel moans. The whole side of her body feels broken. Oh, and he heard! He's coming down! She crawls off the chair but when she tries to stand, her foot gives out and she falls again.

The door opens. "What happened?" he says. He lifts the chair out of the way.

"Don't touch me," she cries.

"You're hurt."

She gets herself up and limps to the other end of the room.

"You've got a sprain," he tells her.

She shakes her head.

"I'd better take a look at it," he says.

He notices the window. Stepping around the books he goes over and reaches up to open the curtains wider. As he does this, his T-shirt comes loose from his belt, and his stomach bulges out like a loaf of bread.

"Nancy can look at it," she whimpers.

"Nancy will be a while yet." He wipes a finger under each of his eyes. He clears his throat. She wonders, astonished, if he's crying. Finally he says, "You can't break these windows. They're covered in a special film." A glance in her direction. "I'm just going to go upstairs to get some bandage."

She listens for the door to close at the top of the stairs before taking the note from her pocket and sticking it under the toy chest. Then she quickly gathers up the books and puts them in the shelf. Her arm and leg are red and scratched. What if he wants to rub antiseptic cream on her or make her soak in a bath? She yanks the duvet off the bed, wraps it around herself, and sits on the sofa. She'll let him bandage her foot, she decides, but that's all. Maybe it *is* sprained. It hurts.

"The rain's letting up," he says, coming through the door. No mention of the duvet. He drags the chair over and sits in front of her. He's wearing cologne. Musk, it smells like, the same as Mika wears. He must be on his way out, she thinks, and her fear eases slightly.

But at his touch, she begins to shake. He cups her foot in both hands, like you'd hold a bird. "It's swollen," he says. "How does it feel?"

"Okay," she murmurs.

"I should have brought down some ice."

"I don't want ice!" She wants him to just hurry up and finish.

"All right. No ice." He sets her foot on his knee. And now, all of a sudden, *he's* shaking . . . so hard that he can barely cut the bandage. He wraps it too loosely and has to start over.

What's the matter with him, she wonders. Her own shaking stops.

"It shouldn't be too tight," he says.

"It *is*," she says.

"Sorry." Bubbles of sweat dot his forehead. He unwraps what he's done and starts a third time.

"When my mom finds me," she says, "you'll be arrested and go to jail."

He feels around in his pocket for something. Metal clips. He attaches them, then takes her foot off his knee. "There you go," he says. He runs the back of his arm over his forehead.

The bandage is still too tight; her whole foot throbs. "What did you kidnap me for?" she asks angrily.

He looks at her. She looks away, frightened again. She tucks her bandaged foot under the duvet.

"It's what Nancy told you," he says. "You were in a

dangerous situation. At the motel where your mother works. At your house. Certain men . . ."

The bandage roll has dropped to the floor, and he picks it up and presses it between his palms. His legs still shake a little. "You're a very beautiful girl," he says, glancing at her. "There are men who would like to take advantage of that. Do you understand what I'm talking about?"

She isn't sure. "No," she says.

"They want to hurt you. For their own pleasure."

Oh, she thinks. For sex. She thinks of Elliott, the unemployed drunk man from across the street who yells, "You don't love me anymore!" at her mother. Her mother just laughs. All the neighbours put up with him and say he's harmless. But once, when she ran over there to get Happy's ball, he jumped out from behind the hedge and growled, "How about a kiss?" and tried to grab her arm. His dirty fingernails left a scratch. She didn't tell her mother because her mother would have gone crazy.

"Do you mean Elliott from across the street?" she asks Ron.

He blinks a few times. "I couldn't say."

A notion strikes her. "Do you work for the government?"

"No, I don't. Why?"

She shrugs. If he *was* a spy, he wouldn't tell her. But he wouldn't be worried about the police, either. Or maybe he would, she reasons, if his mission was top secret. But she really doesn't think he's a spy. "Who are they then?" she asks.

"I haven't got names."

"Not Mika who lives in my house." Her throat tightens. "You don't even *know* Mika."

His eyes are on her lips. She jerks her head to the side.

"Not Mika," he says. He stands. "Nancy will be back soon with your new clothes. And maybe"—he's glancing around the room—"you'll let her put some ice—"

"How long do I have to be down here?"

He picks up the Barbie doll. "I don't know."

"A week?"

"Longer." He adjusts the crown.

"Two weeks?"

"Longer than two weeks."

"But I'm supposed to go to music camp!"

The look of surprise that crosses his face gives her hope. "It's been paid for and everything!"

"I'm sorry." He frowns at the doll.

Tears prick her eyes. "I want to go home now. I don't *care* about the men."

"Nancy won't be too long." He puts the doll on the toy chest and leaves the room, Tasha running out after him.

Rachel buries her face in the duvet and cries. Not for very long, though. She's tired of crying. She undoes the bandage and wraps it again so that it's looser.

She's trying to remember all the men she has ever met. There are so many. Of all the video store customers and neighbours and people from the bar, only Elliott pops up as bad. Eventually the idea of slave drivers occurs to her. Lina's older brother, who was born in Mauritania, says that slave drivers from Africa are stealing dark-skinned girls off the streets and shipping them out of the country in orange crates. The police won't do a thing about it, he says. When Rachel told her mother this, her mother said, "Lina's brother has an overactive imagination." But what if it's true?

The more Rachel thinks about it, the more true it seems.

It explains, for instance, why Ron never went to the police. And why he can't tell her the men's names. If he doesn't come right out and *call* them slave drivers, maybe that's because he's worried she'll start screaming and he won't know what to do. He's a very sensitive person, it seems to her . . . crying about the window, shaking the way he did.

She feels a twinge of guilt to think how hurt he looked when she told him he was going to jail.

THE CALL comes in not five minutes after the news conference.

Celia and the deputy chief of police are drinking coffee in the dining room. The powder-fine fingerprint dust, which started out black and white—black for the light surfaces, white for the darker ones (but now, having endlessly risen and resettled, is ash grey everywhere)—has been ineffectively wiped off the table, leaving a silver sheen. Celia rubs X's in it. She is trying to compose herself. By the end of her statement her voice had disintegrated to a cracked whisper. She didn't break down, though. She didn't need the deputy chief to take her arm, although he did.

His name is Martin Morris. He's a tall man with a long, worn face and heavy-lidded eyes full of some private misery. And yet his voice is deep and reassuring, and listening to him now (he's saying that several radio stations interrupted regular programming to broadcast live) she thinks maybe it isn't misery, it's exhaustion. He has told her he's an insomniac. She wonders how *she* looks, how she looked on the TV. On the slim chance that Rachel sees her, she hopes she came across as in charge. How awful to think that instead of comforting Rachel she's giving her something else to worry about. Whenever there's a small crisis, a cheque bouncing or the car not starting, Rachel is the levelheaded one. As she, Celia, begins to lose it, Rachel's face takes on this long-suffering expression no nine-year-old child should have access to.

"I can't vouch for the networks," Martin Morris says. He's still talking about live coverage. "CTV potentially, on their all-news station."

"So the call could come any time now," Celia says.

The call to Mika's cell—that's the number she gave. Even so, when the phone in the kitchen rings at exactly that moment, and despite the fact that it's been ringing all day, she gasps.

Big Lynne answers. "Fox residence, Constable Shriver speaking," she says in her loud, no-nonsense voice. A pause. "That's right." And then, "I'm here. Who's calling?" Another pause. "I can promise that."

In the silence that follows, Morris scrapes back his chair.

"Can you tell me . . ." Big Lynne starts.

Morris comes to his feet. Before he reaches the doorway Big Lynne is there. "Pablito," she says to Celia. "Does that mean anything to you?"

"Oh, my God," Celia says.

"She's alive," Big Lynne says.

The room goes black.

When Celia regains consciousness, Morris has left, and Big Lynne is pressing a wet sponge to her forehead.

"Boy," Big Lynne says, "did you go out like a light."

"Where is she?"

"We don't know."

"I thought the calls were traced." Celia pushes away the sponge. "I thought it was instantaneous."

"It is practically, but the call was made from a phone booth. At the Gerrard Square Mall. Pape and Gerrard. It was a woman. She said Rachel is fine and being looked after by people who just want her to be safe and would never hurt her. She said tell the mother 'Pablito,' that Rachel told her to say it."

"Oh, God. Oh, thank God."

"You pray for miracles and sometimes you get them."

"It's our word. You know? Our secret word."

"I figured as much."

"How long before the police get there?"

"Any patrol cars in the area will be there already."

"But the woman won't be."

"Listen, she went to a crowded place. Somebody might have seen her acting suspiciously. I'd be surprised if she hasn't been picked up on one of the surveillance cameras."

"They'll be able to get her fingerprints, right?" Celia is thinking that the kind of woman who would abduct a child will have a criminal record.

"Sure, if she left any. They might even get DNA. You can get it off the mouthpiece, from saliva. Not a lot of people know that. Come on. I'll play you the message. Can you stand? Are you okay?"

They go into the kitchen. "Here, sit," Big Lynne says, pulling out a chair. She jabs a couple of numbers into the phone and hands Celia the receiver.

Two rings, and then, "Fox residence, Constable Shriver speaking."

"Where Rachel Fox lives?"

"That's right."

"Okay, I'm only going to say this once, so don't interrupt me. Rachel is alive, she's doing good."

There's a jumbled knocking sound, as if the receiver was dropped.

"Hello?" (From the woman.)

"I'm here. Who's calling?"

"Don't talk, okay? Just let me tell you. First off, I need a promise that it won't get out to the media that you got this call."

"I can promise that."

"Okay, so, here's a word. Pablito. You tell it to the mother and she'll know I'm not fooling around. Pablito. Rachel told me to say it. Like I said, she's doing good. She's with people who only want her to be safe. They would never hurt her, don't worry about that. But if this gets out to the media or whoever, then, I don't know. Seriously. Something bad could happen."

"Can you tell me—"

Dial tone.

Celia holds the receiver away from her ear, her relief shaken by the threat. "What does she mean, *something bad could happen*?"

"Well, by *people* she most likely means herself and her husband or boyfriend, and maybe she made the call behind his back, so if he finds out, she's in trouble."

"Will he find out?"

"Not from a police source."

"But why would she call?"

"Maybe Rachel got to her. Or she's feeling guilty."

"So they don't want money."

"*She* doesn't."

"But why would they take her then?"

Big Lynne opens her hands. "Hard to say."

"She sounded scared."

"Is the voice familiar?"

"I'm not sure . . ."

"Do you want to hear it again?"

"Yeah."

On it comes. The accent is East Coast or northern Ontario. The word *seriously* jumps out at her, the way it breaks into an anxious quaver, almost a laugh.

"Anything?" Big Lynne asks.

"Let me hear it again."

This time *seriously* merges with the whole jittery tone of the message. Still, there's something. "I should look at those lists," she says, referring to the lists, now in police hands, of motel and video store customers.

"We can have them faxed," Big Lynne says.

Celia stands and starts to move around the kitchen. Where has she heard that raspy, nerve-wracked voice before? She mentally rummages through the neighbourhood. Meanwhile Big Lynne radioes an officer at the mall and learns that surveillance cameras are being seized and roadblocks set up in surrounding streets. Celia pictures the woman slinking down a garbage-strewn alley. She tries to conjure a mental image of Rachel's face to assure herself that the fear in it is bearable. Nothing comes, nothing has come for hours. It's all right, though: Rachel is alive and being looked after by people who would never hurt her. Why would the woman say it if it wasn't true? Why would she risk making the call? "Are the forensic guys still upstairs?" she asks.

"No. Why?"

"Maybe I'll lie down now."

Her apartment is undisturbed. The computer has been taken, and there's fingerprint dust all over the place, but everything else is as it was: scattered sheet music, overflowing ashtray. She goes into Rachel's bedroom. On the floor is a pile of dirty clothes that haven't made it to the laundry. She kneels and brings a white cotton jersey to her face. She imagines a test where there are a hundred piles of clothes and if she finds the pile with Rachel's smell she'll find Rachel. A million piles, it wouldn't matter, she'd pick the right one.

"You're alive," she says. She falls forward as the relief begins to burst out of her in convulsive gasps. When she can catch her breath, she says, "I knew you were, I knew it." She rolls onto her back. A feeling of tranquility comes over her. She recognizes that it is temporary and fragile and maybe not even real, but it's enough for now. She sleeps.

Chapter Nineteen

*R*ON SAID HE wanted to sleep in the shop and get up every few hours to listen at the door, but Nancy took a dim view of that. She told him Rachel would hear him moving around and it would scare her.

"What if her foot's bothering her?" he said.

"Her foot's fine," Nancy insisted. "Don't worry about it. Don't go down there."

When she comes out of the bathroom after brushing her teeth, he's lying on the bed. He's still in his boxer shorts, she's glad to see. She smelled cologne on him earlier, and since he never wears cologne except when he wants sex, she thought—surprised and frankly disgusted—that he was in the mood. But his shorts are the opposite signal, so he must have lost interest. She's wearing underpants and a T-shirt. For her, the idea of wanting to have sex ever again is impossible to imagine.

She pulls her half of the sheet up to her waist. A second later she throws it off. In spite of the open window and rotating fan and the rain they had earlier, the room is stuffy. Neither of them suggests switching on the central air conditioning because then the basement gets cold.

"I forgot to let Tasha in," he says suddenly. He starts to sit up.

"She's with Rachel," Nancy reminds him.

He lies back down. After a moment he says, "I suppose she'd prefer a piano."

"A keyboard is what I told her," Nancy says. "A piano wouldn't fit down there anyway, right?"

"It'd fit, an apartment-sized one. The problem is carrying it. I couldn't do it myself."

And even if she had two good legs, Nancy doubts she'd be any help. "Well, that settles that," she says.

She thinks about how Rachel is also limping, for the time being anyway. She heard what happened from both Rachel and Ron, and yet she can't rid herself of the guilty feeling that *her* limp somehow got passed along, like a cold. "We're lucky she didn't kill herself," she says, "falling off that chair. Poor thing, she was only trying to see out."

"She was trying to break the glass."

"You can't blame her."

"I don't."

"It's like a fake room," Nancy goes on. "Windows, but they're painted over, they don't even look real. A big, expensive TV but it's only for movies. I don't get why you can't hook up the satellite, then block the stations that have news."

Ron is silent.

"There's a way of keeping the volume down, too, isn't there? So she can't turn it up?"

"Yeah, there is."

"So what's the problem?"

"I never thought of it."

"Jeez, Ron."

"I'll do it tomorrow."

"First thing."

He pats her knee. "First thing."

A red glow fills the room from the neon plumbing-supply sign next door. Nancy wonders if she left any lights on in her apartment. She remembers about the present under her sofa and says, "It's your birthday."

"Yeah," he says. "I was thinking how long my mother's been gone. Twenty-six years."

Nancy lifts a hand to ward off that information. His mother dying on his birthday has always struck her as a bad omen. On top of which, at any mention of his mother's being dead she is reminded of the envelope she found about a year ago. She was searching his kitchen for shish-kebob skewers, and at the back of a cupboard under a pile of old receipts she found an unsealed manila envelope that had MOTHER written on it but there was nothing inside except for six pieces of paper covered in scrawls. The scrawls had names: *Commander* and *The Victor* and other names she doesn't remember. None of them made any sense or had anything to do with a mother. Did he mean *his* mother? She never asked. Aside from not wanting him to know that she'd looked in the envelope, she had a feeling the answer might be creepy or just plain sad. His childhood, what little of it he has ever talked about, was worse than hers in a way. At least she was never lonely.

"I bought you a present," she tells him. "But I decided not to bring it over."

"My present is how great you've been. I couldn't have done this without you, Nance."

You *did* do it without me, she thinks, restraining an urge to confess what she did without him—the phone call. He'd be stunned. And then he'd . . . what? Pack up and move Rachel somewhere else? She counsels herself to let sleeping dogs lie. There has been nothing about it on the radio, and there would have been by now if the media had found out.

"We're going to get through this," he says.

She turns to face the wall. "Just don't go downstairs."

She wonders if she still loves him. She imagines him in prison and the other prisoners kicking him in the head, calling him a fat fuck, and that tells her. But she supposes she knew she loved him when she came up from the basement and said, "You have to buy Rachel a keyboard," and he said, "All right," no questions, no argument, and she remembered he was only trying to protect Rachel from abuse and for a few minutes she was ashamed about having made the phone call behind his back.

Funny how she keeps forgetting about the landlord. It could be the name: Mika . . . she pictures a little dog. And then there's the rage Rachel flew into, defending him. Would Nancy have defended her father like that? Well, not like that (in her house the girls didn't lose their tempers) but she remembers how upset she got the time her uncle Barry called him an evil bastard. She was almost fifteen before she worked out that her father didn't pick her because he loved her the most, he picked her because she was the scared one, the one who wouldn't tell.

Ron is quietly snoring. Not that she thinks he's asleep. She hopes Rachel is. She offered to sit with her until she fell asleep, but Rachel wasn't interested. "I've got Tasha," she said, which Nancy took to be a good sign—how close the two of them had already gotten.

"You wait," she said, "she'll crawl right under the covers." And then, at the door, she added, stupidly, "Sweet dreams."

Rachel was nuzzling Tasha. Without looking up, she murmured, "I don't think I'm going to have sweet dreams."

That made Nancy cry a little as she climbed the stairs. It wasn't just how depressed Rachel sounded, it was how excited she'd been only a few hours before . . . and friendly, squeezing Nancy's hand while Nancy filled her in about the phone call. She wanted it word for word, so Nancy did her best to remember everything: the policewoman's name (she said "Constable McIvor," though that wasn't it) and how she said, "Rachel's doing good," and so on.

"Did Constable McIvor believe you?" Rachel asked.

"Sure, she did. Because I told her *Pablito*. I said, 'You pass that along to the mother and she'll know I'm not fooling around.'"

"Yes!" Rachel cried, then covered her mouth with her hands.

"It's okay," Nancy said. "He can't hear us in here."

They were in the bathroom, their supposed reason being that Rachel was trying on her new clothes in front of the mirror. Nancy had brought down an ice pack, and now she got Rachel to sit on the toilet while she sat on the floor and unwrapped the bandage. There was an ugly bruise and still a bit of swelling, so she applied the ice. "Brace yourself," she said, but Rachel didn't seem to feel anything, she was too caught up in imagining her mother and Mika's relief. She had them drinking wine from one of the bottles Mika put aside for special occasions. She had them eating, finally, after almost no food since last night. She wondered what they'd be having for supper. Spaghetti, she decided. "That's what we have on Saturday nights," she said, "Mika and me, if I don't go to the motel. I'll bet my mom isn't going to work. Not tonight."

"Spaghetti and meatballs?" Nancy asked.

"I'm a vegetarian, I told you already." She wiggled her foot. "That's enough," she said about the ice.

"So you're *all* vegetarians."

"My mom almost is. She eats fish. I don't. But I'm not a vegan because I eat cheese and eggs. They don't hurt the animal." She was back to her chatty voice. "Mika eats veal. It used to really bother me, but he explained how eating lots of meat is part of his culture. He's from Finland."

"Finland, eh?" Nancy wrapped the foot back up and began examining the scratches on Rachel's arm and leg.

"She's alive, she's alive," Rachel sang.

"Who?"

"Me. That's what my mom's saying—'She's alive, she's alive.'"

Her mood held for another couple of hours. She tried on the clothes and shoes, or at least *a* shoe, on her good foot. It was a bit roomy but she said she didn't care. The purple jeans were a hit; she asked if she could keep them when she left. "They're *yours*," was how Nancy answered. To get off the subject of leaving, she looked at her watch. "Hey, supper-time," she said, although it was only ten after five.

Upstairs, it gave her no pleasure to report that Rachel liked the clothes and wasn't in pain. It annoyed her to see Ron sitting at the counter, tinkering with a motor and listening to music on the radio, while, because of what he'd done, people's lives were in turmoil. "From now on," she announced, "I'm a vegetarian. I'm never touching meat again. And I'm never buying it either. You can buy your own meat."

"I don't need meat," he said. "I'm on a diet."

"And I'm eating my meals in the basement. With her."

"Good idea." He offered to set up the card table.

"*I* can set it up," she snapped.

"It's in the furnace room," he said, ignoring her tone.

She found herself infuriated. "You act like everything's going along just fine! Well, it's not!" And then she lit into him for waiting outside the door while she was in with Rachel: "It's like you're an armed guard. Like you'd shoot her if she left. Why don't you let me have my own key?"

"You might leave it lying around."

It was true, she might. "I'll wear it on my chain," she said, fingering the eighteen-karat gold necklace he gave her last Christmas.

"All right. But then don't leave *that* lying around."

"I'm not a complete numbskull."

She went to get the card table.

As soon as she told Rachel that Ron wasn't waiting outside, Rachel asked to hear about the call again. "The policewoman answered . . ." she prompted.

"After two rings," Nancy said, flipping open the legs of the card table. As before, she skipped over the warning about keeping the media in the dark, saying, instead, that she finished off with, "Rachel sends her mother all her love."

"I thought you just hung up!" Rachel cried.

"I got that in first," Nancy said, wishing she had.

During supper Rachel stayed chatty and wound up. She

talked about a boy named Leonard who walked her to and from school and took piano lessons from her mother. She said that she also took piano lessons and practised an hour every night after supper.

"We'll have to get a piano down here," Nancy said, carried away by Rachel's mood. "Or a keyboard maybe. Whatever will fit."

"Keyboards are expensive."

"Listen, Ron wants you to feel at home."

It was the wrong thing to say. Rachel barely spoke after that. She huddled into herself and shrugged off Nancy's suggestion that they watch a movie together. Nancy read through the movie titles, trying to entice her. Finally Rachel said, "If I wanted to watch anything right now, it would be TV. But it doesn't even work."

"Is that what's bothering you? No TV?"

"What's *bothering* me is I'm here." She scowled and picked at her bandage. "Do you know who the men are that want to hurt me?"

"Not by name." Other than Mika, there were only the men who drank at the motel, and Nancy had a feeling Rachel wouldn't take them seriously.

"Are they slave drivers?"

"Slave drivers?"

"My friend's brother, he's from Africa. He says the slave drivers that live there come over here and kidnap girls that have dark skin and send them *back* to Africa."

"Okay," Nancy said uncertainly. Should she go along with this? Would it make things easier?

"I thought maybe they're slave drivers."

"Well, maybe they are."

Rachel looked up. "Really?"

"Ron hasn't actually told me." She straightened the pile of DVDs in her lap.

"He doesn't want to upset you probably."

"Yeah, probably."

"What will they do if they can't get me?"

Nancy sighed. She wanted to comfort this kid, not terrify her. But if she said, "Give up and go home," she'd just have to invent another gang of bad guys. "Wait around," she said finally.

"For how long is what I wonder."

"Oh. A while."

"Ron said more than two weeks."

"He did?"

"I think three weeks. I think they'll wait around for three weeks." She nodded. She intended to stick with this idea. And she was through talking about it. "I should have a bath," she said, coming to her feet.

"I'll run it for you," Nancy said.

"Can we wash my hair?"

"You bet we can."

Later, Nancy told Ron about the bath but not about washing Rachel's hair.

She can hardly tell it to herself. You hold a little girl's head under the tap. She's naked in the tub, her eyes are squeezed shut, she trusts you. But she isn't yours. She shouldn't be anywhere near you, as a matter of fact. If there are words for how that can make you feel, Nancy doesn't have them.

Besides, it's none of his business.

* * *

WHILE RON waits for Nancy to fall asleep he holds himself motionless, although his heart is drumming and itchy rivulets of perspiration trickle down his chest and ears. Sex might help but he feels her resistance and he respects it. Not for the first time he is struck by the irony that he has stayed with Nancy all these years partly because she can't have children, and yet what attracted him right from the beginning was her maternal instinct.

In her new incarnation she's scarcely recognizable. Her little face, normally so eager, is pinched with purpose and judgment. Not always reasonable judgment. She'll admit that Rachel needed rescuing from that Mika bastard, then five minutes later she'll say, "You shouldn't have taken her." He's trying to be patient. He can understand how hard it might be for her to accept that only a day ago Rachel was living through the same nightmare that she herself, at the same age, barely survived.

There's also the fact that Rachel's mother has a hold on her sympathies. She met the woman once, unfortunately, and found her to be *really nice*. "Who could love a child more than her own mother?" she asks.

Me, he thinks. I could. But he knows better than to say so. "She's the love of my life"—what if he said that? What if Nancy had come back early today and caught him slumped on the counter, sobbing? She'd have been scared to death. No explanation other than that he was losing his nerve would have made sense to her.

It isn't his nerve he's losing, it's his grip, his emotional equilibrium. The thought of Rachel in the basement is agony. He's almost better off going down there because then he sees her for the scared little human being she is, and all he wants is to make her feel safe. If killing somebody would accomplish anything, he'd do it. He'd kill Mika in a minute, not that Rachel would thank him.

He reminds himself that it has been only twenty-six hours. In a few days the tension will ease off, they'll all relax, and Rachel will be in a better position to see her old life for what it was. Right now *he's* the enemy. *He's* the one she hates. Thinking this, his eyes fill, and for a few seconds he's on the verge of breaking down again. He retrieves the memory of her foot in his hands, and that helps. Except now he has to go down there.

"Nance?" he whispers.

Silence.

"Are you asleep?"

He gets out of bed and leaves the room. Once he's in the kitchen he breathes more freely. Despite what Nancy said, he doubts that Rachel can hear him through the three-and-a-half-inch fibreglass insulation. And even if she can, a few muted creaks aren't the kind of noise that disturbs a sleeping child.

He feels his way to the shop, where he switches on a light. A towel is under the counter, and he gets it and wipes his face and chest. It's much cooler down here. He looks at the door to the basement. Is she warm enough? He'd better check. He picks up the key and takes a few steps, then stops, shocked by the ease with which he almost talked himself into barging in on her.

And yet . . . What if she's in trouble, moaning in pain?

He opens the door and steps onto the landing. Before he knows it, he's at the bottom of the stairs. He remembers Tasha and counts himself lucky that she hasn't woken up and started barking. He presses his ear against the door to the room. Nothing. Good, he thinks forcefully, pushing aside his disappointment that there's no need for him to enter. He sits on the bottom step.

She's not even ten feet away. She's wearing the pink nightgown Nancy bought her. He stands. He sits. He begins rocking back and forth, big swings of his torso as if physical momentum alone could decide whether he should go in or stay put. And yet even as he surrenders to the sensation of consciously abdicating responsibility he knows which side of him will prevail and when it does, when the rocking stops, it's as though he has passed through fire. *This* is why he needs to be down here, he tells himself. To test his love.

"Pssst!"

He jerks around. Nancy is on the landing, motioning violently for him to come up. He gets to his feet. The joy evaporates. Why didn't he send Nancy home hours ago? He can't remember. He can't remember why he was so adamant about having her move in.

He enters the shop and shuts the door. He isn't looking at her, so when the first punch strikes him in the ribs he thinks he's been shot: a sniper through the window. He grabs onto the counter, one arm raised against what there's no mistaking now—the hard fast jabs pelting him like rocks. "Hey!" he's saying. "Hey!"—trying not to yell. Finally he gets hold of her wrists. For a moment they stare at each other. Her face leaps with fury.

"You promised not to come down!" she hisses.

"I didn't promise." Her body slackens and he releases his grip. He thinks she's going to collapse but she only hobbles sideways. "I was worried about her," he says. "I haven't spent any time with her, not really. You two have spent hours together. I've spent what? Ten minutes?"

"So?"

"I wanted to . . . see how she is." A tide of exhaustion has him groping for the stool. He sits.

"You're why she wet the bed," Nancy says. "Why she crawls under it."

Her fists clench, and he braces for another battering. Where did she learn how to throw a punch like that?

"Don't you get it?" she says.

"No," he admits.

"Because you were never scared of somebody. Of somebody coming . . ."

Her voice catches, and he is moved. "Nance," he says. "You know I would never hurt her."

"*She* doesn't know."

"Oh, God." He walks out from behind the counter and takes her in his arms. She presses her forehead against his chest.

In bed he holds her until she's asleep and then he rolls over and looks at the picture on his bedside table. There's enough light that he can make out the frame and the crack in the glass. The picture itself he can imagine, although it's only because his mother died twenty-six years ago today that he even tries to impose her on the cocky stance and stubborn jaw, the bony knees. A long time ago the girl in the picture became somebody else to him.

Chapter Twenty

*J*ENNY'S SCHOOL WAS in Burlington, just down the street from where her mother worked. Since Alcan's head office was on the way to Burlington, the plan was for Ron's father to give them both a ride, although it would mean that he'd have to leave an hour earlier and Ron wouldn't get his usual lift to school. Ron didn't care. For one thing, he'd gotten used to being alone in the house. Also, he wanted to take apart Mrs. Lawson's vacuum cleaner, and on Monday morning, as soon as he heard the car doors shut, he wheeled it out of the broom closet and turned it on.

There wasn't much suction, partly because, as Ron knew, the exhaust on these old Hoover Constellation models was designed to blow onto the floor and form a cushion of air. He cleared out the intake tube and adjusted the fan belt, and matters improved. He decided against telling Mrs. Lawson. The last thing he wanted was to have her thinking he'd fixed her vacuum for her sake, for the sake of impressing her.

That night she heated up chicken stew from a frozen batch she'd brought in a cooler the day before. Ron, remembering how her husband had died, scrutinized every spoonful for bones. So, he noticed, did Jenny. After supper Ron's father asked if anyone wanted to play gin rummy, but Mrs. Lawson said Jenny had homework to do, and when Jenny left the table, Ron felt awkward. The partnership between him and his father, so clearly broken with a woman in the house, now seemed like a game he'd made the mistake of taking seriously.

"I've got homework, too," he said.

On his way past Jenny and Mrs. Lawson's room he glanced in. Jenny sat very straight at her desk, her back to the door. He went down to his room and lay on his bed and wondered about her. Was her "Moving Day" story true . . . was she really happy to be here? Did she miss her father? Her horse?

He rolled onto the floor and dragged out from under his bed one of the suitcases in which he kept his old toys. Beneath all the tanks and trucks and soldiers he found a Shetland pony, partly melted from the time he tried to see how the plastic would burn. He threw it back in, searched around some more and dug out Geronimo's black stallion, Midnight.

Downstairs they were watching television. There was a wailing sound—on the TV, he thought—but then he realized it was coming from Jenny's room. He crawled across the floor and pressed his ear to the adjoining wall. "Go to sleep," Jenny was saying, "go to sleep now, go to sleep." And then the wailing sound again. "Oh, all right," she said, "I'll heat up your bottle."

He stood and went out into the hall. Silence. He went down to her room.

She was sitting in front of the dollhouse. Without looking around she said, "Do you want to play?"

He stepped across the threshold.

"You can be the father," she said.

"Those shingles are real cedar," he told her, moving closer. He'd noticed them earlier.

"I know." She got up on her knees. "It's all real. The chimney is real brick. They make little bricks especially. And when you do this—" She pushed a button on the fireplace. "Look! Fire!"

Fake fire, but still. He set Midnight down and peered in. No wires were visible.

"Okay," she said importantly, "look at this." She flicked a switch on the stove and the burners turned red. "And there's food in the fridge." She opened it. "Ketchup and milk and juice and a roast of beef and everything a person would eat."

Her arm bumped his as she reached into the dining room. On came the chandelier. "Everything works," she said. She tipped a rocking chair that had an old-lady doll in it. The chair rocked hard, the old lady keeled over. She grabbed something and pressed it into his hand. It was a chimpanzee. She'd taken it from a crowd of tiny stuffed animals propped up on one of the toy beds. "My mother told me your mother used to collect stuffed monkeys," she said.

It was a perfect replica of his mother's favourite chimpanzee, right down to the orange segmented fingers and the red vest and cap.

"Your mother was a scatterbrain," she said.

"She was not," he said angrily. Where had she heard that?

Jenny looked puzzled. "What's a scatterbrain?" she said.

"I have to finish my homework," he muttered.

He put the chimpanzee back and went to stand but

Jenny cried, "Hey!" She had picked up Midnight. "I didn't see him! What's his name?"

"Midnight."

"I think he should be Misty." She snatched up a man doll and thrust it at him. "Put him on Misty. He's outdoor father."

Ron didn't think to refuse. He spread the doll's legs and set him in the saddle. Because the knees wouldn't bend he could only secure him by leaning him forward and pinching the arms on either side of the horse's head in a jockey's pose. Jenny seized a woman doll from the kitchen and pranced her out of the house. "Oh, Phil," she said in an actressy voice. "You promised to mow the lawn."

Ron waited. The man looked so small and insecure on Midnight, though he was smiling happily. He had brown wavy hair and wore blue jeans and a blue-and-green check-ered shirt.

"He has to answer," Jenny said in her own voice.

"I'm riding my horse," Ron said.

"All right, darling. Don't be too long."

Ron cantered Midnight to the end of the carpet.

"Okay," Jenny said. "Leave him there. Now you're in-door father." She handed him a blond man wearing a navy bathrobe and smoking a pipe. He had a sleepy, heavy-lidded smile.

"Can't the other guy go in?" Ron said. The man's smile disturbed him.

"Don't be silly." She pointed to a bedroom. "Okay, lie him down. Turn on that lamp." Ron obeyed. Jenny switched off the downstairs lights and hopped the woman up the stairs. In the doorway the woman paused to say, "How many times do I have to tell you not to smoke in bed?"

Ron tugged at the pipe.

"It doesn't come out," Jenny said briskly. She placed the woman beside the man. "Oh, darling," she moaned, and turned her doll and pressed it against Ron's. "Hold him!" she ordered because Ron's hand had flown right out of the house. "You have to hold him," she said. "They're sexing!"

Ron sat back on his heels. For the first time since he'd come in here he was aware of Jenny's proximity.

"Hurry up!" she said, a blush overtaking her face.

His mouth felt parched as he reached in and held the man. That was all he had to do; Jenny's doll did the pushing and moaning.

"Hey, Buddy!"

It was his father, calling from downstairs. Ron jumped up and ran into the hall. "Yeah?" He still had the man doll.

"*Wild Kingdom* is on!"

"I'm doing my homework!"

"Just letting you know!"

He returned to the room and dropped the doll on the carpet. Nothing of the panic he felt constricting his face showed on Jenny's. She looked only irritated as she plucked the woman off the bed and walked her into the baby's room.

"See you later," he said.

No answer.

At breakfast she was her silent, unfriendly self. It surprised him that she could pretend nothing had happened; it elevated her in his eyes. After everyone had left the house he went into her room. The man dolls were where he'd left them, one lying across Midnight, the other on the floor nearby. The woman doll was leaning against the refrigerator, her head twisted backwards. He picked her up and picked up the indoor man and rubbed them together. Nothing. He twisted the woman's head to the front and tried again, this time saying, "Sexing," and now he felt a thrill but it was dis-appointing compared to what he'd felt last night. He needed Jenny, he guessed. Without her, the dolls were just dolls.

That evening he stayed in his room and started putting together his new model airplane. Although Jenny chattered away next door, he fought the temptation to go over. He sus-pected she knew better than to talk to anyone about the sexing, that wasn't what worried him. It was his father's finding out he'd played with dolls at all. If Jenny gave up waiting and came to his room, he'd tell her he was busy. "Can't you see I'm busy?" he practised under his breath, using different tones of voice. But she didn't come. Why? Was she mad at him? Had she even thought about him at all?

DAYS WENT by and then weeks and she kept to herself. He figured he'd let her down. Or maybe she just didn't like him. She barely spoke to his father, either, except when she had a new story to read. (Since "Moving Day," there'd been "Guess What? I'm Part Chinese," "How to Make Friends," and "The Tragic Death of White Star," about a racing horse that broke its ankle and had to be put to sleep.) Mostly she stayed in her room, or she and her mother sat at the kitchen table and worked on her flash cards. Every Saturday after lunch they visited people they knew in Burlington. On Sunday evenings they lay on the sofa together and watched *The Wonderful World of Disney*. It unsettled Ron how they clung to each other with their legs and arms entwined. If his father also found this behaviour peculiar, he never let on.

She began to be the girl he dreamed about at night, the girl who was in danger but didn't realize it and couldn't hear him yelling. He'd been having these dreams for years but until now the girl had always been faceless.

One night he woke up from such a dream, and there she was. "What?" he said, frightened.

"Shhh." She wore a long white nightgown. She moved into the horizontal bars of light coming through his blinds. "They're sexing," she whispered.

"Who?" He thought she meant the dolls.

"My mother and your father."

"What are you talking about?"

"Come on! You can hear them!"

Still uncomprehending, he got to his feet and followed her into the hall, then stopped at the sound of birdlike cries coming from his father's room. Jenny, who was right outside the door, covered her mouth with her hands.

The cries jerked higher. There was a deep male groan, after which the cries broke off. Jenny hurried back to where he was. She tugged his sleeve. He pulled away.

The rescuing thought that the man in there wasn't his father came and went. He returned to his room, shut the door, and sat on the edge of his bed.

Jenny giggled.

She was lying under the covers. He jumped up. "What are you doing?" he whispered. "Get out of here!"

"I'm scared," she said in a small voice. He knew she wasn't. All he could see of her was the glint in one eye and the suggestion of her face, a darker whiteness than the pillow. He wondered if she and her mother were sex maniacs.

Mrs. Lawson must be, or else why would his father let her into his bed? It was quiet down there now. Were they finished? His skin felt pricked all over by pins or sparks.

"For goodness' sake," Jenny said, "are you going to stand there all night?"

She sounded like the woman doll. Stirred—and shamed—he yanked at the covers. "I said get out of here!"

"Don't, don't," she whimpered.

"What if your mother comes back?"

"She won't."

"How do you know?"

"Because she stays with him for . . . I don't know . . . an hour sometimes."

"What are you talking about?"

"They used to sex all the time at our old house."

He couldn't quite let himself hear this. "Maybe they're going to get married," he said.

"My mother is never getting married again," she said. "Ever." She pulled the covers back up around herself. "Are you coming to bed or not?"

He climbed in and lay at the very edge of the mattress, turned away from her. Spears of light from a passing car shot through the blinds onto the wall, where they leaned and fell, then drifted upwards.

"We could play," she whispered.

Up near the ceiling the spears zoomed off.

"Okay," she said, "you're Phil and I'm Carol. Our baby is called Wendy and our horse is called Misty." She shunted closer. "Wendy fussed all day long," she said in the woman doll's voice. "I hope she hasn't got the croup."

Ron had no idea what the croup was. He said, "Me, too."

"You have to speak lower," she said.

"Me, too," he growled.

"I don't know what I'd do without Misty. He's such a comfort to me." Her arms slipped around Ron's waist.

He ejaculated, although because it was his first time, he thought he'd got so keyed up he'd wet his pants.

"Now you say something," she said, nudging him.

"I've . . ." He struggled for breath. "I have to . . ."

"What, darling?"

"Go to sleep."

"Aren't you going to kiss me first?"

"Stop it, Jenny. I mean it."

She withdrew her arms and climbed out of bed. "Okay," she said. She still seemed to be in the game but as a squeaky-voiced little sister who cheerfully did what she was told. "Nighty-night," she whispered from the hall.

He waited until he heard her door shut before turning on his light. He'd already figured out what had happened, and he wondered if some evil force had entered the house and taken possession of all its inhabitants. Except that he didn't feel evil, but maybe you weren't supposed to, maybe the evil force vanquished guilt. Which would explain how his father and Mrs. Lawson could have sex only a few feet away from their own children. *They used to sex all the time at our old house.* If it was true, it must have been before his mother died because, since then, his father had never once gone out after supper.

And even this prospect, for all its awfulness, failed to disgust or offend him. He was barely able to hold it in his mind. He turned to face the wall on the other side of which was Jenny.

He couldn't believe how normal everybody was at breakfast. Jenny read a book about Welsh ponies and kept checking her watch. She looked at him woodenly when he asked her to pass the milk. Of course, his father and Mrs. Lawson were old hands at putting on a show, he knew that now. Still, it amazed him that they gave nothing away. When his father squeezed by Mrs. Lawson to get to the fridge, all she did was say, "Oops, sorry."

After everybody had left, he rummaged through Jenny's desk. There was a pad of paper, some markers, four decks of flash cards, and a harmonica. He blew on the harmonica. He considered writing her a note that said, "Dear Carol, hope to see you tonight, your husband, Phil." But what if Mrs. Lawson found it? Jenny's nightgown was hanging from a hook on the back of the door, and he went over and stroked the soft flannel. It dawned on him that he had better start wearing shorts under his pyjama bottoms, just in case. Maybe Jenny knew what happened to boys—she knew more than she should—but if not, he couldn't imagine telling her. What he *could* imagine was her saying, "Hey, why are you wet?" Then he'd have to jump off the Bloor Street Viaduct. To make certain he died instead of turning into a human vegetable, he would jump from the highest point.

She didn't show up that night or the next. He had a good idea why. Both nights until past two o'clock he lay awake with his door ajar, and no sounds came from down the hall.

On the morning of the third day he caught her by herself as she was going down to breakfast. She was wearing another of her old-fashioned, baggy dresses, this one red velvet with white bows at the wrists.

"Hey," he whispered, leaning over the banister. "When do you think we can play again?"

Without turning, she cocked her head. "Pardon?"

"You know," he said. "Phil and Carol."

"Oh," she said, starting to blush. "Well, the trouble is, I don't think your father likes my mother anymore."

"What do you mean?"

"He just doesn't like her." She touched her birthmark.

"Why not?"

"How should I know?" And on she went, down the stairs.

She came to him that night. He must have fallen asleep as soon as he closed his eyes because the last thing he remembered was pulling the covers over his shoulders.

"Phil? Phil?" She was lying behind him. "Are you awake?"

"Hi, Carol."

Before he was even properly facing her, she had her arms around him. She clung and squirmed. "Oh, darling, darling, darling," she whispered. He grasped handfuls of nightgown.

When it was over, she went still, as if sensing the change in him. He held her by her shoulders. She felt alarmingly flimsy, like one of his model airplanes. He asked if she was sure her mother wouldn't go back to their room. She said, "Uh-huh." She sounded groggy.

Already he was getting excited again. "Better not fall asleep," he said in his regular voice.

Her body tensed. "I won't," she said crossly, and pulled herself free.

"What's wrong?" Could she tell he was excited?

"Wendy needs her bottle."

He had a flash of cunning. "But, darling," he said in Phil's voice, "aren't you even going to kiss me good night?"

The kiss was a hard pushing together of their closed lips. It hurt more than he'd thought kissing a girl would. As his arms started to go around her, she wrenched back. "Good night, good night, good night," she snapped from within another baffling flare of temper. She slid her feet to the floor.

She showed up the next five nights in a row. Provided he talked like Phil and called her darling, she was happy to kiss him. In Carol's voice, she said, "I love you so much," and in Phil's voice he said he loved her, too. He wished he had the nerve to say it in his own voice.

Before and after school, when he had the house to himself, he looked through her closet and dresser drawers. He laid her underpants, dresses, and tights on the double bed she shared with her mother, putting the dresses above the underpants and the tights beneath, to make a line of girls. Back in his own room he imagined enemies for her—werewolves, assassins, cannibals—then killed them with his G.I. Joes. He decided that he would marry her as soon as she had finished high school. She'd be nineteen by then, he'd be twenty-two. A lightness came over him to have this resolved; he felt cleared of an enormous guilt he hadn't been entirely aware of. What *she* felt, he couldn't guess. During the day she hardly glanced at him, and he understood that if he wanted to keep their game going, he was to keep his distance.

SHE FAILED to show up the next three nights, even though he heard Mrs. Lawson in his father's room. What was the matter? Had he upset her? Was she tired of him? He couldn't bear not knowing. On the morning of the fourth day he waited for her outside the bathroom door and when she emerged he said in his man's voice, "I missed you last night, Carol. I hope Wendy isn't sick."

Instantly she fell into character. "Oh, she's just going through a fussy stage."

"I hope I see you tonight."

"I need my sleep, you know," she said, though not so dismissively that he lost hope.

She came just after midnight. He pretended to be asleep and let her kiss him awake. By simply saying, "Aren't you boiling hot, darling?" he got her to take off her nightgown.

She had shut the door, as always, and they weren't even talking, and yet her mother must have suspected something because she threw the door open and flicked on the overhead light.

"Oh, my God!" she cried. She rushed over and dragged Jenny off of him.

"You're hurting me!" Jenny cried. She hung limply in her mother's grip. Mrs. Lawson snatched up the nightgown. Through *her* nightgown her body showed, the thin, flat-chested shape of it. Naked Jenny and naked Mrs. Lawson, one taller than the other, that was all. Ron, who wasn't naked, pulled up the covers.

"What's going on?" His father stood in the doorway.

Mrs. Lawson wrapped the nightgown around Jenny's middle. "Go to your room!" she said, giving her a push. With tight, stumbling steps—the nightgown was tripping her up—Jenny headed out, past his father.

"He had her on top of him," Mrs. Lawson said. "Naked." Her voice was clipped now, matter-of-fact. She spoke as someone who had seen this coming.

Ron's father looked at Ron as if perplexed to find him there, in his own bed. "Okay," he said to Mrs. Lawson. "I'll take care of it."

"You'd better," she said.

His father waited until she was in her and Jenny's room before asking Ron what had happened.

"Nothing," Ron said. Under the glaring overhead light his father's bald spot shone like glass, like a glass lid.

"Nothing," his father said. He looked up at the model airplanes that hung from the ceiling. "Okay," he said, switching off the light. "We'll deal with this tomorrow."

Next door, Jenny and her mother were talking in quiet voices. Ron was too terrified to get out of bed and listen at the wall. *You'd better.* What was it Mrs. Lawson wanted his father to do? Hit him? Call the police? If the police came, he'd sneak out the back door and jump off the Bloor Street Viaduct. It helped to imagine his suicide and the aftermath, all the guilty parties.

His father didn't wake him for breakfast. He woke him as everyone was leaving the house. "We'll talk tonight," he said. Instead of going to school Ron went to the ravine and walked for miles along the Don River, whose dereliction— the odour of sewage, the stranded plastic bags and half-submerged shopping carts—provided a sad, companionable comfort. He had figured out that he probably wouldn't be sent to jail. What was more certain was that Jenny would never come to his room again. He doubted she'd even want to. He wondered—and this compounded his dread—if she'd write a story about what the two of them had got up to.

Dusk and hunger finally drove him home. The light was off in the front hall but he perceived the emptiness. Except for the television, the floor lamp, and his father's chair, the living room had been cleared out as well.

"Is that you, Buddy?" Ron went to the top of the basement stairs, and there his father was at the bottom, pushing up a mattress. "Grab that end," he grunted.

Little was said as they worked. Mrs. Lawson had hired a truck and two men and had moved her furniture to her sister's place in Barrie—his father told him that much. Where she and Jenny were now, he couldn't say. "Nope," he answered as to whether he thought they'd ever come back.

For supper he ordered pizza. They sat on their old chairs at their old kitchen table, which compared to Mrs. Lawson's seemed cheap and rickety. The pizza cutter was missing, though it had been theirs. Ron's father used scissors. "You know what you did was wrong," he said. "You know that."

"I'm probably going to marry her," Ron said. "When she finishes high school."

His father set a slice of pizza on each plate. "You'll get over her long before then."

"I'll never get over her."

"Sure you will. Believe me, I know what I am talking about."

He seemed to be on the verge of offering up some of his words of wisdom, of taking the two of them back to where they'd been before Mrs. Lawson and Jenny. Ron waited, but there was nothing else. They put their heads down and concentrated on eating.

Chapter Twenty-one

IN THE SECOND-FLOOR bedroom that serves as his office, Mika presses an ice pack to his temple and studies the chart he has been putting together. His cell phone is on the desk by his left hand, and as he reads he nervously flips the case open and shut. True, the woman phoned on Celia's line, but that doesn't rule out the possibility of one of the other abductors phoning *him*. The not-so-veiled offer to pay for Rachel's release still stands, after all.

Happy and Osmo slump at his feet. They are anxious and despondent and won't be comforted. Every once in a while Osmo gets up and turns in a circle, and Mika, his concentration broken, glances at the television set he keeps tuned to the twenty-four-hour news station. If there's nothing on about Rachel, he looks at the bookshelves for the sake of satisfying himself that they're free of fingerprint dust. A police-hired firm is arriving in a day or so to clean the entire house, but despite persistent nausea and vertigo (the aftereffects of the concussion), Mika took care of this room on his own.

He sets down the ice pack and checks his watch. Ten

fifty-five. Under the A.M. column of his chart he writes *11:00*. The day is *Monday*, the hour *61*. Hour by hour, he's tracking the investigation and media coverage. A child vanishing during a blackout would be a big story no matter what; make the child gorgeous, and it's huge. On Saturday the picture Mika took of her in her white-lace dress filled the front pages of all three daily papers, and yesterday the *Star* had an entire "Rachel" section in which neighbours were interviewed, various experts consulted, and pertinent aspects of the case itemized, including details of Mika's fall down the stairs and Chief Gallagher's unequivocal statement—more of a relief to Celia, it seemed, than to Mika—that "Mr. Ramstad has been cleared of all suspicion and is now helping to facilitate the investigation."

Throughout these articles Rachel's looks are underscored. "The Face of an Angel" was the *Sun*'s headline this morning, over another full-page photo. What do the editors mean to suggest? That the disappearance of a more normal-looking child would be less newsworthy or terrible? Maybe Mika is being too cynical. Rachel *does* have the face of an angel and, as he tells Celia, if ever there was a time when the media's fixation on beauty could prove useful, it's now. Let the media be enraptured is his primary feeling. Let them enrapture the public, let the public fall in love with Rachel, let the public become so personally invested in seeing her found safe that not even their own brothers and sons will be above suspicion.

People take for granted it's a man they're looking for. The woman's phone call is still a secret (a false-alarm bomb scare is how the police are accounting for their activities at the Gerrard Square Mall) and one of the reasons Mika is scouring the newspapers and listening to radio and TV reports is to assure himself it remains that way. He has heard the recording, the woman saying they would never hurt Rachel, but could she really speak for the man or men or cult that, with her phone call, she betrayed? He confesses nothing of his misgivings to Celia. She is trying so hard to imagine Rachel in reasonably safe hands. When she learned that the woman's DNA had failed to produce a match, instead of being discouraged, she said, "Okay, she hasn't got a criminal record, she's not a criminal, that's good."

Right now, Celia is searching the Don Valley with a group of volunteers. Mika had thought, after hearing about the phone call, that the ground search would be called off. But as a lead investigator explained to him, calling it off after only two days would have the media demanding to know why. On top of which, and more importantly, the phone call doesn't preclude the discovery of physical evidence—an item of clothing, or even of Rachel herself.

"Abductors have been known to let their victims go," he said.

"Wouldn't she run straight home?" Mika asked.

"If she was in a condition to."

If she was in a condition to. With these dreadful words now at the front of his mind, Mika is more frustrated than ever that he's still not feeling steady enough to take part in the search.

There are other ways to be useful, however. Yesterday afternoon he and Jerry Osborne, Celia's boss at Tom's Video, arranged to post a fifty-thousand-dollar reward—twenty-five thousand each—for any information leading to Rachel's safe return. The announcement was made public at a 4:00 P.M.

news conference, as Mika has noted on the chart. A reward entering the picture so early in an investigation is unusual, but the feeling of Chief Gallagher is that, while the abductors may not trust a ransom offer, there's a chance that one of the greedier or less involved participants could be lured out with the more legitimate prospect of a reward. For the news conference he said simply, "We have no leads and no suspects. We're hoping fifty thousand dollars will do something to change that."

While grateful for his discretion, Celia began to fret that the phone call would be leaked anyway. Mika couldn't blame her. "The whole police force knows," he reminded Gallagher.

"They also know what's at stake," Gallagher said. "Many of them have kids of their own." He put a hand on Celia's shoulder and promised her there would be no leak, and he sounded so persuasive and looked so invincible with his large jaw and pale, deep-set eyes (even when he was smiling, which he certainly wasn't now, he gave an impression of barely contained ruthlessness) that Celia was reassured, and Mika wondered if he didn't have some illicit, rarely resorted-to stratagem up his sleeve.

On his chart, under *Thoughts*, Mika wrote: *Best course of action in event of leak—outright denial?*

Tomorrow afternoon Celia will be making another plea to the abductors, this one scripted with the help of Chief Gallagher to appeal directly, though not too obviously, to the woman caller. So Celia will be saying that she is the only family Rachel has and that a little girl Rachel's age needs to be with her mother. She'll beg the abductors to be merciful and to do the right thing. In Mika's opinion the tone is perfect: he can't imagine that the suspicions of the other abductors will be aroused, but neither can he imagine how the woman—if she hears the message—will remain unmoved.

Eleven o'clock. He turns on the radio.

". . . continues for nine-year-old Rachel Fox, the little girl who went missing from her downtown Toronto home during last Friday's blackout. In spite of a fifty-thousand-dollar reward offer and a massive effort that has brought together hundreds of volunteers plus scores of search-and-rescue experts, Chief of Police Tim Gallagher confirms that there are still no concrete leads. Earlier this morning police personnel spent several hours at the Victoria Park waste transfer station, separating household garbage from clothing. A few items that may or may not be related to the case were retrieved."

Mika knew this was going on. He entered it under 8:00 A.M. Now, with a trembling hand, he enters the details: *A few items retrieved at transfer stn.*

Keeping a record, he says to himself. It's the slightly embarrassed explanation he gave Little Lynne when she brought him coffee and he saw her looking curiously at his chart and clippings. To confess that by creating an overall picture he's hoping to detect a clue—an unexplored avenue of investigation perhaps—would have sounded arrogant, he felt, especially to a police officer.

"Whatever helps you get through," was Little Lynne's response, and he thought, Yes, there's that as well.

He comes to his feet and goes to the window. Pushing up a slat of the blinds, he peeks out. The crowd across the street is larger than it was an hour ago. One woman, conspicuous for her girth and yellow straw hat, has been front and centre since dawn, sitting on a folding beach chair. No one else is familiar. For the most part people stand and gaze and move on, like visitors at an exhibition. Last night a group of children from Rachel's school held a vigil, and a few votive candles still stubble the curb. Above all this, along the telephone wire, pigeons hunch their square shoulders and make small shifts of position.

He turns back to the room. The dogs are awake, watching him. He closes his eyes and attempts to recapture a sense of Rachel. But it's gone . . . it left the moment he heard she was alive. He imagines this is because the forces of terror necessary to bring it about aren't quite as potent as they were.

He sits at his desk and presses a hand to his throbbing temple. He thinks, nothing prepares you for loving a child. Even when you know that you love her, you still may not have any idea how much because the feeling is so ordinary and instinctive, like a love for life or truth.

If only he'd let her give him the flashlight. If he'd had the flashlight, none of this would have happened. "Stupid, stupid," he mutters. That Celia forgives him is a miracle. Not for a second does he forgive himself.

Chapter Twenty-two

AT BREAKFAST ON Monday morning Nancy asks Rachel what she thinks the best model of electric keyboard is.

Rachel doesn't know.

"Well, Ron won't settle for anything less than top of the line," Nancy says. "I can guarantee you that."

Rachel's heart races. She has always wanted an electric keyboard. When Ron leaves to go to the music store, she lets Nancy talk her into drawing pictures on the card table. She's nice to her. She says, "You smell good. Like cold cream."

Nancy touches her face. "I must've forgot to wipe it off."

There's another smell coming from Nancy, a bad breath smell, but Rachel isn't going to mention that. "Why do you use cold cream?" she asks. "You don't wear makeup."

"I use it instead of soap, right? I've got really dry skin."

Rachel looks at Nancy's wrinkled face. "You know what smells exactly like cold cream? Magnolia blossoms."

"I've never been to the South."

"Magnolias grow right here in Toronto. I guess they grow in the South, too."

"Have you ever been South?"

Rachel shakes her head.

"Would you like to go some time? To Florida or some place like that?"

"I'd like to go to Disneyworld."

"One day you just might," Nancy says. "You never know, eh?"

Rachel shrugs. She used to have a grandfather in Florida, but he died. She studies her drawing—it's the lamb at Riverdale farm—and decides it isn't any good. She looks over at Nancy's drawing, which is either a horse or a dog. "Can we watch TV now?" she asks.

All day yesterday, from the minute Ron hooked up the satellite, she lay on the sofa and watched TV. Nancy tried to get her to play board games, but Rachel didn't feel like it. "Being kidnapped makes you tired," she pointed out. She kept falling asleep and dreaming about the slave drivers. In one dream their leader was Lina's uncle, Mr. Hakim. He tried to get her to drink a potion. Waking up, she was relieved for a few minutes to be somewhere Mr. Hakim would never look.

She goes over and sits on the sofa, leaving room for Nancy. "Okay, let's see," Nancy says. She picks up the remote, then puts it down again. "That's him," she says, hearing something Rachel didn't, and she leaves the room. A minute later she returns to ask if Rachel is okay with Ron coming in.

"I guess," Rachel answers. Still, at the sound of him on the stairs, she limps into the far corner. It isn't that he scares her, or at least not as much as he did, it's that she doesn't want him checking her sore foot. But all he does is glance in her direction and say, "Glad to hear you're feeling better."

He has the speakers. He puts them down, then brings

in the keyboard. He takes his time deciding where everything should go and what furniture needs to be moved.
Rachel wishes he'd hurry up because she has to pee. Finally
she can't hold it any longer and she slips into the bathroom
and turns on the tap to cover the noise. When she comes
out, he's playing notes and sliding the volume up and down.

"It's top of the line," Nancy tells her. "Just like I said. All
the bells and whistles." For some reason she's talking very
fast. She gives Ron a nudge. "Let Rachel have a try."

Ron steps aside. Rachel walks over, forcing herself not
to limp. She brushes her fingers along the keys.

"You can change the settings," Ron says. He goes to
show her, and his hand grazes her shoulder.

She flinches.

"Sorry," he says.

"Like, you can make it be a harpsichord or a grand piano
or jazz organ, or whatever," Nancy says, still talking fast.
"Go on, sweetie, sit. The stool's adjustable. You just crank
the lever there on the side."

Rachel sits. She presses "Rock Piano" and plays a pair of
C-major chords, then tucks her hands under her legs. "I can't
play in front of people," she says, meaning in front of him.

"Oh, okay," Nancy says. "We'll get out of your hair."

"I won't be a second," Ron says and goes into the
bathroom.

"What's the matter?" Rachel whispers to Nancy.

"The matter? What do you mean? Nothing. Nothing's
the matter."

"You're talking really fast."

"Am I? Oh, well, I'm just so thrilled. I'm thrilled for you,
that's all."

"But you sound upset."

"Don't be silly."

The toilet flushes, and Ron comes back out, rubbing his hands together. Rachel hopes he didn't dry them on the towel.

"Okay, sweetie," Nancy says. "Have fun."

She and Ron leave the room.

Rachel waits until she hears the shop door close before pressing the button for "Classical Piano" and playing the first few bars of the piece she's working on at home—the Bach Minuet in G Minor. She wonders if Nancy is upset because the keyboard is top of the line and Ron wasn't supposed to spend so much money. Or maybe when she was in the bathroom he told her about her bad breath and that hurt her feelings.

It exasperates Rachel to think this. "Everybody around here is so sensitive," she thinks. Her throat aches. She wants her mother. She wants her mother to have a top-of-the-line keyboard.

WHEN RON pushed the toy chest back a few inches to make room for the keyboard, Nancy found herself looking at a folded piece of paper that had the word *HELP* written on it in orange marker. Without Ron's noticing, she picked it up. Rachel, at the time, was in the bathroom, so she didn't notice anything either.

Now, standing behind the garbage shed (she told Ron she was going out for a smoke), Nancy rereads the words *They are liars* as if she could see them in a less wounding light. Calling Ron a liar she can understand, but why include *her*? Aren't she and Rachel supposed to be allies?

Frankly, she's surprised Rachel still wants to escape, considering the slave drivers she thinks are prowling the streets. And how did she think she was going to get the note outside? Was she going to bide her time and wait for Nancy to screw up?

Nancy presses the note against her chest, against her fantasy that Rachel was starting to feel at home. It's just that she seemed almost cheerful this morning, talking about magnolia trees and the South, so when she said she'd like to go to Disneyworld, Nancy began to wonder if Ron's plan for the three of them to live in Florida might not be so far-fetched after all. She pictured the palm trees and the pretty stucco bungalows.

She tells herself that Florida might be in the cards yet, some grimy, motel-room version of it. Because whatever happens, Rachel can't go home. Nancy still wishes Ron had phoned Children's Aid instead of bringing her here, but she has come around to agreeing with him about the landlord. Her change of heart happened yesterday when she was hav-ing a shower. In her mind she saw a man with his hands on Rachel's body, and she knew, as definitely as you know you'll never kick an animal, that she'd never send a child back to an abuser.

Something else comes to her, now, another revelation: keeping Ron out of the basement has been a mistake. Look how Rachel cringed when he accidentally touched her arm. Unless Rachel gets to know him better and find out how gentle he really is, she'll always be cringing.

Nancy reads the letter again. The writing is heart-meltingly neat: straight across the page, no slanting off. No spelling mistakes. *They are liars*. Well, we are, Nancy thinks. Let's face it.

She decides to put the note back. As long as she stays awake down there, what harm can it do to let Rachel have her little secret.

Chapter Twenty-three

OVER THE WEEKEND Celia had thought that her best chance of finding Rachel would be to follow her instincts. "Right or left?" Constable Bird would ask, and she'd try to feel a tug in either direction. There were streets where she remembered people having smiled or stared at Rachel in a way that now seemed suspicious, and she would get Bird to pull over while she studied certain houses and strained to pick up a signal: a voice in her head, a shift of light. Anything. Twice she and Bird climbed out of the car and knocked on the front door. At the first place a blind man and his guide dog answered. At the second it was an old woman who spoke no English.

Where was the telepathic power she'd tapped into Saturday morning? She was trying so hard to be aware and in the moment. Maybe she was trying too hard. Or maybe there'd never been any telepathic communication in the first place; it had all been wishful thinking. She felt foolish and inept, a drain on Bird's time. But what was she supposed to do with herself? She couldn't sit around at home, going mad. Bird suggested she join the grid search, and after not much thought she agreed. Grid search. It sounded so reassuringly methodical. She pictured the Earth sectioned off like a soccer ball, and the people and things within each section being there for the finding.

Today, Monday, she is with a group called OVERT, which stands for . . . she forgets . . . something Volunteers something Response Team. Since 8:00 A.M. they've been moving up the Don Valley ravine, spreading out into the parks and wild areas. The debris down here is mostly beer cans and plastic bags and broken bottles, but there are surprises as well. Celia comes across a cardboard box of cement denture moulds, and the man to her left finds a metal Ladies sign that must have been pulled off a washroom door. Around three in the afternoon the same man finds a girl's red tank top. Celia's relief that it isn't Rachel's causes her a few minutes of deafness, during which time she is able to read lips. "I'm all right," she insists. By now she is caught up in the rhythm of the search and is glad when it resumes. On she goes, with the expectation of finding she hardly knows what. Not Rachel (the idea of her waiting under a bush seems too fantastic, too much to hope for), and not anything belonging to Rachel, either. It's more a case of covering ground, getting it out of the way. Shrinking the grid.

At four o'clock the searchers divide into subgroups and go their separate ways. At six thirty, in a park on the east side of the river, Celia's group breaks for supper. She collects an egg-salad sandwich and a Gatorade and walks off by herself to sit on a log situated above a stretch of rapids. She feels like a machine, her hand parts putting food into her mouth part as her eyes mechanically scan the rocks and trees on the far bank. A man who looks like Bill Clinton sits down next to her and starts in on his sandwich.

"How are you holding up?" he asks.

His raspy voice startles her for being so much like the voice of the woman on the tape. "I'm okay," she answers but something in her has ruptured and she adds, "Except I've got to get back home now."

The man goes to look for the person in charge. So organized and efficient are these people that in no time a car is waiting for her at the nearest intersection. The driver, an older man in a Hawaiian shirt, talks the whole way about a cat he lost six months ago and is hoping will show up eventually. "Not that I'm comparing my circumstances to yours," it occurs to him to add. On her instructions he pulls around behind her house, where an officer patrolling the lane opens the car door and then the gate to the yard. Jerry, her boss at Tom's Video, is sitting with Mika on the back stoop. Both men come to their feet.

"I haven't even thanked you," she says to Jerry. She means for putting up half the reward money. He draws her into his arms. A long time ago, during his boxing days, his wife and seven-year-old son were killed in a car accident.

"She's alive," Celia says. She thinks he deserves to know.

"I feel that, too," he says.

"No, I mean she *is*," Celia says. She's crying. She leaves it to Mika to tell him about the phone call.

"Can I have a listen to that tape?" he says.

The three of them go into the house. Big Lynne, who is sitting at the kitchen table and has obviously met Jerry, announces that she has just heard some good news.

"What?" Celia says, stiffening.

"The reward has gone up to seventy thousand dollars. Two separate donors called in and made pledges of ten thousand dollars each."

"Who?" Celia asks.

"We've got their names but you wouldn't know them, apparently. One is somebody Edwards, from London, Ontario, and the other is MacDougall, I think it is. They want to remain anonymous. To the general public anyway."

"That's great," Jerry says.

Is it? Celia has no idea. She was braced for a sighting, another phone call. "Anything else?" she asks.

"The tips to the hotline are up over eight hundred. That's the most there's ever been by day three on a case like this."

Day three. Too much time is passing. Celia tells Big Lynne she wants Jerry to hear the tape, and after a pause to register the fact that Jerry is aware of the phone call, Big Lynne gets up, turns on the CD player and slides in the CD, which is one of several copies made by forensics from the original message.

Jerry listens twice. "I feel like I've heard that voice before," he says.

"Really?" Celia says.

"I'm just not coming up with a face."

"Was it from around here?" Big Lynne asks.

"I don't know. Maybe."

"It must be from around here," Mika points out, "if you've both heard it before. A store customer."

"Except I've gone over those names," Celia reminds him. "Twice."

Jerry says, "They wouldn't be holding Rachel right in her own neighbourhood, would they?"

"It's not being ruled out," Big Lynne says.

She reads to him the police profile of the woman caller: white, midthirties to early forties, native of northern Ontario, high school dropout, tobacco smoker.

Jerry listens to the tape a third time. He shakes his head. He offers to look at the customer list himself, although he says his gut tells him it isn't someone from the store. Celia suggests that while there's still light the two of them walk around and hand out reward flyers. "Something might ring a bell."

They go along Carlton to Sherbourne, south on Sherbourne to Gerrard, then east to Parliament, where they turn north. A few media vans follow but keep far enough back that within a few blocks Celia forgets about them. Jerry hands out the flyers, saying, "Reward's up to seventy thousand." He knows these people: their names, where they live. Celia knows quite a few as well, mostly from the store. Everyone knows her. Even a couple of homeless men make the connection, and when they do their sympathy is so pure and unsparing that Celia has to turn away. She studies the faces of passersby. She hardly expects the woman to be out enjoying herself. Still, she homes in on certain females, certain female voices. She looks up and down the street, at storefronts, at parked cars, hoping to spark a memory.

They call it quits at the corner of Parliament and Wellesley. It has been dark for a while by then; the streets are emptying.

"What we should do tomorrow," Jerry says, "is knock on people's doors."

"The police have done that."

"*We* haven't. You never know who might answer."

"Do you think the woman would?"

"These kind of people, they've got to be cocky, right? But even if it's one of her kids or her boyfriend that answers, it might trigger something."

She reminds him of the press conference at four o'clock. "I'll need be to be back by three."

"I'll keep going on my own."

"What about the store?"

"John's there. Listen, I'm in this for as long as it takes."

They start walking south. In front of one of the Tamil groceries that are still open this time of night, a young girl sits on a milk crate and peels an orange. Why didn't the abductors take her, Celia wonders: she's beautiful, she's unsupervised.

"You can go crazy going down that road," Jerry says.

"What road?"

"Wishing it was some other kid."

"I don't *wish* it," Celia says, only mildly surprised that he read her mind. She comes to a stop and considers him, a still-handsome man with a tanned bald head, massive tattooed arms, and a barrel chest. "How did you get through?" she asks.

"Get through?" But it's clear he understands the question. He rubs his head. "There were some bad years there. My sister . . . you met Jean?"

Celia nods.

"She scraped me off a couple of floors. And then, the passage of time. You don't want to be that person anymore."

They keep walking. Her heart overflows. She stops again and says, "We should get married."

"Celia . . ."

"We *should*."

His gaze descends to her throat. She remembers she hasn't taken off the necklace she wore to the motel Friday evening.

"Rachel's alive," he says. "You hold on to that." He tugs her necklace around so that its single pearl hangs at the front.

Big Lynne is still sitting at Mika's kitchen table, arms folded over her large breasts, eyes pouched with fatigue. "Anything?" she asks. Celia shakes her head. Big Lynne sighs. She gestures at the desk and says she has put Celia's messages in two piles: "The one on the left is your friends, and the other is what came into the command post. People writing down their prayers and good wishes."

Celia thanks her. She says good night. Big Lynne says, "I'll be right here if you need anything, hon." They're like women speaking to each other in a dream. Before leaving the room, Celia takes the CD player.

Nobody has been in her apartment all day, it looks like: the dust is still thick; the footprints—mostly her own—track every inch of bare floor, evidence of her hellish nightlong wanderings. Felix saunters in from the deck, and she fills his bowls before hunting for a cigarette. She finds a half-smoked one in the bathroom, gets it lit, then drops on the sofa and listens to the CD. When the woman says that Rachel is with people who only want her to be safe and would never hurt her, she feels her chest loosen, only to have it tighten at *something bad could happen*.

She presses Start again. This time she talks along, trying to match the woman's pitch. At *seriously* she attempts the quaver. She turns the CD player off and says, "They would never hurt her, don't worry about that," and the next thing she knows she's waking up to the smell of burning.

She grabs the butt and tosses it into the ashtray, then spits on the glowing orange circle in the sofa. She hears the TV in Mika's office. Still trembling, she makes her way down there.

He's sitting at his desk among his newspaper clippings.

"Hi," he says, swivelling around. He turns off the TV. The dogs haul themselves up and wag their tails halfheartedly.

She drops onto his chaise longue. After a while a thought she had earlier in the day returns to her, and she says, "Remember my friend Hannah, who I told you about?"

"The one who died of cervical cancer?"

"Uterine cancer."

"Yes. Right."

"I know it sounds awful but I never really liked her all that much. She liked me, so I was her friend. But she was paranoid. She thought everyone hated her. A lot of people did because she'd phone them in the middle of the night and accuse them of gossiping about her behind her back."

"Did she do that to you?"

"All the time. After Rachel was born, it really started to get to me. I stopped returning her calls. I didn't even call her when I found out she had cancer. I told myself I was too busy. And then one day I was coming out of my dentist's office on St. Clair, I was by myself, and a woman at the bus stop says, 'Hi, Celia,' and it was her. She looked terrible. She had a moustache, this black fuzz on her upper lip, and she was wearing a baggy man's coat with egg all down the front. I said how I'd heard the news and hoped she was feeling better. She said she was going to make it. I said, 'Good,' or something like that. I could have said 'I'll call you' or 'I'll come round to see you.' But I didn't. She just sort of stared at me. And then the bus pulled up and she got on. A week later, she died."

"So now," Mika says, "you're being punished."

"Maybe." She lies back. From this angle the bump on his temple—he has removed the bandage—is disturbingly large.

"If God wanted to punish you, why wouldn't he give *you* cancer?"

"That would be too straightforward. And it wouldn't hurt as much."

He nods. His mouth moves, then he says, "But of all the people who never returned Hannah's phone calls, why . . . why would you be the one who has to suffer?"

"Because she showed herself to me at her unloveliest. At her most exposed. And I turned away."

"*She* got on the bus."

"You know what I mean."

"You aren't being punished, Celia, dear."

Something about how sympathetic he sounds, this warm, rueful moment the two of them are sharing, has her burning with anger. "*Of course* I'm being punished," she says. "I'm being punished because I'm a bad mother. I'm being punished for going to my *dumb* job and leaving her . . ."

With you. The unspoken words clang around the room. He fingers the bump on his head.

"Just leaving her," she says. "Not being home. I don't blame you, Mika. I really don't. I blame myself and always will." She starts to cry.

"Oh, Celia."

"Can I lie here for a while?"

"Of course you can."

Chapter Twenty-four

SITTING AT THE shop counter, looking out the window at
the turquoise sky and at the unmarked van that has been
parked across the road for the past two hours, Ron remembers the evenings he sat on the porch stairs of the house on
Logan Avenue under a sky filled with the same aquarium
light. The prickly sensation gripping his skull was the same,
too, generated back then by a real fear that his father wasn't
coming home. This was in the months after Jenny and Mrs.
Lawson left, when his father stayed late at the office and
phoned Miss Spitz two doors down and asked her to cook
Ron his supper, something Miss Spitz, a retired school-
teacher whose saving grace, in Ron's eyes, was that she
owned an ancient Kirby vacuum with a floor-polisher attachment, seemed glad enough to do.

He comes to his feet and moves around the counter—
stepping over Tasha—for a better look at the van. The windows are tinted, so if someone's inside, staking out the
shop, he can't tell. But why *would* someone be staking out
the shop? In child abduction cases the police don't wait to
have their suspicions confirmed, they kick down doors.

"Getting paranoid in my old age," he says to Tasha.

She watches him with her big, crazy eyes. She is lying on a piece of cardboard between a pair of Honda lawn mowers, both of which are due to be picked up in the morning. He'll have to get to work first thing. Or maybe he should start tonight. He stands there, mentally disassembling the engines, checking the throttle plates. No, he decides, he's too tired. And anyway, he wants to finish going through the newspapers.

He closes the blinds, switches on a light, and walks over to the basement door. Not a sound. He pictures Rachel asleep and is suffused with tenderness. Before the feeling can turn into something else he strains to hold it there, at that safe, protective place. The vision of her pee is what he's up against—he's been up against it since he saw it in the toilet this morning. He wills himself to remember instead the shy droop of her body when she said she couldn't play the piano in front of people. And how bravely she held herself together when he told her about seeing her mother on TV.

This came later, the talk about her mother. They were eating supper. He's still not sure what caused Nancy to reconsider her position about his spending time in the basement, but sometime after lunch she announced that keeping him and Rachel apart was doing everybody more harm than good and that Rachel had agreed to let him eat his supper downstairs.

"I told her you were feeling hurt and left out," she reported. "That did the trick."

Ron nearly wept. To think that Rachel cared about how he felt! At five o'clock he went upstairs and changed into a clean shirt. A half hour later, when Nancy started fixing the trays, he rifled through the corner cabinet and found the linen napkins that had been his mother's. "Her meals should be an occasion," he said, removing the paper napkins that Nancy had laid out. "Something for her to look forward to."

"Do you want me to put on a dress?" Nancy asked.

"A dress?" He turned to her. Despite the three place settings, he hadn't actually been picturing her at the table. She was wearing the same jeans and tank top she'd been wearing since Friday night, but how she looked hardly mattered. *He* was the one who needed to make an impression. "No," he said. "You're fine."

Rachel sat beside him, to his left, and for the first part of the meal he restricted himself to quick glances. Just having her close by, listening to her breathe and swallow, that was enough. He was content to keep out of the conversation, such as it was—Nancy babbling on about vegetarianism and playing the banjo, Rachel responding in monosyllables, made timid, he felt, by his presence. So it surprised him when she caught his eye and said, "You're watching TV and reading the newspapers, right?"

He admitted that he was.

"Okay, so . . ." She set down her fork. "What are they saying happened to me?"

He wiped his mouth with his napkin. "That you went missing," he said carefully. "And that the police are searching for you—"

"Who's for more salad?" Nancy cut in. "Ron?"

He lifted his hand. He could handle Rachel's questions.

She was rolling up the corner of her placemat. "Have they shown my picture on TV?"

She's vain, he thought, amused. "Oh, yes. Lots of lovely pictures."

"Have they shown my mom?"

Her lower lip quivered, and he was taken aback. Was she going to cry? He stared at her, dazzled by the twitches of life under the polished-wood smoothness of her face.

It was Nancy who answered. "They've shown her a few times," she said cheerfully. "Eh, Ron? Talking to reporters?"

With an effort he transferred his gaze to her. "Just once."

"When was that again?" Nancy went on, keeping up a show of lightheartedness.

"Saturday."

"In Rachel's house?"

"Out on the lawn."

"The front lawn."

"That's right." He glanced back at Rachel. Her face was still again, her eyes clear. She asked if her mother had been upset.

"Not that I could tell," he lied.

"What did she say?"

"She said . . ." He cut his eggplant into squares and tried to think of something credible and comforting. "She said, 'I hope my daughter is safe.' She said, 'Whoever has her, please take good care of her.'"

"She wasn't crying?"

"No, she wasn't crying. She seemed to be doing fine. Holding up."

Rachel scratched her throat and looked off to the side, presenting her exquisite profile. He was about to add, "Of course, I don't *know* her," when she turned to Nancy and said, "Can I feed Tasha some of my tofu?"

"You can try," Nancy said.

Ron would have liked to have asked Rachel how she

was enjoying the keyboard, but he sensed she wouldn't welcome a question that obliged her to express any gratitude or pleasure. Besides, her enjoyment was obvious. For most of the afternoon, every time he stood at the door to listen, he caught halting snatches of melody. Or scales. She seemed to practise scales endlessly. But he couldn't risk mentioning this either, in case she turned the volume down so low he'd be denied hearing her at all. So the subject of her piano playing wasn't touched on, not until dessert, when Nancy asked about sheet music: did Rachel need any? "There's this store on Yonge Street where I buy mine," she said. "It's got music for every instrument. Mostly piano, though."

"I know," Rachel said. She patted her lap, and Tasha jumped into it. "My mom goes there."

"Oh, okay," Nancy said.

With two fingers Rachel began to stroke the dog's back. Ron felt himself becoming entranced again. He felt as if his entire life had been spent waiting for exactly this display of delicacy and sweetness and feminine self-containment. He gazed at the blond hairs on her forearm. His breath quickened, and he stood and walked over to the keyboard and made a show of checking the speaker connections.

Nancy started to clear the plates. Apparently she wasn't going to press the matter of the sheet music but Rachel had been considering it. "Maybe the Grade 4 Conservatory book," she said at last. "There's some other books but I have to remember what they are. I'll write the names down for you later."

And then she informed them that she was playing a recital on August 10, and since she was going to be missing music camp she had a lot of practising to do.

"Actually," she said, "I should get back to practising right now."

For a disoriented moment Ron imagined that he would be *attending* the recital. Taking his cue from Nancy, he left the room, still uncertain as to how this piece of news should be handled.

"We go along with it," Nancy said when they were upstairs. "Like we're going along with the slave drivers."

"Right." He kept forgetting about the slave drivers. They came in handy but the idea of them was so absurd.

"Let's just be happy she's settled down for now. We can burn our bridges when we get to them."

"*Cross* our bridges," he corrected. He agreed with her, though.

Nancy should be asleep by now. After putting Rachel to bed she took a couple of Gravol pills and went upstairs.

He checks his watch. Nine thirty. He turns up the radio. Rachel is the lead story: another mention of the fact that this morning a few items possibly related to the case were retrieved from the Victoria Park waste transfer station. Possibly related but not, as only he knows for certain. In a case where there was no struggle, no coercion, and not even a crime scene, there can be no *items*. The phrase *immaculate abduction* leaps to mind, briefly stunning him with its brilliance. He half wishes he could phone it in to the media. He feels, tonight especially, a compulsion to broadcast his extraordinary luck and the sense of destiny it has conferred on him.

The weather report comes on: below seasonal temperatures for the next few days. He may need to get the furnace going to keep the basement warm enough. He turns the radio down, switches on the lamp and takes the day's newspapers out from under the counter. Nancy is avoiding the newspapers (as well as the radio and TV) so he goes through them only when she isn't around.

He starts with the *Sunday Star*, which has a section called "Where's Rachel?" Knowing that he's vulnerable tonight, he avoids the pictures of her. But on the second page there's a big colour shot of her wearing her "Super Star" T-shirt, the one she was wearing that first day he saw her, and before he can stop himself, he's on his feet.

He looks at the door to the basement.

He takes a step. Halts.

Yesterday he promised Nancy that he would never enter the apartment without first getting Rachel's okay. He was only too willing to promise—he needs these kinds of restraints—and he's determined to keep his word.

Like an automaton, feeling the great resisting force of his body's machinery, he changes direction and walks to the window.

The van is gone.

Chapter Twenty-five

 T UESDAY AFTERNOON IS cool and clear, no threat of rain, and this time the press conference takes place on schedule. When it's over, Big Lynne sets out plates and forks and serves the apricot tart she made in her own kitchen the day before. Celia accepts a small piece to prove she isn't starving herself. With her back to the phone (if she looks at it, the woman won't call) she smokes cigarettes and drifts in and out of listening to the others talk about the huge media turnout and whether or not the *Globe and Mail*'s crime reporter suspects the police of knowing more than they're saying.

Eventually the conversation moves on to more neutral topics. Big Lynne and Chief Gallagher discover that they both grew up on dairy farms in large families, and the two of them compare stories of 4-H Clubs and 6:00 A.M. milkings, and Celia reflects without resentment or envy—it's simply a stray thought—that these are people whose lives have never hung, as hers does, by the thread of a single human attachment.

At six o'clock they turn on the TV for a rebroadcast of Celia's appeal. She is disturbed to realize that she never once looked up from her notes to address the woman personally. But the others assure her that looking down is better, more natural.

"Playing up for the camera never works," Big Lynne assures her. "It's like you're acting, and that puts people off."

A few calls come in, from friends and well-wishers. Nothing from the woman. At seven o'clock Chief Gallagher leaves, and a bit later Little Lynne shows up with pizzas and to take over from Big Lynne, who nevertheless hangs around for another hour or so. The waiting goes on until midnight and beyond, with Little Lynne staying up after Celia has gone to bed.

Not that Celia sleeps. She paces and smokes. She has fits of sobbing—into pillows and towels so as not to alarm Mika. Lying on the pile of clothes on Rachel's floor she mentally inventories the faces of every woman she has ever served at the video store. She goes into the living room and listens to the CD of the woman until the voice disintegrates into a meaningless, hideous racket. She opens books and points at the page, and the word her finger has landed on is a message. But no matter what the word, she can't tell whether she should be encouraged by it or frightened. Even *hope* (which she lands on) is inscrutable.

No call comes the next morning, either. It's possible, of course, that the woman isn't listening to the radio or TV. And so Mika designs another flyer, this one featuring a photo of Celia and Rachel hugging each other under the heading "Please Give Me Back My Daughter," and then there's a transcription of what Celia said on the air. An hour later the flyer is being distributed citywide by the volunteers who have been taken off the ground search. Meanwhile

Celia and Jerry continue knocking on doors that the police knocked on a day or so earlier. They work opposite sides of the street or, if they're in an apartment building, opposite sides of the hallway. Where they can, they look in windows.

The only way that Celia manages to stay functional is to enter a state of detached, almost catatonic alertness, a thing she finds she is able to do once she's outside her own home. People look at the flyer and then at her and then at the flyer again and become stricken with sympathy and with their inability to help. Holding herself at an otherworldly distance, Celia asks them to check their garages and lockers one more time. She can barely feel it when the women touch her arm. There are women of the right age and with the right general appearance but they don't have the right voice. There are men who could be the boyfriend of the woman, and Celia peers past them, down their hallways. At one house, a queasy feeling infiltrates her composure and she asks the man if she can look around. "Be my guest," he says, holding his German shepherd by its studded collar, waving her into his grimy, smoke-filled living room. He even opens a locked basement door and then apologizes for the mess, explaining that the police searched the room a couple of days ago.

"Sorry to bother you," she says.

"Hey, no problem," he says. "I'd be going out of my friggin' mind if I was you."

It's almost ten o'clock by then, and Jerry walks her back to the house, where Big Lynne and Mika are waiting to tell her that the television show *Lost Children* phoned and a crew is arriving tomorrow morning to tape a segment.

"It'll air Saturday night at nine o'clock," Mika says, referring to his notes. "The Fox Network."

"They're doing a special about abducted children from other countries," Big Lynne says. "Kids who might have ended up in the States. They want Rachel to be the main story."

"The States? Who says she's in the States?"

"Nobody, hon. Nobody. It's a slim possibility, that's all."

Celia tries to remember if she's ever seen the show. She doesn't think she has.

"There's a sizeable Canadian audience," Mika says. He checks his notes again. "Eight hundred thousand. Of which more than half are here in Ontario."

"We don't have to tell them about the phone call, do we?"

"No, no," Big Lynne says. "Absolutely not. That's top secret."

"Will they want to talk to me?"

"They asked to."

"Well . . . I guess . . ." Celia sets down her canvas bag of undelivered flyers. She feels anxious about taking time away from her door-to-door search. "If it doesn't go on too long."

"You give them as long as you like, hon, not a minute longer. They'll be here at eight sharp so you'd better try and get some sleep."

She tries until 2:00 A.M., then gives up and wanders through the apartment. There's something about being in motion that keeps her a split second ahead of panic. At around three o'clock Mika comes upstairs and offers her a tranquilizer. She declines. She doesn't want to be foggy for the interview. She asks him to lie down with her, though. She thinks that might help. They lie on Rachel's bed and gaze at the ceiling, where three lines of light, which seem to have no connection to the gap between the curtains, cross to form a collapsing H.

"What does it mean?" Celia says.

Mika takes a long time answering. "Nothing," he says finally.

She dozes off. When she wakes up, she's shaking.

"It's all right," Mika says.

"If they kill her," she says, finishing a thought from her dream, "I don't know how I'll be able to kill myself fast enough."

"They aren't going to kill her."

"I need a gun. Do you think Gallagher could get me a gun?"

"Celia, the phone call hasn't been leaked. Nothing's happened."

"I need a gun."

"Why are you talking like this?"

"If she dies—"

"But she won't."

"But if she does, why would I live another minute?"

A siren screams down Parliament Street. She could swim out into Lake Ontario, she guesses. It's only a ten-minute drive to Cherry Beach.

He starts to speak, then squeezes her hand. She turns and looks at him.

"I don't know," he says.

She closes her eyes. When she opens them, it's dawn. She smells coffee. Still barely awake, she shuffles to the kitchen, where Mika is cutting up the apples and plums he found at the bottom of her refrigerator. She sinks onto a chair. "Did you sleep?" she asks him.

"A little." He touches the bump on his temple.

"How *is* that?"

"Fine. I'm completely recovered." He sets the plate of sliced fruit on the table. He has more to say, and she waits, listening to the spatter of rain on the roof.

"If it's all right with you," he says at last, "I'd like to go out with you and Jerry . . . after the television people leave. I can't match the woman's voice to a face, I can't do that, but I'm sure . . . I would recognize it if I heard it."

"If you feel up to it, that would be great."

"The other thing I was thinking is that we should look beyond the grid. I've been asking myself, Why would they be holding her inside the grid when they must know that that's where the most intensive searching goes on?"

"The phone call came from inside the grid."

"To deceive us, maybe."

"But beyond the grid is the rest of the world."

"Let's suppose it isn't. Yes, they may have taken her out of the country, but from what I've read that's rare in cases of abductions by strangers." He's speaking energetically now, without hesitation. "So if we suppose that she's still in Toronto, I think we should also suppose that they're *not* holding her in a high-rise apartment building or anywhere else where the neighbours are too close for comfort. We should be focusing on less congested places. Apartments above stores, that kind of place."

"Houses next to empty lots," she says.

"Down at the waterfront, for instance. In the industrial areas."

"Oh, Mika." She's wide awake now. "This is a really good idea." She feels in the pocket of her bathrobe. "I was sure I had a cigarette in here," she mutters, coming up empty.

"Are you out?"

"Do you have one?"

"Sorry. I meant to buy some yesterday."

She bursts into tears.

"Celia. Oh, God. I'll go see if Lynne or—"

"No . . . it's . . ."

"You're exhausted."

"It's just that . . ."

It's that her hopes are up. It's that last night all she could think of was getting her hands on a gun.

Chapter Twenty-six

*T*HANKS TO GRAVOL, Nancy falls into long, dreamless stupors. At ten o'clock she closes her eyes and the next thing she knows it's morning and the guy who lives above Vince's garage is revving his motorcycle. While Ron goes on sleeping, she gets out of bed and hurries down to the basement.

She has discovered that by pulling the handle toward her she can turn the lock silently. The only sound is the whisper the door makes brushing over the carpet. This morning, Thursday morning, Tasha is in the room. She dashes past Nancy and up the stairs. Nancy goes over to the bed and parts the curtains.

Her newest terror is that to punish everybody—herself and Ron and the mother—to get back at them for their sins, Rachel won't make it through the night. But here she is, only asleep, fists tucked up by her throat. Nancy lets out her breath. Every morning she is stunned all over again that this beautiful girl wound up in Ron's basement. It's like having a fairy in the basement, or a movie star.

She closes the curtains. Before she reaches the door, a small, strangled sound has her rushing back. "Rachel?" she says. Rachel's eyelids are fluttering. What Nancy wouldn't give for the right to hold her.

"Rachel?"

Rachel sighs and rolls onto her other side, facing the wall.

Back upstairs, Nancy lets Tasha into the yard and puts on the coffee, then sits at the kitchen table and takes a look at the chart Ron wrote out last night for the sake of having a clearer picture of how Rachel is passing her time. "It isn't cut-and-dry," Nancy told him, but as they went through Rachel's day together she realized that it *was* pretty cut-and-dry, that, since Monday, things had more or less settled into a routine.

> *8:00–8:30—breakfast**
> *8:30–10:00—watching cartoons**
> *10:00–11:00—drawing**
> *11:00–12:00—playing keyboard*
> *12:00–12:30—lunch**
> *1:00–2:00—watching* Antiques Roadshow*
> *2:00–3:00—playing keyboard*
> *3:00—snack**
> *3:15–4:30—playing cards or board games**
> *4:30–5:30—watching* Cheers, *playing keyboard*
> *5:30–6:00—supper***
> *6:15–8:15—watching DVD movie***
> *8:15–9:00—bath**
> *9:00–9:30—reading**
> *9:30—lights out.*

A single star means that Nancy is usually in the room. Two stars mean that Ron is there as well. Granted, he has only watched a movie with them the one time, and that was last night, but he's hoping it will turn into a regular event, and Nancy can't see why it won't. Rachel was fine. Afterwards, when Nancy asked her if she'd minded that he'd stayed on, she said, "He didn't talk. People talking all through movies is the only thing I mind."

"So you're not so scared of him anymore," Nancy ventured.

"Not if *you're* there." She picked up the *Beauty and the Beast* DVD—it was the one they'd just watched—and said, "He's like the Beast."

Nancy had to laugh. "He *is*, isn't he? Big. And shy. Even the hair!"

"I mean he's weird."

"Oh, okay."

"But don't tell him."

"Hey, he'd never get mad at *you*."

"It might hurt his feelings, though."

"It might," Nancy said slowly. "That's true." On Monday, to win Rachel over to the idea of letting him join them for supper, she'd talked about his mother's dying when he was little and how not being allowed downstairs was hurting his feelings, but she hadn't expected it to be taken so deeply to heart.

She pins the chart to the bulletin board. The coffee is ready, and she pours herself a cup, then steps outside with her cigarettes. In the corner by the fence Tasha is digging a hole, her stubby tail going like a motor. "Tasha, come!" Nancy calls. The dog keeps digging.

"Tasha!"

The dog trots over. There's something in her mouth. She drops it on the stoop.

It's a dead rat, a little grey one. Shaggy coat. Smooth, banana-coloured belly.

"Ah, jeez," Nancy says. She picks it up by the tail and tosses it over the fence. She likes rats. She used to keep them when she was a kid. She hopes this isn't a sign, that's all. It *feels* like a sign: your dog bringing you a dead rat first thing in the morning. Don't let it be a sign, she prays.

RON WAKES from a dream that Rachel is sitting on his lap and kissing him on the lips. He tries to hold on to the sensation of her luscious mouth but quickly loses it to the real world: Tasha barking, the smell of coffee.

He gets out of bed and lumbers down to the bathroom. He'll be fixated on that kiss all day now, as though it really happened. If he could just see her, he knows he'd be set straight. But Nancy doesn't want him going down to the basement without her, not unless there's a good reason. Maybe he could say he needs to check the vents for mould. Or maybe—his hand goes still on the hot-water tap—he could show Rachel a few of his vacuums. It seems to him that she's just about ready for a little educational diversion.

He shaves and showers, his mind wholly occupied by this exhilarating prospect. Which machines would she get the biggest kick out of? The Westinghouse, for sure. She'll never see another machine like the Westinghouse, he can guarantee that. And then the Hoover Model O because it's one of only three left in the world. Maybe he'll bring down the Hercules Dust-Killer as well, show her how they used to generate power with hand pumps back in the 1800s. It'll be a history and science lesson rolled into one.

It'll have to wait until later, though. Edith Turnbull, an

old friend of his mother's, is expecting him to drop off her rewired floor lamp first thing, and then she wants him to take a look at her central vacuum canister.

But that's all right. Thinking about his vacuum cleaners, picturing the best of them in the room again—with Rachel looking on—has given him some breathing space.

NANCY STUBS out her cigarette and goes back inside to fix Ron his new crash-diet breakfast: orange juice, a soft-boiled egg, a piece of toast with margarine, black coffee. Right on schedule, at seven thirty, he comes down.

"I was thinking," he says. He pulls out the chair and sits. "I could show her my vacuums this morning."

"This morning?"

"Not the whole collection. Three or four." He taps his spoon on the back of the egg. "It'll be educational for her. Stimulating as well."

"I suppose," Nancy says. She can always cut it short, if Rachel gets too bored. "Don't you have to go to Mrs. Turnbull's?"

"I'll be back by nine thirty. We can move her drawing time to one of the TV-watching slots."

He eats quickly, gulping his coffee. When he's gone, Nancy makes breakfast for herself and Rachel. It's the same every day now: orange juice, slices of banana and apple, scrambled eggs, porridge with cream and brown sugar. She picks the tray up gingerly, testing her bad leg, then heads down to the basement.

She hears the sobbing before she reaches the bottom of the stairs. "I'm coming!" she calls. But in her agitation she drops the key, and hours seem to pass before she finds it and gets the door open. By now her leg has begun to cramp. She staggers over to the bed and falls next to where Rachel lies curled up on her side.

"What's the matter?"

"The slave drivers . . . they . . ."

"No, no, no." Sensing there won't be any resistance, she draws the hiccuping child into her arms. "You had a bad dream, sweetie, that's all."

"The man, he put me in a cage . . ."

"Shhh. There's no man. He's all gone."

She frees up one hand to punch her cramped leg. With the other, she presses Rachel closer. The sobs seem to be pouring out of Rachel's chest into her own. They seem to be rattling down her body to her aching thigh, where they start to have a soothing effect. When they stop, in that same instant, so do the cramps.

For a few minutes they both lie still. Out in the yard, Tasha barks.

"See?" Nancy says. "You're here with Tasha and me and Ron, safe and sound. It was only a dream."

Rachel wriggles out of the embrace. "I have to go to the bathroom," she says crossly.

She picks at her breakfast and refuses to talk. Finally she throws her fork on the floor and cries, "I *know* it was only a dream! Quit saying that!" Her eyes fill. They look blind, they're so light blue. "I want my mom," she whimpers.

"I know," Nancy says miserably.

"Couldn't I just talk to her on the phone for a minute?"

"Sweetie . . ."

"Couldn't I write her a letter then?"

Nancy tries to imagine what the risks might be. Finger-prints, but those can be wiped off.

"When I was at science camp," Rachel presses, "I wrote her every day."

"Well . . ."

"Please."

"Maybe a short one."

Rachel jumps to her feet.

"But you can't write about me or Ron. Or even Tasha. You can't write about the shop."

"I won't, I won't, I won't!"

"We'd better do it now, before Ron gets back. Let's talk about it first, though. What do you want to say?"

"I want to say . . ." And she launches right in: "'Dear Mom. I love you very, very much. I miss you *so* much. I miss Felix. Don't forget his vaccination shot. I miss Mika. I hope he's all better. I hope Osmo and Happy aren't moping about me like they did last summer.'" Her face darkens. To Nancy she says, "They hardly *ate*."

"That's something for dogs," Nancy agrees.

"'I'm fine,'" Rachel goes on more slowly. "'So don't worry. I have a beautiful room with a big-screen TV and a soft, white carpet and a brand-new electric piano, and—'"

"Hold on," Nancy interrupts.

Rachel spins around.

"Don't say *brand-new*. That means it was just bought, and the police might be able to trace the store."

"'And an electric piano, and I'm practising a lot. When the coast is clear . . .'" She turns on her heel again. "Can I say about the slave drivers?"

"No, better not."

"Why?"

"Well . . ." Nancy fusses with collecting the dishes. "You don't want to scare her, right?"

"Right."

"So I'd leave them out of it, if I were you."

"Okay, I'll say, 'When the coast is clear in two and a half weeks, I'll be coming home, and then—'"

Nancy sighs.

"What?"

"Nothing." Now isn't the time to dash her hopes about going home. "Go on."

"'And then I'll tell you all about my adventures. Love, Rachel. Ex oh ex oh ex oh.' And I want to draw a picture."

Fifteen minutes later Rachel is watching cartoons, and Nancy is in the shop trying to find a stamp, her ears pricked for the sound of Ron's van, although it's still early. A book of stamps turns up in a coffee mug. She rips off two for good measure. Before sealing the envelope (on which Rachel has already written the address) she takes out the letter and reads it again to make sure nothing is given away about the house. The picture is on the other side. At the top it says *I MISS YOU* and then there's a girl, Rachel playing a keyboard. She has purple hair and orange skin. Black tears fall from her eyes. The TV and both windows are shown but, like the girl, they're done in all the wrong colours. Nancy sticks the letter in the envelope and goes to the kitchen to hide it in a side pocket of her purse.

She's coming back down the hall when somebody pounds on the front door.

"Hello!" a woman shouts.

It's Angie.

Nancy limps into the shop. After a few fumbling attempts she gets the door opened.

"Where is he?" Angie says, entering on a gust of perfume. She glances around. "Is he here?"

"He's out," Nancy whispers. The room seems to be tilting. She feels sick to her stomach.

"Why are you whispering?"

"Sorry."

"Look at you. Your worried, scrunched-up face." She presses Nancy's cheeks between her hands. "Why haven't you been returning my calls? Eh? *Eh?*" She gives Nancy little slaps. Her bracelets rattle.

Nancy is puzzled. What calls? Did Angie call *here*? "Oh, right," she says, as the fact of her abandoned apartment drifts back to her. "I haven't been checking my messages."

"So," Angie says, dropping her hands, "I phone Frank and he says you're working for Ron now and living with him, too. Doctor's orders. Obviously your doctor hasn't *met* Ron."

"Yeah, I'm doing the bookkeeping," Nancy says. "Stuff like that."

"Well, it isn't helping. Your limp is worse than ever." She takes her cigarettes out of her purse, then goes still. "What's that? A piano?"

Nancy doesn't answer. She has already heard the keyboard and is hobbling over to turn up the radio.

"Where's that coming from?"

"Next door."

"You can hear it from next door?"

The radio is on the top shelf. Nancy is barely able reach it. She twists the volume knob.

"CALLING FOR RAIN!" a man blares.

"Whoa!" Angie cries.

Nancy twists the knob the other way. "It drives me crazy, hearing scales . . ." She finds the right volume. ". . . all day." She rests her weight on the lowest shelf.

"You're losing it," Angie says. "You know that?" She sticks a cigarette in her mouth. Her red hair, with the light coming in from behind, smoulders at the edges. Nancy pictures her bursting into flames. She pictures the police pulling up and shooting her in the head.

"Oh, my God!" Angie says.

"What?" Nancy says, petrified.

"I almost forgot. You know that girl who was abducted?"

Nancy's stomach turns over.

"Well, don't you recognize her?"

"No."

"She's the girl from the salon that day! Remember? When you brought the chocolates, and her mother caught you?"

"Really?"

"I can't believe you don't recognize her. You've seen the pictures of her, right?"

"Yeah."

"She's a natural blond, even though she's part black. That is *so* exotic. But, God . . ." Back the cigarette goes between her lips as she fishes around in her purse. "Where did I put . . . Oh, here!" It isn't a lighter she pulls out, it's a piece of paper. She steps around the floor lamps. "Have you seen this flyer?"

With a wildly shaking hand, Nancy takes it. There's a

photograph of Rachel and her mother hugging. Above that it says, *Please Give Me Back My Daughter.*

"Look at them," Angie says. "They're so *happy*. I hate to say it but she's probably already dead. Those sickos don't waste time . . ." She tails off. "Are you okay?"

Nancy's gut is heaving. Letting the flyer fall to the floor, she leans over and throws up.

"Shit," Angie says, prancing back. Some of the vomit has landed on her ankle. The rest is sliding down the front of a dehumidifier.

"Sorry," Nancy gasps.

"Where's the kitchen?"

Nancy gestures over her shoulder.

"Do you want water?"

"Ginger ale, maybe. There's some in the fridge."

She picks up the flyer, blood rushing to her head and blinding her for a few seconds so that the photograph seems to develop before her eyes. Rachel is smiling at the camera. The mother is smiling at Rachel. If there is evil in the mother's face, Nancy can't detect it. She gets herself over to the counter and sits on the stool. The flyer, which is powder blue, she folds into a small square.

"I could only find one glove," Angie says, coming back into the room. She has a bucket of water, a roll of paper towels, and the ginger ale. A yellow plastic glove is on her right hand. "You aren't pregnant, are you?" She sets the glass on the counter.

That almost makes Nancy laugh. "It must be some kind of bug," she says, and wonders if this isn't the case—she feels hot and achy. "I hope I don't give it to you."

"I never get sick," Angie says. With one foot she shoves a box out of the way, then sets down the bucket and kneels in front of the dehumidifier. "What a piece of crap. Why didn't they just throw it out?"

"You'd be surprised what people want fixed."

Nancy sips her ginger ale. She is very aware of the coldness of the glass under her fingers and the tingling sensation inside her mouth. She looks at Angie's big curvy hips in her flowered pants and at the strip of white skin where her blouse has ridden up. At her beautiful, manicured hand, the one without the glove, pressed flat on the dirty floor. Every time she thinks about it, she can't believe she has a friend who's so sexy and strong. You should hear how Angie orders around her mafia boyfriend! And yet she's caring, too, and loyal. All through Nancy's bad times, Angie was the only person Nancy could count on. Could she count on her now? What if she just blurted it out, what if she said, "Oh, by the way, Rachel Fox is in the basement"?

Angie throws the dirty paper towels into the bucket. "Listen," she says, "I don't know what's going on around here . . ."

Nancy sits straight.

"But if Ron's trying to keep you hidden away, all to himself, you're crazy to let that happen."

"I'm not hidden away," Nancy says. She holds the glass of ginger ale with both hands, stunned by how close she came to confessing. "I'm in a *shop*. Where people are."

"Yeah, right. Look at them all. Frank feels the same, you know. That Ron is bad for you. He thinks you're getting beat up, actually."

"He *said* that?"

"He said you act like his sister did when she was getting beat up."

"Ron couldn't beat up a worm! If anybody's getting beat up around here, it's him!"

"Well, good. Good for you."

"It isn't good for me. Jeez."

Angie comes to her feet. "Are you going to be sick again, do you think?"

"I don't know."

"Go lie down."

"I will."

"If you weren't acting all weird, all nervous and freaked out, then I'd keep my mouth shut about Ron."

"I always act all nervous and freaked out," Nancy says, half joking.

Angie sighs. Either she thinks this isn't true at all, or she has just realized it is. She picks up the bucket. "Come and get your nails done one of these days. On the house."

As soon as she's gone, Nancy secures the bolt lock and closes the blinds. Then she goes over and opens the basement door a crack. Rachel is still playing the keyboard.

Thank God for that keyboard, Nancy thinks. She digs into the front pocket of her jeans, feels her lighter and her psychic pouch, and removes them both. Like most of the things in her life before Rachel, the pouch seems pathetic, not that she discounts its powers. Her fear of losing Ron is what she can't believe, how she clamped on to the idea that he was picking up women in bars. It's little girls he likes, not women.

Her breath catches; she has shocked herself. Why would

she think that? Ron can barely *look* at Rachel, he's so shy. Except . . . except he *does* look at her. When they were watching the movie last night, every time Nancy glanced over at him his eyes were on Rachel. Every time Rachel turns around, his eyes are on her bum.

Nancy shudders. This is crazy. *She's* always looking at Rachel, isn't she? At her mouth, her hair, at her bum, probably, and it has nothing to do with sex. And if Ron isn't interested in sex with *her* anymore, well, the feeling's mutual. She shakes her head to clear it of disgusting ideas. You've got a fever, she tells herself. It's the fever talking.

She tosses the psychic pouch into the garbage and lights herself a cigarette. Back behind the counter she fingers the flyer with a sharpening suspicion that if she unfolds it and sees the picture again, something in her will crumble—and maybe she *wants* something in her to crumble.

Sandy, her dealer, used to pass her the baggie of meth in a powder blue envelope, like an invitation to a tea party. His hand sliding across the table to her hand in the glassed-off smoking section of Coffee Time Donuts. She places her hand over the flyer, and the sweet feeling of giving herself over to some huge, heartless force comes back. She shuts her eyes. On the radio a woman is saying, "Our next caller is Ellen, from Toronto. How are you today, Ellen?"

Ellen coughs. "Sorry about that," she says. "I'm getting over a cold."

"So, Ellen," the host woman says. "Are the children of single mothers at greater risk than children living in two-parent families?"

"Absolutely," Ellen says. "If there'd been a father around, then Rachel's mother wouldn't have had to work two jobs."

Nancy twists in the stool and looks up at the radio.

"Presuming the father *had* a job," the host woman says.

"Well, yeah," Ellen agrees, "but most fathers *do*. So if he'd been around, then either him or the mother would've been at home when the lights went off. And if the landlord fell and knocked himself out, that wouldn't have been Rachel's problem."

"You're jumping to a lot of conclusions," the host woman says. "Anybody—the mother, the father—*anybody* could have fallen and hit their head in the pitch dark."

Good point, Nancy thinks. She can't quite understand what she's hearing. Is Ellen blaming Rachel's mother?

Ellen coughs. "Sorry about that. Yeah, but they said the landlord had been drinking, so—"

"Who said that?"

"It was on the news. On TV, I think."

"You're giving me a rumour, Ellen, and I'm not in the business of spreading potentially harmful rumours. Next on the line is Maria from Orangeville. Go ahead, Maria. You've got thirty seconds."

Maria says, "I feel really badly for the mother. I just want to get that out up front. I mean, it's a parent's worst night-mare what she's going through, and I'm praying for her."

"We all are," the host woman says.

"But, well, I just think she could have made wiser life decisions."

"How so?"

"Well, for instance, I read in today's *Sun* that the reason we haven't heard anything about the biological father is that she doesn't even know his name."

"I read that, too," the host woman says. She sounds sad.

"You know? I mean, before you have sex with strangers, and I don't think that's right but it happens, at least take responsibility for your own protection. Because sooner or later you're going to get pregnant and bring a fatherless child into the world."

"You're taking a risk in more ways than one," the host woman says.

"The health risks and on and on," Maria says. "But what I'm getting at is, there's a side of the family, the *father's* family, that hasn't been there for Rachel her whole life."

"That would certainly seem to be the case, I'm afraid. As to whether or not any of those family members would have been in the house on the night of the blackout, we can only speculate. Thanks for your call, Maria."

"No child should be an accident," Maria gets in.

Holding on to the shelf, Nancy switches the radio to a station where there's music. She wonders if it's true about the mother not knowing the father's name. Ron is always saying that the mother is stupid and selfish. What if he's right? What if, in spite of how much the mother loves Rachel, she has lousy maternal instincts? Nancy looks at the square of blue paper in her hand. She opens it. The picture and the words blur together. She thinks about the letter Rachel wrote, and right now—with her head swirling and her skin on fire—she can't imagine actually driving to a mailbox and dropping it in. Risking everything for a woman who maybe never deserved Rachel in the first place.

Chapter Twenty-seven

*T*HE *LOST CHILDREN* people are in Celia's apartment, setting up their equipment, when Laura arrives and somehow manages to talk her way past the police officers stationed on the porch. And then Mika, not knowing any better, invites her into the house.

At the sight of her, Celia feels her whole body clench. The reason she hasn't been returning Laura's calls is that Laura can be overbearing and hysterical. She can be spectacularly generous as well (for two months she let a homeless woman sleep in her second bedroom) but it's this other side of her, the high-strung, interfering side, that Celia can't imagine taking on right now. She looks at Mika. He blinks and looks at his shoes. Laura says, "Hi, Celia," in a small voice, and Celia goes over and hugs her, pulling away when Laura starts to cling.

"You're busy," Laura says, stepping back so that a man with an armload of cable can get by.

"I have a few minutes," Celia says.

They go into Mika's kitchen. Laura has brought a vegetable lasagna, and she hands it over to Little Lynne. She waits for Celia to sit before sitting herself. She's subdued, not herself at all. An opened pack of du Maurier Lights is on the table, and when she picks it up and sets it down again, Celia says, "Go ahead."

"That's okay," Laura says.

"Oh. Right." Laura is a rabid nonsmoker. That's something you should know about a close friend. Celia *does*, of course, know it. She pulls out a cigarette for herself. "You don't mind."

"God, no."

They look at each other. Laura's eyes fill, and Celia looks away and reaches over to the counter for some matches.

"Celia, what can I do?" Laura asks.

"You can hand out flyers."

"I have been. So has everyone on my street. Everyone wants to do something."

Celia lights her cigarette. Whenever she is reminded of how people all over the city are giving their time and money to help out, she feels a vague alarm. This onslaught of generosity from strangers. How can she be grateful enough? And if she isn't grateful enough what will happen? Her anxiety is of an accruing debt, some complicated moral interaction understood by everybody except for her and for which, whatever happens, Rachel will end up paying.

"I don't know how you do those press conferences," Laura says. "The one on Tuesday? I could tell it was killing you, but you were so good. Did many people call in afterward?"

"Yeah, a lot of tips came in. But no real leads yet." She turns, hearing someone in the doorway.

"Ready when you are," says a man from the TV show.

Celia puts out her cigarette.

"Is it all right if I wait?" Laura asks.

Celia looks at her again. The threat of tears has passed. "Sure," she says, softening. "Have some coffee."

The man leads the way up to her apartment. People and equipment crowd the living room, but he takes her past all this out onto the deck where the host—Celia met him downstairs—is seated on a kitchen chair. "Sorry to keep you waiting so long," he says.

"That's okay."

The man who came to get her says, "If you could just sit right there." He's indicating the sofa. Not the middle of it, where the gash is, but to one side of that. She sits on the gash.

"Do you mind moving a little to your left," a woman in earphones asks.

"I'm better here," Celia says. She doesn't see how showing rips in her furniture will get Rachel home any faster.

There's a silence.

"How about *I* do the moving?" the host says and shifts his chair.

Celia tugs her skirt over her knees. She's wearing a sleeveless white blouse and a blue jean skirt. No lipstick, hair combed flat. A technician comes over and clips a tiny microphone to her collar. A makeup lady powders her face. The host, meanwhile, crosses and uncrosses his legs. He's a dark, compact man with quick brown eyes. *He* is dressed like a fashion model: black shirt unbuttoned at the neck, black pants, black boots. Big Lynne told her that his son was killed by a pedophile, and as he glances around, then lifts his chin to the makeup lady, Celia wonders how many months or years went by for him before he began to care again about the way he looked.

"Nervous?" he asks.

"No," she answers truthfully.

"Good. This isn't *60 Minutes*, there's no angle or agenda on my part or on the part of the show. All we're hoping for here is to help bring Rachel home to you safe and sound. All right?"

She nods.

To start with he asks her to describe Rachel as a person, what she likes to do when she isn't in school, what she wants to be when she grows up. He moves on to the life she and Rachel lead: the piano lessons, the video store. He helps her. He clarifies, for instance, that Mika isn't just her landlord and frequent babysitter, he's a trusted friend. He makes no reference to his own son, not even indirectly, and she begins to think that he won't, that the subject is off-limits. But then, after she says, "Every waking minute I'm holding my breath," his face seems to age twenty years and he says, "I know that feeling," and instantly she's on her guard. She doesn't want her feelings to be feelings he knows. *His* child died. She sits back, as if with the same smoothness that he conducted the interview he could pull her into his hell.

But he sits back, too. He's done. Unclipping his microphone, he smiles and says, "Good job." He asks if they can film the drawings in Rachel's bedroom.

"Whatever you think will help," she says.

"You're a brave woman, Celia," he tells her. "I pray that what we're doing here today contributes to bringing Rachel home to you." His hand bolts across the space between them and they shake. Even the reassurance in his grip unsettles her.

Downstairs, the kitchen radio is on, and Mika, Little Lynne, and Laura are all listening.

"I just think she could have made wiser life decisions," a woman caller says.

Celia pauses, unnoticed, in the doorway.

"How so?" the host says.

"Well, for instance, I read in today's *Sun* that the reason we haven't heard anything about the biological father is that she doesn't even know his name."

"I read that, too."

"Here we go," Little Lynne says grimly.

"You know?" the caller says. "I mean, before you have sex with strangers, and I don't think that's right but it happens—"

"Oh, fuck *off*!" Laura says, slapping the table.

"I can't listen to this," Mika says. Little Lynne reaches for the dial.

"No," Celia says. "Leave it."

They all spin around.

"Celia—" Mika starts.

Celia holds up a hand for quiet.

The caller is speaking: "What I'm getting at is, there's a side of the family, the *father's* family, that hasn't been there for Rachel her whole life."

"That would certainly seem to be the case, I'm afraid. As to whether or not any of those family members would have been in the house on the night of the blackout, we can only speculate. Thanks for your call, Maria."

"No child should be an accident."

Little Lynne turns it off. "Sorry, Celia. There are always a few holier-than-thou types out there."

Celia walks over to the table and sits. She isn't offended.

"They make me sick," Laura says. "You're a monster if you have an abortion, no matter how young and alone you are. But if you decide, okay, I'm going to *keep* the baby, you're a bad mother because there's a side of the family that isn't *there*. They can't have it both ways!"

"It's true though," Celia says.

"What is?" Mika says.

"About no family being there."

"That isn't your fault," Laura says.

"*My* family. My father. Rachel's grandfather. Last Christmas she wanted us to go visit him in Florida and I told her he'd died. Can you believe that?"

Mika shrugs. "Maybe he has."

Celia looks at him. "You know what else? A part of me was relieved that my mother died when she did so I could have Rachel all to myself."

"You weren't *relieved*," Laura says quietly.

"I'm even jealous of you sometimes," Celia says, still addressing Mika.

"It's natural enough."

She shakes her head. Only she knows how greedily she loves her daughter. Seeing her across a room or in the playground at school, what's her first thought? Mine, she's mine. It isn't just amazement. Something miserly and famished runs underneath: the worst of herself, the worst of her mother in herself. A genetic fault line maybe. But that's hardly an excuse.

Chapter Twenty-eight

"*A*MEN," RON SAYS in response to the caller's declaration that no child should be an accident. He pulls up in front of the shop but keeps the radio on to hear the news. The lead story is about the steelworkers' strike. Rachel is next—the same report as an hour ago: a second candlelight vigil held last night; DNA samples being taken from staff and patrons of the Casa Hernandez Motel.

He turns the van off. That the mother doesn't have ten illegitimate kids is what he finds surprising in all this. Although maybe she does and they're living in foster homes. Or maybe Rachel is the only one she didn't get around to aborting.

He grabs his toolbox and climbs out of the van. Across the road, Vince, who is climbing out of his truck, calls, "How's it going?"

"Not too bad," Ron answers.

"You've been closed a lot this week."

Ron tenses. Since when did Vince start noticing his Closed sign? "Running around on house calls," he says.

"I was just out on a call in Mississauga," Vince tells him. "It's raining like a sonofabitch out there."

"It'll be hitting us soon," Ron says, relaxing. Vince is being neighbourly, that's all.

The shop blinds are down, the overhead lights off. Behind the counter Nancy sits holding a cigarette she makes no attempt to conceal.

"What are you doing?" he says.

"Oh," she says foggily. "Sorry." She drops the cigarette on the floor.

"That's not dope, is it?" he says, crossing the room.

"What? No, no . . ." She slides off the stool and grinds the butt under her foot. "Listen, Ron. I think I have the flu. I need to lie down."

"Is Rachel all right?"

"Yeah, she's fine. She's playing the keyboard."

He lowers the volume on the radio. "I don't hear anything."

"She was a minute ago."

He checks his watch. According to the schedule she should be watching cartoons.

"All of a sudden I felt woozy," Nancy says.

In the dim light her face is chalky. He switches on the lamp, and she's even whiter. He notices the piece of paper she's holding. "What's that?"

"Oh. A flyer about Rachel."

She gives it to him. He quickly reads it over. "Where'd you get this?"

"Somebody dropped it by."

"Who?"

"I don't know. They left it. . . ." She waves in the direction of the door. "It was in the mail slot."

"Really?" That flyers begging for Rachel's release are

being distributed beyond the official grid is worrying. On the other hand, volunteers go where they want; it doesn't necessarily follow that the search has widened. "They didn't knock?" he says.

"No. Nobody knocked."

He scans it again. "'I am the only family Rachel has,'" he reads out loud. He snorts, then decides not to get himself worked up. "So," he says, "Rachel's fine."

"Yeah, yeah."

Her indifference takes him aback. "I should look in on her," he says.

No response. He assumes she's mustering her opposition.

"I can ask her if she wants to see the vacuums," he says.

"Oh. Right."

"You don't have to be there, do you?"

"It's up to her." She steps around the counter. "I need to lie down. Wake me in an hour."

He balls up the flyer. For all its troubling implications, it has given him an idea, which is that to pique Rachel's interest in the vacuums he should first show her one of his pamphlets. He gets the most recent version off the shelf and opens it on the counter. He'd forgotten about the author's photo, but there it is. His smile is insanely wide. His hair is slicked down flat.

He finds a pair of scissors and cuts the entire panel off. Better to lose the section on Eurekas than to leave a hole in the panel and have Rachel wondering what it was he didn't want her to see. He skims the rest of the pamphlet. There's the odd word she might stumble on, but by and large the language is simple enough, intended for the general public.

She's kneeling in front of the dollhouse.

Hi," she says. His heart pounds, not just at the sight of her in her white skirt and blue-and-white sailor jersey but at the sight of her *there*, where he has placed her a hundred times in his imagination. "Can I come in?"

She cranes to look past him.

"I'm afraid Nancy's feeling a bit under the weather," he says, stepping over the threshold. "She might have the flu. How are you feeling?"

"Fine." She shifts her weight so that she's sitting on the foot she hurt. She thinks he's asking about that.

He closes and locks the door.

"Did Nancy go out?" she says.

"Out?"

"Did she, like, go shopping?"

"No." He wonders what she's getting at. "Nancy's here. Taking a nap."

Her hair is pulled back into a ponytail, and he is treated to the spectacle of her small, protruding ears. Her only defect, objectively speaking. It is unbearably sweet to him that she shows them off by wearing pearl studs.

He gestures at the dollhouse. "See that red button? Above the fireplace?"

She twists around.

"Push it," he says, moving closer. "See what happens."

She sticks her hand into the living room and gives the button a quick tap. The logs glow red. A second later the mantelpiece candles come on.

"Isn't that something?"

She nods.

In her other hand she's holding the mother doll. "Have you given her a name yet?" he asks.

"No."

"How about the baby, does she have a name?"

"No."

"Where's the father?"

She points to the office. The father is sitting behind the desk. What could be more natural than for Ron to get down on the floor, pluck the father off his chair and have him say something? Have him say, "Honey, isn't it time to feed the baby?" Or, "How about I fix us some supper?" He takes a step closer. As if reading his mind, Rachel lays the mother doll on the veranda and flicks the switch that turns off all the lights.

"Enough of that, I guess," Ron says. "For one morning." He sounds anything but nonchalant. He slaps the pamphlet against his thigh and only then remembers he even has it. "Oh," he says, gathering his wits. "You might find this interesting. It's about my collection. I don't know if Nancy has told you, but I collect and fix historical vacuum cleaners, some of them over a hundred years old." He offers her the pamphlet. After a moment's hesitation she takes it and pulls it open. "That one you're looking at," he says, "that's the Constellation."

"It's like a spaceship," she murmurs.

"That's what I always thought. I thought they should have called it Sputnik. Would you like to see the real thing?"

She shrugs. "Okay."

"I'll just be a minute." He hurries to the door. "You have a look at the pamphlet, see what other ones you want me to bring down."

When he returns with the Constellation and its box of attachments, she's sitting on the sofa, the pamphlet spread across her lap. "It's starting to rain," he announces, pushing the door closed with his foot. He's out of breath. He sets the box on the side table. The machine he puts on the floor in front of her.

"Do you like the colour?" he asks.

She nods.

"It's called Aqua," he says. "For aquamarine. Fifty years ago you saw a lot of aqua around. Aqua fridges and stoves, aqua cars. It was a real popular shade back then. So—" He clasps his hands. "The Hoover Constellation, model eight-two-two. A classic example—I go into this in my pamphlet—a classic example of form over function. Do you know what that means, form over function?"

She shakes her head.

"It means nice to look at but not very good at its job. The problem with the Constellation is the exhaust. Somebody had the bright idea that the exhaust should blow out onto the floor under this metal ring." As he leans down to demonstrate he finds her bare legs only inches from his face. He drags his eyes to the metal ring but now he's forgotten what he was talking about. "Here," he says. "I'll plug it in."

Of all his mid-twentieth-century machines the Constellation produces the most satisfyingly smooth whirr (which he considers ironic, given its disappointing performance). He lifts the switch with his toe, and after a few seconds of not looking at her, just listening, his mind clears. "So what happens," he says, returning to his earlier thought, "when you have the exhaust blowing onto the floor, is that the machine is easier to drag around, sure, because it's sitting on a pillow of air. But you pay for that little feature on the suction side." A reckless impulse takes hold of him and he says, "Would you like to give it a try?"

"You mean vacuum?"

"There's a bag inside, ready to go."

She stands. He passes over the handle, not quite believing that he's about to let her dirty one of only four unused Constellation bags in his possession.

"Should I do the sofa?" she asks.

"Why not?"

Before he can instruct her, she has started. She uses firm, straight sweeps, up and down. He should intervene—she's pushing too hard on the bristles—but her purposeful little hips have him captivated. When she says something over her shoulder it comes to him like a voice in a storm.

"What?" he says.

"Look—" She shows him the brush. "The fuzz isn't going *in*."

He stares at her pointing finger.

"See? The fuzz is all *here*, and it should be going in. Right?"

"Right." He switches off the power. The sudden silence is jolting. "That's what I was telling you about," he says, opening the box he brought down. "About the pillow of air. . ." He takes out the drapery brush and the bags. "How that . . . ah . . . gets in the way of . . ." He takes out the instruction booklet. "Where's the crevice tool?" he mutters. "It should be in this box." He paws through the remaining attachments. "Don't tell me . . ." The sweat begins to drip

down his forehead. Did he accidentally throw it out when
he was emptying the storage space? Without all its attachments, the machine is next to worthless.

"Stay right where you are," he says. "I'll be right back."

WHEN THE thud of his footsteps fades altogether, she lays
the vacuum cleaner handle on the sofa and walks to the
open door. He has left the door at the top of the stairs open
as well.

In her amazement it doesn't occur to her to escape. All
she can think is, now's her chance to sneak her note outside. She gets it from under the toy chest. She refolds it so
that the word *HELP* shows, then tucks it into the waistband
of her skirt and leaves the room. She tiptoes up the stairs.
Just inside the shop she pauses to listen. Ron seems to be at
the back of the house; she hears what sounds like furniture
being moved back there. She makes her away around the
lawn mowers and lamps. So that she doesn't bump anything
she presses her elbows to her sides.

The front door is unlocked. She steps onto the concrete
porch. It isn't raining anymore. Cars and trucks zoom by,
splashing water. Pigeons drop from the hydro wires to peck
at an orange pizza box.

Where should she put the note? Across the road there's a
man leaning against a truck and talking on a cell phone. She
decides to give the note to him. She descends the stairs. She
passes Ron's van, knowing it's his because it says *Ron's
Appliance Repair* on the side.

The man is getting into his truck. She walks faster. The
pigeons scatter ahead of her, onto the road.

"No!" she cries, worried that they'll get hit. She waves her arms to bring them back.

The note falls out of her skirt and is run over by a motorcycle.

It's all she can do not to dash out into traffic. She doesn't, though. She waits until it's safe.

So where does the car come from? It's suddenly there, an inch away from her leg. Behind the windshield is a black man in a turban. His door opens. He climbs out.

"Are you all right?" he says in a foreign accent. "Did I hit you?"

She steps back onto the curb.

"Little girl, did I hit you?" He moves closer.

She turns and runs.

The shop door is stuck. She bangs on it with her fists. She starts to cry.

Through the glass she sees Ron charge out from the hallway. He opens the door and scoops her up. Kicks the door shut. He carries her down to the basement. Kicks that door shut. He lays her on the bed. She can't stop crying. "They saw me!" she cries. "They saw where I am!"

"It's okay," Ron says. He strokes her face. "You're okay. I'm here. Ron's here."

WHAT WAS that loud noise? Nancy listens, rigid with fright. Except for the drone of voices from the shop radio, the house is quiet. She sinks into the pillow.

She was having a terrible dream: the flyer and the letter Rachel wrote to her mother this morning and the *HELP* note under the toy chest—they were getting all mixed up. She opened the flyer, but it turned into Rachel's letter, and she thought, Holy Christ, these are all over the city! She looked at it again and it was the note, it said *HELP* in orange marker, and she thought, *These* are all over the city. And they were. She looked outside, and there were notes everywhere, on telephone poles, on car windshields. *HELP, HELP, HELP* as far as she could see.

She should get up. She's so tired though. Just a few more minutes, she tells herself.

AFTER A while Rachel becomes aware of him stroking her face. His hand shakes, but he's gentle. She sees the silver button on his cuff and is reminded of the silver snaps on Mika's blue jean shirt.

She misses Mika. She's glad it's Ron who's with her, though. She can't imagine Mika grabbing her and kicking the door shut. Mika would have wanted to know what the matter was. He might even have gone over to the slave driver and said, "May I help you?" Once, he caught a homeless man yanking out his lilies by the roots, and instead of yelling at him he went over and said politely, "May I help you?"

She needs to use the bathroom. She tells Ron, and he stands to let her off the bed. He checks his watch.

"Are you going upstairs?" she asks worriedly.

"I'll stay if you want."

She nods.

In the bathroom she tries to think what it was about Ron that used to frighten her. She can't remember. When she comes out, he's crouched in front of the dollhouse.

"Usually in the morning we draw," she tells him.

She draws the customers from the motel: the pink-haired old woman, the black man who shook her hand, and so on. Ron draws a vacuum called a Hoover Model O. It takes him a while to get going—he keeps crumpling up his page and starting again. He says he'd like to show her the real thing, and she remembers how upset he was about the Constellation's crevice tool and asks if he found it.

"No." He frowns at his drawing.

"You'll find it," she says. "You'll find it in the very last place—" She freezes.

Somebody is knocking on the shop door.

She jumps up.

"It's only a customer," he says. He reaches for her hand. His knees start to jiggle. "Don't worry," he says.

When the knocking stops, she pulls her hand away, slowly (it's so easy to hurt his feelings), and sits back down.

"What would you do if a slave driver broke down the door?" she asks.

"An alarm would go off," he says. "But if the guy was stupid enough to hang around, I'd grab the wrench I keep under the counter and swing it at him."

"Is it a big wrench?"

He opens his hands as wide as his body. "It's heavy. It could do some damage."

"What if he had a gun?"

"I'd throw the wrench at his head and disarm him."

"What does disarm mean?"

"Get his gun."

"Would you shoot him?" she asks hopefully.

"If I had to."

"Would you kill him?"

"Maybe."

"What would you do with the body?"

"Bury it in the backyard."

"But wait until it's night," she says. "So nobody can see. And then—oh, I know!—you could plant a bush over the place and people would think that's why you were digging!"

"Even better, I could lay down patio stones."

"Yes! Patio stones!"

He holds up his picture. "This doesn't do it justice."

"It's good," she says, impressed. He has drawn little squares of shine on the metal part and made a shadow on the wall behind.

"You should really see the real thing."

He looks at her. His eyes beg, like a dog's. She doesn't want to see another vacuum, though—he might get all excited again and forget about the slave drivers. "How about we watch TV?" she says.

As he's flicking through the channels there's a noise from upstairs, a thud. She covers her mouth with her hands.

"That's just Nancy letting in Tasha," he says. He pats her leg. And there go *his* legs again . . . the jiggling. After a minute, Nancy and Tasha can be heard coming down the stairs. He turns off the TV. Rachel moves down the sofa— she has a feeling Nancy won't like Ron and her sitting so close together.

"Door's open!" he calls.

Tasha runs in. Nancy comes over, fluffing her hair with her fingers. "Everything okay?" she says. One side of her face is wrinkled from the pillow.

"We had a little incident," Ron answers. "I left the door open by mistake and Rachel went outside and a slave driver was there."

Nancy's mouth fall opens. "Where?"

"On the porch!" Rachel cries. Telling the truth will only cause trouble—they'll want to know what she was doing down by the road. They'll ask if she was trying to escape. Thinking this, it comes to her that she *could* have escaped. She begins to whimper with confusion, with frustration. "And then the door was stuck!" she cries. "Ron . . . he had to open it. He carried me down!"

"Oh, sweetie," Nancy says. She sits. Ron stands. Nancy rubs Rachel's arm. "That must have been scary. What did the guy look like?"

"He was black, and he was wearing a green turban." Now she's thinking that if she *had* tried to escape, the slave driver might have followed her.

"You never saw him before?"

"No, I never saw him. He went—" She makes claws of her hands.

"Jeez."

Did she mail the letter? Rachel wonders. Nothing in Nancy's face tells her.

"I should open the shop," Ron says. "Don't worry, Rachel. I've got my wrench." He smacks his fist against his palm.

She imagines the green turban caving in, the slave driver flying across the pavement. "Okay," she says.

"You LUCKY bastard," Ron says out loud. Things couldn't have turned out better if he'd left the doors open deliberately. If he'd *hired* the guy in the turban.

He supposes he can assume, by now, that the guy failed to recognize her.

The shop phone rings. He stares at it until the machine

picks up. He looks toward the window. Nobody there, no strange cars. He goes over and slides back the lock. He pictures her terrorized face on the other side of the glass and wonders at his speed and decisiveness. She weighed nothing. He touches his shirt where she buried her face. Still damp, though whether from his own sweat or from her tears he can't tell.

Children produce so much fluid when they cry! Laying her on the bed, seeing her drenched face, his only impulse was to clean her up. He couldn't control his trembling, and he wasn't unaware of the fact that the police might be on their way. But wiping away her tears claimed all of his attention. He used the edge of the bedsheet and then, as she calmed down, his fingers. She closed her eyes. He kept on going, wiping her cheekbones, under her nose, along her lips.

He makes his way to the counter and finds the towel. He dries the back of his neck. It's what happened a little later that he's thinking about now. He was sure she wouldn't flinch when she felt his hand on her knee, and he was right. He figured she barely registered it. Except she did. She did register it. Because when she heard Nancy on the stairs, she tugged her skirt down and moved away from him. Like a girlfriend when the wife turns up.

She *knows*, he thinks.

A buzzing starts up in his ears. A barrage of images crowd his vision, and he stumbles into the stool. "Wait a minute," he mutters. "Wait a minute, wait a minute . . ." The images retreat.

What does she know? That she turns him on? That, like Mika and every other man in her life, he's going to take advantage of her?

All along, maybe even before he brought her here, he had faith that they would reach a stage where they could be physically comfortable with each other, the way fathers and daughters naturally are. He didn't think it would happen so soon, but he was confident that when it did he'd be a satisfied man. From never touching her to feeling her little body collapse against his, getting treated to innocent flashes of skin, kissing her good night, kissing that gorgeous pink mouth . . . how could it not be enough? Every father of a beautiful child must be tempted, he thought—he still thinks. So his theory as to why most of them don't yield (presuming most of them don't) was that they don't have to, they aren't desperate. Every day they can count on their measured-out dose of contact.

The thing is . . . He starts pacing. The thing is, he's no longer sure he ever really believed this. The thing is, his hand on her knee *wasn't* enough. And she *isn't* innocent—far from it, she comes with more experiences behind her than he can bear to imagine. There's a good chance she's not even a virgin.

His pacing has brought him into the kitchen. He returns to the shop and stares at the basement door. What does any of it mean, except that he's going to have to fight even harder? Do the resisting for both of them.

There's a way of thinking about her that helps. If, instead of dwelling on a specific part of her body, he has her hunching in a chair or limping across the room, or even if he remembers certain facial expressions—the guarded twinges that telegraph her ticking mind—his love tends to win out.

"All right," he says, as if everything's settled. He hears Nancy climbing the stairs, and he goes and sits on the stool.

"So what happened?" she says.

"I was showing her the Constellation, and I got distracted. It was unbelievably stupid."

She looks at him. She's still very pale. "*Both* doors," she says. "You left *both* doors open."

"But she came back. That's the important thing."

"What about the guy in the turban?"

"I guess he didn't recognize her."

Nancy keeps looking at him. Finally she shakes her head. "Well, she can't get over how you *scooped her up*. She keeps saying, 'Ron's real strong.' She says you should eat *all* your meals with us."

He feels his heart skip. "Is that okay with you?"

"With me?" She heads for the kitchen. "It's what *she* wants that matters, right?"

Chapter Twenty-nine

ALL FRIDAY AFTERNOON, while she and Jerry and Mika knock on the doors of the derelict and stranded houses below River Street, Celia has it in her mind that if Rachel isn't found today, she'll phone her father when she gets home. She'll do the right thing, win back God to her side. But as she's eating supper her nerve begins to fail. She tries to imagine the conversation ("It's Celia." "Who?" "Celia, your daughter." Silence) and decides it won't hurt to put the call off until the next morning.

"He's probably unlisted anyway," she says to Mika.

"Let's see," he says. He looks up the Florida area codes in the phone book and dials Fort Lauderdale information. There's a William C. Fox on 14th Avenue.

"So you think this is a good idea," she says as he hands her the number.

"It's up to you, Celia."

In her apartment she finds the vodka bottle and has a swig. She punches the number with a pen that says "Fox Network."

Five rings before he answers, his husky, slightly high-pitched "Hello" unmistakable.

"Dad. It's Celia."

"Celia!"

She's taken aback by how pleased he sounds. "Your daughter," she says.

"Of course! Celia!" He loudly clears his throat. "What a wonderful surprise. How are you?"

"Awful, actually."

Now comes the silence.

"Is it your mother?"

"Mom died nine years ago. Didn't anyone tell you?"

"No. No, nobody did."

"I thought one of your old friends would have."

"Well, I've been out of touch."

Celia lets that go.

"How did she die?" he asks.

"She had a stroke."

"That's how her own mother went."

"Dad, I'm calling about something else."

"All right."

She takes a breath. If she doesn't get it all out at once, she won't get it out at all. "I have a daughter. She was born a day before mom died. Her name's Rachel. Rachel Lauren. Last Friday she was abducted from the house where we're living. We don't know who took her. There's a huge search going on here in Toronto. We're pretty sure she's alive but . . . I should have told you about her before."

"Celia. I don't know what to say. I'm so sorry."

"I thought you should know."

"I should. I should." Another lengthy throat clearing. Then, "I'm afraid I'm not very mobile."

She thinks he's saying he doesn't own a car.

"I'm in a wheelchair," he goes on. "I wouldn't be much use in the search."

This is a small shock. Not so much the wheelchair (he's seventy-two) but his feeling that he should come up and help. "There are hundreds of searchers," she says. She asks him how long he's been in a wheelchair.

"Ten years it would be now. It's multiple sclerosis."

"Oh, God."

"I manage all right. But this . . . this abduction business. You must be in a terrible state. Do you have a husband to help you out?"

"No." She starts to cry.

"Celia," he says. "Celia. You don't deserve this."

How does he know she doesn't deserve it? When he thinks of her, who is the little girl he remembers? When she thinks of *him*, it's as if she's flipping through a book of photographs featuring a person she met and liked but can't claim to have known very well. (Somebody famous maybe, since he was handsome: a tall man with very white teeth for the time and lots of blond hair.) There he is, washing the dishes, his shirtsleeves rolled up, his watch on the glass shelf above the sink. There he is, painting the dining room ceiling, all that hair bunched under a baseball cap. Between the pictures is nothing, no rippling out of memory or impressions. With the real pictures, the ones in the photo album, she at least knows from things her mother said how old he was when the picture was taken, what the circumstances of his life were: working at the car dealership, for instance, where he couldn't bring himself to waylay potential customers out in the lot. Her mother never understood why a man of his retiring nature went into direct sales. Long after he had run off, she said to people, "Bill likes to keep himself to himself," as if his absence were simply an extension of that character trait. The only memories Celia has of him ever talking to *her* are from his Sunday-night phone calls when he doled out questions about school and choir practice and she said, "Fine," and her mother stood in the kitchen doorway, flushed and picking her nails, pathetically hopeful. Even at eight years old Celia knew he was never going to leave Hazel Beals and come home.

"Do you need money?" he asks. "I'm not in the lap of luxury down here but I could—"

"No. There's money."

"Well . . . and the police are doing everything they can?"

"They seem to be."

"It's a terrible thing."

"I just wanted you to know you have a granddaughter." She wipes her nose on her sleeve. "When she comes home, maybe we'll visit you."

"That would be wonderful. What did you say her name is?"

"Rachel. Rachel Lauren Fox."

She senses him absorbing the "Fox"—his unwitting contribution. "Rachel Lauren," he says. "Very pretty."

"I'll call you with any news."

"What's your number there? Hold on, let me grab a pen."

The phone drops and for a moment the line seems dead. She wonders what he was doing when she called.

"All right," he says.

She gives him the number.

"You'll find her," he says. "You hang on tight."

"I will. Good-bye, Dad."

"Good-bye for now."

You hang on tight. She'd forgotten he used to tell her that at the end of his Sunday-night calls. This is her first thought. Her second is, he sounded glad to hear from her. More than glad . . . relieved. As though all these years he's been waiting for her to pick up the phone. But then why did he stop phoning *her*? She thinks of the things she didn't ask. If he's still with Hazel, or if Hazel is even alive. If he has other children, not by Hazel, who would have been too old, but by someone else. She grips the receiver. She looks toward the door, and Mika is there.

"How did it go?" he says.

She places the receiver in the cradle. "Good."

But another thought is pushing at her. A dread. What if all she gets is one family member at a time? She had her mother, then she had Rachel—not even a full day's overlap. Now she has her father. Unless she loses him again, she won't get Rachel back.

"You told him what's happening?" Mika says.

She nods. She isn't going to burden Mika with her new fear. He'll want to talk her out of it and he won't be able to. Nobody could. Nobody could convince her that the world doesn't work that way. The truth feels intensely private to her right now. She doesn't expect logic or even sanity, she's only trying to pay attention.

Chapter Thirty

*W*HEN NANCY REMINDS Rachel that on Thursday she called Ron weird, Rachel lifts her chin and says, "I meant *sensitive.*" A moment later she adds, "Anyway, that was *before.*"

Before she found out how "strong" and "brave" he was. And "smart" now, too. "He can fix any vacuum that was ever made," she informs Nancy.

Nancy knows she should be glad about the turnaround, and at first she was. Two days later she frankly wishes things could go back to how they were. The so-called rescue and Ron's promise to throw his wrench at the slave driver are all Rachel can talk about. She has him bring the wrench down and let her feel how heavy it is. She draws a picture of it half buried in the slave driver's neck, so much blood streaming out behind that Nancy thought she had him wearing a red cape. There are endless pictures of Ron: Ron holding the wrench, Ron throwing the wrench, Ron driving his van, Ron fixing vacuums. She gives him huge arms and a flat stomach. The pictures of him with the wrench she tapes to the wall across from her bed.

Ron pretends not to be as thrilled as he obviously is. He says, "She needs to see me as a hero right now. It's a stage, it'll pass."

In the meantime he gets to have her run up to him, crying "Ron!" every time he enters the room. He pats her head and smiles, showing his teeth. He has a new, high-pitched laugh. Meals are taken up with him telling her about his favourite topics: bird migration, World War II, and Ives McGaffey, the inventor of the vacuum. Nancy has heard it all before, many times, and even when it was new to her she drifted off. Rachel, though, seems hypnotized. She gazes at his face. When *she* talks, it's always to him, even if she's answering a question Nancy asked. She wants him close by but if he stays too long she worries that he isn't guarding the shop. "Should I go up?" he asks. She pushes him over to the door, then pulls him back. Then pushes him to the door again. He lets himself be thrown around.

She still believes she's going home in a couple of weeks. That hasn't changed. Her plan is for Ron to sneak her outside in a box.

"Any slave drivers still in the neighbourhood will think you're an air conditioner," Ron says, playing along. Afterwards, to Nancy, he says, "I can go through the motions, at least. Put her on a trolley and wheel her as far as the parking lot."

"And then what?"

"And then I see some slave drivers—she can't see anything, she's in the box—and I wheel her back inside."

"Big hero."

"Do you have a better idea?"

"Me? I don't have *any* ideas."

"Maybe in two weeks, she'll want to stay."

"Are you kidding?"

"Look how far we've come in just eight days."

"Look how far you've come, you mean."

She tries to form a new bond between herself and Rachel through music. She brings down her banjo and plays the songs she's been working on: "Billy Boy," and "Yellow Bird." Rachel listens politely, then asks her if she has ever played the guitar.

"I don't have a guitar," Nancy says. "Anyways, I like the banjo. The sound, right? The cheery sound."

"I like the guitar," Rachel says.

Nancy goes into the bathroom and cries.

She has never felt so lonely. Just to get Rachel's attention—and to knock Ron down a peg or two while she's at it—she talks about the letter Rachel wrote her mother and thinks is in the mail. She says she hopes Ron never finds out. "He'd be furious," she warns. It's true, he would be. With Nancy though, not Rachel. As to whether or not Nancy really will mail the letter, she can't decide. She has sliced open the envelope, and several times a day she studies the picture to reassure herself that there's no hidden message. She turns the page over. *Dear Mom,* she reads. *I love you very very much.*

Chapter Thirty-one

WHILE CELIA WAITS for Mika to return from the printer's with more flyers, she sits at the dining room table and listens to the CD of the woman. She's still hoping to come up with a face or a location, but she also listens now for the reassurance. *They would never hurt her, don't worry about that.*

The kitchen phone rings regularly: people calling about the *Lost Children* program, which aired last night. Big Lynne takes messages. One call, though, has her walking into the dining room and putting a hand on Celia's shoulder. Celia stops the CD. "Hold on," Big Lynne says, then covers the mouthpiece and says to Celia, "It's a guy named Robert Jones. From New York City. He thinks he might be Rachel's father."

A loud noise rushes through Celia's body.

"Do you want to talk to him?"

Celia reaches for the phone. "Hello?"

"Celia?"

"Yes."

"I apologize for bothering you at such a terrible time."

"Who did you say you were?"

"Robert Jones."

Jones. "Are you black?" she asks.

"Yes. I'm black."

"Are you an architect?"

"Architect? No. No, I'm an investment broker."

"You never studied architecture?"

"No, I never did."

The tension drains from Celia's chest.

"I'm calling," he says, "because I saw the show last night, and you look a lot like a woman I dated ten years ago, when I was living in Toronto. Her name wasn't Celia, it was Shelagh . . . Shelagh Conroy, but she'd changed it once before, and I thought she might have changed it again."

"I'm not her."

"All right. Well, that's—"

"Good-bye," Celia says, and hands the phone back to Big Lynne.

An hour later she and Jerry and Mika are waiting out a downpour in a donut shop on Dundas Street West. A sign above the tiers of donuts says No Smoking but the place is empty and there are tin ashtrays on the tables, so she lights a cigarette.

She's been telling Jerry about the phone call. "I was braced," she says, shifting her backpack of flyers to an empty chair. "Rachel is always going on about how, one day, a black man from New York City is going to get in touch and hook her up with her father, so I was thinking, okay, here it is."

Jerry reaches across the table for some napkins, which he uses to wipe his bald head. "It could still happen."

"A couple of million people watched the show," Mika says.

"I don't mean that," Jerry says. "I mean exactly what she predicted could still happen."

"Oh, she's convinced it will," Celia says. "It's as if she's *seen* it."

Jerry shrugs. "Maybe she has."

Celia and Mika look at him.

"I believe kids have visions all the time. Flashes of the past and future, lost souls. All that stuff. Kids are new to the world. Eternity clings to them."

"Did Ben have visions?" Celia asks gently. Ben was his son.

"Yeah, he did. He saw these reptile guys with green scales. He took it for granted they were aliens. Who's to say they weren't?"

"The shape of life a thousand light years away," Mika volunteers.

"Exactly."

Celia turns in her seat to blow smoke. Across the road, at a rooming house, water pours thick as an arm from a downspout. A crease of light between the closed curtains of a ground-floor room keeps catching her eye. But when she and Mika knocked on the door, nobody answered.

"I don't know if this qualifies," Mika says, "but . . ."

In the pause, while Mika gears himself up, Jerry pulls out some more napkins.

"When I was five or six," Mika resumes, "I was on a camping trip with my father and I saw very clearly an image of a skull and crossbones in front of our flat outside Helsinki . . . where we were living at that time. My father told me I was only imagining things. So I believed him. Then two days later, we arrive back home . . . and . . . in the middle of the lawn is a pesticide sign with the skull and crossbones picture. While we were gone, a company sprayed our lawn by mistake. They were supposed to have sprayed a place on another street."

"It qualifies," Jerry says.

"It hardly seems possible, though," Mika says. "Does it?"

"Anything's possible," Celia says.

And that, she thinks, is the nightmare. The worst-case scenario is just as possible as the best-case. There are a thousand possible explanations, tens of thousands of possible suspects. The possibilities of doing the wrong thing, thinking the wrong thought, you can't even measure.

Chapter Thirty-two

*N*ANCY COMES UPSTAIRS and announces, "She wants *you* to read to her."

"She does?"

"Don't look so surprised."

He's fixing a Cuisinart four-slice toaster. He pulls the knob off the carriage lever and removes the front-end cap. "What do you think?" he asks, trying to keep his voice casual.

"I think you better go read to her."

"Are you going to be there?"

"She only wants you."

"Okay, well, I'll just wash my hands."

In the bathroom he takes off his shirt and runs a damp facecloth under his arms. The summer evening beyond the window—cars changing gears, the drooped, tropical silhouette of an ailanthus frond—reminds him of getting ready for dates back in high school, his elevated hopes. "Take it easy," he warns himself in the mirror. There are no hopes here, other than to earn more of her trust and affection. He gargles with mouthwash and dabs his neck with cologne.

When he comes downstairs, Nancy is holding the refrigerator door open. "We need milk," she says. "And I told her I'd buy some chocolate ice cream."

"I'll get it later," Ron offers.

"I'll get it. Tasha needs a walk." She shuts the fridge and walks toward him, limping a little. He steps back so that she won't smell the cologne.

"How's the leg?" he asks.

She turns and looks at him. "What?"

"Your leg. How's it doing?"

"The same."

He waits until he hears the shop door slam before going down to Rachel. She's in bed, sitting up with the covers pulled to her waist.

"Hi," he says. She's wearing the pink nightgown.

"Hi."

The bed curtains have been tied back to allow her to see the drawings of him on the far wall. The *Ron wall,* she calls it.

"Do you have the book you want to read?" he asks.

She slips it out from under the duvet. "*Amazing Grace.* Have you read it, Ron?"

"I can't say that I have."

"It's good."

He sits next to her and lifts his legs onto the duvet. The book is thrust into his hands.

"That's Amazing Grace." She points at the cover. "He used to be a famous race horse but now he's sick, and Annie . . ."

As she chatters away, Ron stares at the nest of pleated skin over her knuckle. Everywhere on her body are these morsels of superfluous beauty.

". . . which is as far as we got." The finger moves to

indicate that a page has been turned back. "Right there. Chapter Three."

"Chapter Three," he says, and with shocking trust she settles into the crook of his arm. The candied scent of baby shampoo wafts up from her damp hair. His heart rattles in its cage. "'Annie took the stairs two at a time,'" he reads. "'She had to reach Belinda before Sarah did. Sam laughed—'"

"No!" Rachel cries. "You missed a whole part!"

"Sorry." He clears his throat and goes back to the beginning. "'Annie took the stairs two at a time. She had to reach Belinda before Sarah did.'" The sweat is starting to collect along his hairline. He wipes it with his finger. "'Sam laughed—'"

"You missed it again! Ron!"

"Sorry."

"It's because you're shaking. Why do you shake like that?" She gazes up at him. She's as innocent as a flower.

"I don't know."

"Because you're sensitive?"

His eyes fall to her mouth. A machine roar fills his skull. Her lips are moving, she's saying something. He bends closer to hear. Closer. He smells the toothpaste on her breath. She smiles. "Rachel," he groans, and she twists away and snatches the book out of his hands. He sits back, terrified.

But she's only taking over the reading. Through the dying roar in his head he hears, "'Baron was the last of the livery horses.'" She twists around again. "What's a livery horse?"

He disengages himself and comes to his feet. "A livery horse . . ." His glance skims the room: the dollhouse, the drawings of a man with huge arms and too much hair. "A livery horse . . . is . . . it's a horse for hire."

"Why did you get up?"

He looks at her. She seems gaudy all of sudden. Her fat pink lips. Her yellow hair. "I heard something," he says maliciously.

"Oh." She hunches. She shrinks back to perfection.

"It's probably nothing." His anguish is enormous. "But Nancy has gone out, so maybe I should go check."

"Are you coming back?"

Other men would have slipped her a drug. He shakes his head, furious at the thought of how low other men sink, what they get away with.

"Okay," she says. "I'll see you in the morning."

TASHA TROTS through the puddles, shattering the reflection of streetlights. Nancy sucks on a cigarette. At the intersection she wakes up to the fact that she's heading for Mac's Milk, which has a mailbox out front, rather than for Laird Variety, which doesn't. She takes this for a sign that the letter in her purse is destined, finally, to be sent.

She ties Tasha's leash to a bike rack and enters the store. Standing at the counter, waiting for the person ahead of her to buy lottery tickets, she watches the security camera. She wonders if the police are able to trace a letter to a certain box or at least to a certain neighbourhood.

Back outside, she looks for more cameras. There don't appear to be any, although in the dark it's hard to tell. She unzips the side pocket of her purse and removes the envelope, worried for a moment that it isn't sealed. But it is. At some point today she must have taped it. She opens the mailbox. Drops the letter inside.

"Shit," she says a second too late: she forgot to wipe off

her fingerprints. Oh, well, she thinks. She unties Tasha and
starts walking. She refuses to feel guilty. Ron can flex his
muscles and show off his wrench, but *she's* the one who's
keeping Rachel from falling apart. If that means taking big
risks, too bad.

She stops. Something she didn't register half an hour ago
has just struck her: Ron was wearing cologne. She smelled
it on him. *Ron was wearing cologne.*

HE SITS on his bed and picks up the framed photo. "Jenny,"
he says, willing himself to see her in the girl's narrow eyes
and belligerent chin. He can't do it. He sees his mother.

"I've never been happy," he says to her. He scans over
his life, wondering if this is true. He supposes it's more accurate to say he has never been lighthearted. Or carefree.
Carefree—no part of him finds any connection with that
word. His mother used to tell him he was born watchful.
From watchful to secretive to feeling like a freak of nature,
maybe it's a natural progression. In high school he refused
to donate blood in case the doctors found some grotesque
component that gave him away. His highest claim for himself is that he's a connoisseur of beauty, but even at his
most awestruck there's a thin, sour poison always pooling
underneath. Even with Rachel.

The front door slams. He puts the picture on the bedside table and goes downstairs. Nancy isn't around; she
must have headed straight for the basement. He fills a glass
with cold tap water and thinks about the mickey of rye he
couldn't bring himself to throw out. It's in the cupboard
above the stove. He's still fighting temptation when he hears
Nancy coming through the shop.

She halts just inside the doorway. She's ghostly, her eyes black sockets. "You have to tell me," she says. "I have to know. Do you have sexual feelings for her?"

"What?" He sets his glass on the table.

"Why are you wearing cologne?"

"I didn't smell very good. I was sweating all day."

Those black holes stayed fixed on him.

"Did Rachel say something?" he asks.

"No. Why?"

His blood starts flowing again. "I'm just trying to figure out what brought this on." He goes over to her, extricates the plastic bag from her fingers and puts it on the counter. "You look awful. I don't think you're over that flu yet."

She lets him take her hands. But her gaze slides to someplace over his shoulder. "I feel like you have sexual feelings for her," she says.

"I don't."

Her eyes come back to his.

"I love her," he says. "The same as you love her. But because of what your father did to you, you can't . . ." He feels himself growing angry. "You can't believe a man can love a little girl without . . ." He drops her hands. "Jesus Christ."

"You shouldn't wear cologne then."

"Fine." If she only knew what he had just walked away from down there. Paradise. Paradise is what he walked away from. "Fine. I won't wear cologne."

"Okay. Good." She looks past him again, as if distracted by a more pressing thought. "I'm going to bed."

He waits until she's at the top of the stairs before he empties his glass in the sink and fills it with whiskey.

Chapter Thirty-three

*T*HEY SPEND MONDAY in the Dupont-Davenport area,
Jerry knocking on doors north of the railway tracks, Celia and
Mika working the south side. The next day Jerry comes down
with a bad cold, and it's just Celia and Mika. They decide to
concentrate on the industrial strips at the very periphery of
the official search grid. They drive from place to place, then
get out and walk along little out-of-the-way streets they never
knew existed.

By late afternoon they're making their way up Laird Avenue, north of the bridge. Only a few promising places are left.
The first is a shabby redbrick house with a parking lot out
front and what might be an apartment on the second floor.

"Hold on," Mika says. He takes out his cell.

"Who is it?"

"The battery just died." He slips the cell back into his
pocket and looks at the house. "Ron's Appliance Repair," he
says, reading the sign above the door.

NANCY IS in the kitchen, fixing supper. Ron is in the storage
space, searching through a box of gaskets.

"Hello?" a man calls from the shop.

Ron recognizes Rachel's mother immediately, although she seems ten years older than when he saw her at the motel. "Sorry," he says, walking over to the radio and turning it up. "I didn't hear the door."

"That's all right," the man says. "We were wondering whether . . ." He reaches into his canvas bag, and Ron places him. "Whether you would post one of our flyers."

Ron accepts the flyer, pretends to read. He glances at the mother a few times, as if comparing her to the picture. "Sure," he says. "Be glad to. I'll put it in the window."

The mother looks where he's indicating. "I've seen your van on my street," she says in a tone of having just realized.

"I've done a few house calls in Cabbagetown," Ron says. "You must be going through hell. I'm sorry."

Her gaze has shifted to the basement door. "Is there a cellar?"

"Yep." He nods. "A good-sized one." His pulse is high and shallow in his chest.

"Is that the door to it?"

"It is."

"Do you mind if we have a look?" This from the man. Mika.

"Downstairs?" Ron says.

"If you don't mind."

"I don't mind." He plunges his hands into his pants pockets. "Provided I can find the key. I've got a collection of vintage vacuums down there, so . . ." He walks over to the counter and opens a drawer. "Extremely rare, some of them." He opens another drawer. Rummages around. A voluptuous sensation of terror and surrender is slowing his movements. "Now where would I—"

The phone rings.

Taking advantage of the distraction, he picks up. "Ron's."

"It's me," Nancy hisses. "Act like it's an emergency."

"What?"

"Act like you just heard somebody was in a car accident."

"When?"

"Right now! Say, 'Jesus.'"

"Jesus."

"Yeah, and you've got to rush to the hospital. So now you're listening to the directions."

"Okay." He checks his watch. "Fifteen, twenty minutes." He finds a pen and writes some numbers. "Five, two, seven . . . Okay. See you soon."

"Now hang up."

He puts down the receiver.

"Everything all right?" Mika says.

Ron takes a moment, as a shocked person would do. He lets the murderous hatred he feels for this man glaze all other feeling. "A friend of mine has been in a car accident."

The mother touches her throat.

"It doesn't look good," Ron says. "I've got to go."

"Of course," Mika says. He and the mother make their uncertain way to the door. "Maybe we'll drop by another . . . time."

"I'm usually here," Ron tells him. "Good luck."

"Good luck to your friend," Mika says.

Ron follows them out, gets in the van and drives as far as Eglinton and Yonge before turning back. To be on the safe side—they might not have left the neighbourhood yet—he parks in the lane.

Nancy is sitting on the kitchen floor, still holding his cell.

"That was genius," he says.

"She knows."

"Who?"

"The mother."

"She probably wants to look in everyone's basement. Anyway, I called her bluff."

"She felt something. Rachel is right under where she was, and she felt it."

The certainty and doom in her voice give him pause. A mother's instinct—there's something to that. "We might have to move her to the spare bedroom then."

"Are you kidding?"

"Just for the next few days."

"What about the window up there?"

"Stick a sheet of Mylar over it. Hang some shutters."

"Hang some shutters." She gets herself standing. "This is all way too crazy."

The cell beeps.

"Oh, jeez," she whimpers.

"Leave it," he says.

She flings it to the floor. "I can't do this!" she cries.

"You can."

"I can't! I can't!" Stepping over the still-beeping cell, she grabs her purse and hobbles past him.

"Where are you going?"

"I don't know."

"You shouldn't drive." He trails after her into the shop. "You're too upset."

"Fucking door," she mutters, trying to open it.

He reaches around her and slides back the bolt. "She'll wonder where you are. She's scared enough as it is."

"Oh, yeah?" In her furiously closed face the tears fight to escape. "Well, whose fault is that, eh?" And then she's outside and limping to her car.

He locks the door. The mother and Mika aren't anywhere to be seen, but across the road Vince is standing in an empty bay of his garage. He waves. Ron lifts a hand. The two of them watch Nancy reverse into the cement barrier and drive off on screeching tires.

Chapter Thirty-four

*T*O BYPASS THE crowd out front Mika has taken to parking either on Sumach or Winchester so that they can approach the house from the lane. This evening, before they're half-way across the yard, Big Lynne opens the porch door. "Oh, God," Celia whispers but then sees that the policewoman is smiling.

"There's a letter from Rachel," Big Lynne says.

Chief Gallagher and Deputy Chief Morris are in the kitchen, having themselves just arrived. It seems that the letter was mistakenly delivered to an apartment building down the street and only found its way to the house a little over an hour ago. "We're lucky the tenant wasn't on vacation," Gallagher says. He explains how Big Lynne thought she recognized the writing on the envelope and therefore made a comparison with the writing in one of Rachel's homework books.

"That geography one you showed me," Big Lynne tells Celia. "And sure enough. I tried to phone on Mika's cell."

"The decision was made to open it," Gallagher goes

on. "We couldn't know how time-sensitive the message might be."

"Sure, of course," Celia says.

Gallagher takes some papers from a manila folder. "The original is with forensics. These are copies."

Mika reads his standing. Celia sits at the table. She reads the last part out loud: " 'When the coast is clear in two and a half weeks, I'll be coming home and then I'll tell you all about my adventures. Love Rachel.' "

"When the coast is clear . . ." Mika says.

Celia looks up. The air between her and Gallagher seems to buckle as he reaches for a copy of his own. He says, "Forensics has to weigh in, but assuming that the person who mailed the letter is the same woman who made the phone call, it's safe to say she's willing to take substantial risks. So it could be she has an escape strategy and Rachel is in on it."

"In two and a half weeks. That's quite specific," Mika says.

"Maybe our woman knows that in two and a half weeks whoever else is involved will be away from the premises."

"The other possibility," Morris says in his soft baritone, "is that she's telling Rachel certain things to keep her spirits up."

"Which is good in itself," Big Lynne says.

"What's the postmark?" Mika asks.

"Toronto. Yesterday." Gallagher opens another file. "There's also a drawing."

It says *I MISS YOU* across the top in capital letters. Under that is a picture of a purple-haired, orange-skinned girl playing a keyboard. Black tears run down her face.

Celia lets her own tears fall. Mika grips her shoulder. "She got her streaks after all," he says, referring to the hair, and Celia gives a pained laugh.

Gallagher says, "On the wall, between the windows, it looks like she's drawn a *P* and then, further down, an *M*."

"Well," Celia says after studying her copy. "Sort of."

"You don't think they're deliberate?"

"They're not like her writing at all."

"No, but maybe she's sneaking them in. Trying to tell us something."

"A street name," Morris suggests. "Parliament. Metcalfe."

"Maybe," Celia says doubtfully. "I mean, we should check those streets again. But she isn't . . . she isn't that crafty."

"The keyboard is a Yamaha," Mika says. "That little circle there? It's the Yamaha logo."

"How accurate are her drawings in general?" Morris asks.

"She's a realist," Mika answers. "Not with colour, obviously, but with form and substance she draws exactly what she sees."

"So the windows would have bars."

"Definitely."

"And they'd be high up on the wall."

"She's in a basement," Celia murmurs.

"Ah," Mika says. "Right."

And yet neither of them thinks of Ron's Appliance Repair. They get caught up in the previously unconsidered idea— proposed by Morris—that because of the keyboard and big-screen TV, the abductors could be holding Rachel in a more middle-class neighbourhood than anyone had assumed. They

rethink their door-to-door search plans and get sidetracked by
street maps and strategies.

They get sidetracked by the easing of their worst fear.
By the force of their relief.

NANCY IS crying so hard that she puts on the windshield
wipers. When she realizes how crazy this is, she pulls over.

She has ended up on Cherry Street, almost at the lake.
She restarts the car and drives the last quarter mile to the
parking lot. Everything before her eyes—the trunks of trees,
the falling-down dock house, the crumpled stretch of sand,
the glittering dark blue water—seems stamped with dread.
She opens her purse and finds the joint she tucked in with her
cigarettes last Sunday. "Yeah, right," she mutters, remembering
Ron's "We have to stay clearheaded." How clearheaded is *he*,
saying they should move Rachel upstairs? Voices travel through
the grates in that house, especially between the shop and the
two bedrooms. But even if Rachel's mother makes it to the
basement without Rachel's hearing her, what's she going to
think when she finds an apartment down there all decked out
for a nine-year-old girl?

Nancy can't believe Ron hasn't asked himself the
same questions. So now his only choice is to move Rachel
out of the house. Sneak her across the border, drive to
Florida. At this very moment he could be loading the van.
No, the car—the van has his name on it. Nancy wonders if
he's expecting her to come back in time, or if he even
wants her to. Maybe he's hoping she'll be too late and he'll
have Rachel all to himself.

She puffs on the joint. In her mind she sees a certain

motel room: the closed drapes and soiled light. There's a double bed and a man in boxer shorts sleeping on his side. He's holding a little girl to his belly. He's snoring. The little girl is eating Smarties. Her reward, he said.

WHEN RON opens the door, Rachel and Tasha both come running over.

"Ron!" Rachel cries.

He lays a fatherly hand on her head. Her hair feels alive, pushing back against his palm.

"Aren't we having supper soon?" she says.

"We're a little behind. Nancy isn't feeling well, so I'm doing the cooking. It'll be another fifteen minutes or so."

"What's the matter with her now?"

"Her leg's acting up."

"I *told* her she should get a prescription." She traipses over to the keyboard and sits. "I'm practising my arpeggios."

Upstairs he pours himself a rye and drains the glass. He pours himself another and goes to the kitchen and lets Tasha out into the yard. He surveys the counter. There's a spinach salad already made and some slices of tofu in the frying pan. Four skinned, cooked potatoes on the cutting board. He starts chopping these up. If Nancy isn't back soon, he'll phone her apartment. He can't imagine her staying away for longer than a few hours when she suspects him of having sexual feelings for Rachel. It's easier to imagine her going to the police, but he's betting she won't. Even if she's prepared to crucify him, the only person she now trusts to take care of Rachel is herself.

She was right about the bedroom. It's a bad idea. He's not as convinced as she is that the mother will turn up again, but he can't rule out the possibility. They're going to have to leave, probably tonight. And go where? Florida is out; the U.S. border crossings will be on alert. West, he thinks. Manitoba, Alberta. Pack the car with a few essentials, make the maximum withdrawals on his debit and Visa cards. He'll wait until the last minute to tell Rachel. He'll say . . . what will he say? A gang of slave drivers is prowling the neighbourhood.

She's standing on the other side of the door. She holds it open, then shuts it behind him and watches approvingly as he sets down the tray and turns the key. Any barrier between her and the slave drivers has her approval now.

"Sorry it took so long," he says.

"Potato salad," she says. "Yummy."

"I hope it is."

"It will be, and you know why?"

"Why?"

"Because *you* made it, and *you're* yummy!"

His heart starts jumping.

He focuses on laying out the meal: the plates and cutlery, her glass of apple juice, his rye and water. Only when she picks up her fork does he relax again. Watching her eat has a mollifying effect on his nerves, although it's also a great sensual pleasure. There's something about seeing her put food in her mouth that gratifies and relieves him, as if she were a starving creature he has brought back from the brink. She chews conscientiously, working her entire face. When she swallows, she makes a soft gasping sound at the back of her throat.

Conversation is all about the torturing and killing of the slave drivers. This has been the case since Sunday. For a minute or two she'll tolerate a change of subject, then it's right back to him sawing off a slave driver's legs with hedge trimmers (his weapons having multiplied to include anything lying around the shop), baking a slave driver's eyeballs in one of the microwave ovens, and so on. "What else have you got up there?" she asks eagerly. "I've got a soldering iron," he says. "Do you know what that is?" Given the abuse she suffered before coming here, he understands her need for revenge fantasies. Even Nancy, who hates this kind of talk, can see how revenge fantasies might be therapeutic.

Tonight, when the meal is over, Rachel gets him to bring down the wrench. Usually he just swings it at the air, but tonight she wants him to hit the stuffed monkey, whose name, she informs him, is Lyle. "Here comes a slave driver!" she cries, throwing Lyle into the air. "Take *that*!" she screams.

Ron feels the strangest sadness to see the monkey, with his gentle smile and floppy sausage limbs, go catapulting into the wall. On the other hand, it exhilarates him to use the full force of his body and to have her jumping around screaming. Lyle is indestructible, or appears to be, until the fifth or sixth strike, when his stomach rips apart and a wad of foam bursts out.

"Uh-oh," Rachel says, picking him up. She looks at Ron, stricken.

"Nancy can sew him back together," Ron says. "Or I can pin him with safety pins. For the time being."

"No pins," she says sternly. She sits on the sofa and cradles the monkey to her chest. "Poor Lyle," she coos. "Poor little Lyle."

Ron drops the wrench on the bed. "Would you like to watch a movie?" he asks hopelessly.

She cocks her head. "What time is it?"

"It's . . ." He checks. "Almost seven."

"Can we watch TV?"

"Sure. Sure we can."

"Can we watch *Everybody Loves Raymond*?"

At first she stays over on her side of the sofa. She's quiet. Feeling guilty, Ron imagines. But then Raymond's wife pours spaghetti sauce on Raymond's lap, and she laughs and stretches out her legs.

Now her bare feet are pressed against Ron's left thigh. He keeps his eyes on the television. When she laughs again, he begins to stroke her calf. She acts as if she doesn't notice. Maybe she doesn't. He feels the fine blond hairs under his fingers. He runs his hand down to her ankle. Squeezes her foot. Amazingly he isn't shaking. He concentrates on experiencing her foot as if it were a separate organism and the entire object of his desire.

He's no longer paying attention to the TV, so it startles him when she pulls her feet away. "Time for my bath," she says, jumping up. She tosses Lyle on top of the other stuffed animals. "You have to run it for me, Ron."

"What?" he says.

"My *bath*."

"All right." He stands, teetering a little. He wonders if he's drunk. Gripping the bedstead, the door frame, he makes his way to the tub.

"Don't forget the bubble bath!" she calls.

Is she getting undressed? *Now* his legs tremble. Please don't let her be naked, he thinks—a feeble, insincere prayer against the onslaught of his arousal. By the time he turns off the taps his shirt is drenched with sweat.

He goes into the other room. She still has her clothes on. "Have you read this, Ron?" she says, holding up a book.

"No."

"Do you want to read it to me after?"

"You have your bath, and then if Nancy's feeling better she can read it to you." He seems to be moving toward the door.

"Will you come and say good night?"

"I will."

"Don't forget your wrench!"

The evening sun spreads his shadow across the lawn mowers and microwaves, all the clutter he should have stopped taking in days ago. He phones Nancy. Gets her machine again. "Call me right away," he says. "It's urgent."

A tremor of fear goes through him as he puts down the receiver. What if she's at Angie's? Does she have the willpower to keep her mouth shut around that woman? He doubts it.

He'd better start packing right now. Right now. He hauls himself upstairs and drags his suitcase out of the linen closet. Jeans, shirts, underwear, socks—he throws everything in. He gets what he needs from the bathroom, throws that in. He carries the suitcase downstairs. His mind swerves to the shop. He'll have to post a notice: "Closed for Family Emergency." He'll have to change the message on the answering machine.

He checks his watch: five to eight. They'll leave when it's dark. Maybe Nancy will be back by then. He takes a nip of whiskey. Hours seem to have passed since he ran Rachel's bath. He'd better go down, he thinks, say good night. Let her get some sleep before the commotion starts.

She isn't in the bed. She isn't anywhere. For a sickening moment he's sure she has escaped.

"Ron?" she calls.

She's in the bathroom.

"It's only me," he says.

"I'm still having my bath!"

His vision tunnels. He feels his legs moving. It's not a question of choice.

He reaches the door, which is open. What he sees is her naked, skinny, golden body climbing out of the tub.

"Can you get the towel?" she says.

He lifts it off the hook.

"That was a long bath, eh, Ron? All the bubbles are gone."

He dries her shoulders. Her back. She turns in a circle, shivering. He drops the towel and picks her up under her arms.

"Hey!" she laughs.

He carries her over to the bed. "I'm still wet!" she cries. He can hardly hear her over the roaring in his skull. He lays her among the stuffed animals.

She thrashes and squeals. She screams with laughter. She's like something primitive and embryonic, fighting for air. She tries to cover herself but he yanks the duvet from her grip. Her arms furl. She goes still. Her face blooms up at him, wide with fright. He lets go of the duvet and looks around—bewildered—for the real threat.

It can't be him.

The roaring dies away. He looks back at her. She's huddled under the duvet, only the heel of one foot showing.

"Oh, God, Rachel," he says. "Don't be scared."

Not a twitch from her, not a sound.

"I want you to get dressed," he hears himself say. "And then come upstairs."

THE POLICE station is on the northeast corner. On the northwest corner is an empty lot. Nancy pulls into it and parks.

"Bastard," she moans. She punches the steering wheel. In that same instant the sun, sinking behind her, flares off the chrome of a paddy wagon and hits her in the face.

A sign, she thinks.

She climbs out of the car. She stands there for a minute, assembling her nerve and letting go of everything else. Then she starts limping toward the station. Toward the hard, dark years she always knew lay ahead.

$\mathcal{N}$EITHER OF THEM speaks. Rachel kicks the dashboard and bites her bottom lip.

He told her that all the slave drivers had fled the neighbourhood. A "contact" informed him, he said, making it sound official. Then he left open both doors and waited for her in the shop. A few minutes later she came up. She was wearing the clothes she'd arrived in—the red tank top and white skirt—and she had Lyle, the stuffed monkey, whose lacerated belly she covered with her hand. Her feet were bare.

"What about shoes?" he said.

She shook her head. She was looking past him. "Are you *sure* they're gone?"

The realization that it wasn't too late, that he didn't have to do this, entered his mind and slinked off. He opened the front door. "A hundred percent sure."

She swallowed.

"Come on." He had to get the both of them out of here. Now or never.

She crept forward.

"Let's *go*."

On the porch she hugged the monkey to her chest and peered around. He began to lock up, then thought, Why bother? He waved to Vince, who was closing his garage and who stared but didn't wave back.

It *still* isn't too late, he thinks, not with any hope, only because it's a fact. He glances over at her. Her face is pressed to her window. She's breathing fast. He remembers when he brought her to the house and was afraid she might hyperventilate. He'd like to tell her he's sorry about the duct tape. All the things he'd like to tell her are wedged in his throat behind the one pure thing he'll never get to say to her now.

"Hey!" she says, sitting straight. "That's my school!" She looks at him. "Where are we going?"

He doesn't answer. She turns back to her window.

"Hey," she says again just before he pulls over.

They're half a block away from her house. A police car is parked out front. A dog sits on the lawn.

"I see Osmo!" she cries. She starts to unbuckle her seatbelt.

"Rachel—"

Her distracted gaze swings around.

"Can I ask you to do something for me?"

"What?"

He removes his sunglasses. "Don't let men touch you," he says. "Ever again. Don't sit on their laps, don't let them hold your hand." He's looking deeply into her face and for a second he thinks he glimpses the inscrutable, self-possessed woman she will grow into. "Even men you know."

"Okay."

"I'm serious."

She nods. "Okay."

The seatbelt unbuckles. She opens her door.

"Good-bye, Rachel."

"Oh!"—flashing him a bright, social smile—"Bye, Ron! Thanks for saving me!"

And then she's out of the car and running into the long late-day shadows.

NORMALLY, AT sunset, Mika would be on the porch. But he has a difficult time ignoring the scrutiny of the crowd across the road. Even standing here, knowing he's visible through the screen door, puts him on edge.

He's watching his dogs. They're uncharacteristically vigilant, both of them jerking their heads at every noise. Osmo, who never leaves the porch by herself, is on the lawn.

"They're looking for her," Mika says, hearing Celia come up behind him.

Celia peers around his shoulder then opens the door and steps out. The dogs give her a glance. She sits on the sofa, making herself mostly hidden from the crowd, although the sensation of being stared at doesn't bother her much anymore.

Her heart is still beating quickly, from the letter. She studies the dogs. What do they know? Turning back to Mika, she says, "You did tell them that it's going to be another two and a half weeks."

"They have no concept of weeks."

"I don't either." She sighs.

He goes out to join her. He's remembering what Deputy Chief Morris said about how the woman could be telling Rachel things to keep her spirits up. He lays a hand on

Happy's head. As he does, Osmo starts barking and Happy leaps off the porch.

Celia stands. Both dogs are yelping now. Mika rushes onto the lawn. "Osmo!" he yells, grabbing the dog's collar. Celia parts the branches of the lilac bush to see what's setting them off.

There's a girl, running toward the house. She's thin, with wild yellow hair. A red tank top.

Chapter Thirty-six

WHEN THE DOGS begin to bark, Ron turns around and drives back the way he came. Tears warp his vision. He wonders why he never bought a gun, why he never anticipated this moment. Jumping off a bridge, his old fantasy, seems too dramatic to him now. He guesses carbon monoxide is his cleanest, simplest bet. A hose to the exhaust, the van parked out behind the shop.

He pulls into an alley and cuts the engine. Did he cry this hard over Jenny? Or his mother? He can't remember. He grips the steering wheel. His life begins not to flash before his eyes but to glide, processionally. He sees faces and rooms and chain-link fences and model airplanes and picture tubes and motors. He sees every vacuum he ever refurbished. He sees Nancy grimacing in her sleep.

Poor Nancy. He unclips the pen from his shirt pocket and tugs a business card out of his wallet. On the card's blank side he writes, *Nancy Dunphy had no part in the abduction of Rachel Fox. I misled and used her.* He adds his signature, then puts the wallet and card on the passenger seat, which is still warm. He lets his palm rest there. When the heat begins to feel like his own he starts the engine and drives off.

People will say it's because he couldn't face the consequences.

It isn't that. It isn't the thought of jail or the trial.

It's the thought of the world without her.

It's love.

Acknowledgments

FOR THEIR COUNSEL and support I am grateful to Christopher Dewdney, Beth Kirkwood, Marni Jackson, Virginia de Vasconcelos, Jacqui Brady, Iris Tupholme, Sara Bershtel, Antje Kunstmann, Riva Hocherman, Richard Beswick, Christie Blatchford, and Police Constable Christopher Martin. I am particularly indebted to Superintendent Gary Ellis of the Toronto Police Service.

About the author

About the book

Read on

Ideas,
interviews
& features

Author Biography

BARBARA GOWDY was born in Windsor, Ontario, the third of four children. When she was four years old, she moved with her family to Don Mills, a suburb of Toronto that would inspire the settings for much of her fiction.

For many years, Gowdy studied piano and even considered becoming a pianist but eventually decided that she didn't have the talent to pursue that career. While working as an editor at the publishing house Lester & Orpen, she found herself writing characters into her clients' non-fiction and took this as her cue to start writing professionally.

Her first book, *Through the Green Valley*, a historical novel set in Ireland, came out in 1988, and the following year she published *Falling Angels* to international acclaim. Her 1992 short story collection *We So Seldom Look on Love* was a finalist for the Trillium Award for Fiction. Four years later, the title story from this collection was adapted into *Kissed*, a film directed by Lynne Stopkewich and starring Molly Parker. Two other stories in the collection have been made into films, "Presbyterian Crosswalk" (*A Feeling Called Glory*) and "The Two-Headed Man." In 2003, *Falling Angels* was also adapted to film, with a screenplay by Esta Spalding. *The White Bone* was recreated for the stage by writer Sean Dixon for Toronto's Summer-Works Theatre Festival.

Gowdy's books, including four bestselling novels—*Mister Sandman* (1995), *The White Bone* (1998), *The Romantic* (2003) and *Helpless* (2007)—have now been published

MAY TRUONG

Barbara Gowdy

2

in twenty-four countries. Her stories have also appeared in a number of anthologies, including *Best American Short Stories, The New Oxford Book of Canadian Short Stories in English* and *The Penguin Anthology of Stories by Canadian Women.*

Gowdy has been nominated for many prestigious literary awards. She has been a finalist for the Commonwealth Writers' Prize and a repeat finalist for the Scotiabank Giller Prize, the Governor General's Award, the Trillium Award and the Rogers Writers' Trust Fiction Prize. In 2003, *The Romantic* earned her a Man Booker Prize nomination. She is a recipient of the Marian Engel Award, which recognizes the complete body of work by a Canadian woman writer in mid-career.

Ben Marcus praised Gowdy's literary realism in *Harper's Magazine,* singling her out as one of the few contemporary writers who has "pounded on the emotional possibilities of their mode, refusing to subscribe to worn-out techniques and storytelling methods."

Gowdy appears regularly on television as a commentator on literary matters and has taught creative writing courses at Ryerson University. In October 2006, she was appointed a member of the Order of Canada. Her original screenplay, titled *Green Door,* has been made into a short film, to be released in 2008.

Barbara Gowdy lives in Toronto.

How I Write
by Barbara Gowdy

I didn't start writing until my early thirties. Back then, I worked on an IBM Selectric II typewriter. It featured a twirling type ball and a sticky "lift-off" correction tape—all very high-tech, I thought. I was writing what turned out to be my first published novel, *Through the Green Valley* (a title I did not choose and never quite understood, although it's true to say that since most of the novel is set in Ireland and Wales, green valleys do show up here and there, and characters do occasionally travel through them).

In the final year of the five years that the manuscript took to complete, I graduated to a computer. I forget the model, but that computer crashed about twice a day, and its printer pounded and clacked like a cotton gin. Nevertheless, I was hooked. I loved that you could get rid of mistakes by simply banishing them to the ether. (Gone were the faint shadows left by the Selectric's lift-off tape.) I also loved that you could do checks for repeated words. How many times is it okay to use an adverb such as "morosely" or "happily" in a 90,000-word novel? Once, I'd say. All my subsequent books have been composed on a computer: a luggable, then a portable, then a desktop, then a laptop. Currently, it's a Macintosh PowerBook G4.

Away from the computer, I do no writing at all. I don't keep a notebook or diary, and I almost never jot down stray thoughts. I've come to trust that my narratives unfold only in one place and under one circumstance:

> That computer crashed about twice a day, and its printer pounded and clacked like a cotton gin.

at my desk, with my mind turned to the job at hand. The odd time that I have recorded an idea on a scrap of paper and later tried to insert it into a story, the fit was bad somehow, the tone wrong, or the idea less arresting than I'd imagined.

I'm fastidious. I like a clean, uncluttered desk. Come to that, I like a clean, uncluttered house. When I sit down to write, the first thing I do is mentally scan my surroundings for any screaming mess that requires my immediate attention. More often than not, I land on something. So there goes a half hour while I rearrange the linen closet or collect maple keys from the front porch.

Back at my desk, I eventually type a word. Another word. An entire sentence. I go on for maybe forty-five minutes, then stop to return phone calls and emails. For me a full day's writing amounts to five hours, half of them eaten up by rewriting. I avoid dwelling on the novel's plot or the years it will take to finish. I just try, one word at a time, to get through the day—*through the green valley* of the day. The miracle is, you plod away like this and you end up with a book.

> For me a full day's writing amounts to five hours, half of them eaten up by rewriting.

An Interview with Barbara Gowdy

How did you first become interested in the theme of child abduction?

I found myself wondering, What is the worst thing that could happen to a person? The answer I came up with was losing a child. Not to death, but actually losing a child, finding yourself faced with the unspeakable fact of her disappearance. So I decided to try to write a novel about that. The challenge became how to make the story readable, how to offer hope to the character of the mother and to pull back on the tension.

You have described the book as a suspense novel and also—this might be surprising to some readers—as a "love story."

Ron, the abductor, is desperately in love with Rachel, the little girl. His is a misguided love, clearly, an unrequited love, a hopeless, illegal love, but it's pure and true in its way.

Why did you decide to tell the story from multiple points of view?

Ian McEwan and David Gilmour tell their marvellous stories from the points of view of the male parent, whereas my novel is told from the point of view of the abductor, the abductor's girlfriend, the little girl, the mother and the mother's landlord. This makes for what Lawrence Durrell called a stereoscopic narrative: a narrative that lights the characters from various angles. I felt I needed

66 Stereoscopic narrative: a narrative that lights the characters from various angles. 99

6

to do this in order to break out of what could have been—for me, at least—a claustrophobic story. Also, I was afraid that a single point of view might restrict the reader's ability to sympathize with other characters.

What research did you conduct while writing *Helpless*?

I got in touch with a superintendent of the Toronto Police Force, the guy who literally wrote the book on child abduction, and from him I learned about the massive and intricately orchestrated operation that starts up when a child disappears. I also researched vintage vacuums, because Ron, the abductor, collects old vacuums, which he stores in his basement. I found, as I suspected I would, online sites devoted to vacuum cleaner collectors. The men who are interested in them are like the men who obsess about vintage cars. They keep the vacuums at peak performance and highly polished. The big thing is to have unused bags in your collection. Ron has a Constellation model with four unused bags. I also thought that interest in extreme cleanliness and newness could be linked to children. Children are new machines, they're clean, they're not suppurating and dying. For Ron, anyway, the obsession with vacuum cleaners and the love of little children are linked.

Do you feel you have obsessions that reveal themselves through your writing?

When I taught creative writing, I used to tell my students to write not what they know but what they're obsessed by. They'll use what ▶

❝ For Ron ... the obsession with vacuum cleaners and the love of little children are linked. ❞

An Interview with Barbara Gowdy *(continued)*

they know anyway, for settings and anecdotes. I seem to be obsessed by attachment, the need for humans to attach themselves to other humans, and how helpless we all are before this need. Also, I'm concerned by who it is we find worthy, what sort of human being. What are our yardsticks? How qualified are we to judge? In *Helpless*, for instance, Ron could be seen as heroic, because though he has pedophilic feelings, he does not act on them. To have feelings as strong as his, and to have the object of your love so close and to repress your feelings, could be considered heroic, or it could be considered appalling and disgusting just to have those feelings in the first place. I tend to come down on the side of judging people by their behaviours, not their thoughts.

> I seem to be obsessed by attachment . . . and how helpless we all are before this need.

Is it this decision not to act on his feelings that makes Ron, as you have described him, "not a typical abductor"?

It is definitely not normal for a man to abduct a young girl and then to treat her adoringly and gently, as Ron does. Normally, the girl is used and then quickly disposed of. But that horrible narrative is not one I had any desire to pursue. Ron, very much like Lewis Carroll, the creator of *Alice in Wonderland*, loves little girls. He is an aesthete, a connoisseur of young female beauty. He is convinced that he is abducting Rachel to save her from abuse in her home. At the same time, he knows he has inappropriate feelings for her. Lewis Carroll also harboured such feelings. In his diary, Carroll referred to them as "unholy thoughts," "unwanted thoughts." As far as we know, he never acted upon them.

Was it difficult to tread a middle ground between creating a sympathetic character in Ron and letting him off the hook?

My editor in New York asked me, "Do we have to like the guy?" and I said, "No, but he has to be real." I couldn't bear to have Rachel abducted by a monster. I wanted to make him someone who hadn't yet fallen. I wanted him to have a moral dilemma. That's more interesting to me. If a character has already fallen, there's no dilemma.

What differences have you observed between the reactions of male reviewers and female reviewers?

Most of the reviews I've received from women have been great. They've said there is so much tension, and they were grateful that Ron is dimensional. A few male reviewers have said the same thing, but most men say, "This book has no tension because Ron's a human being." I think interest in young girls, a passing interest, a flash of interest, is so prevalent and so frightening to men that they want to hate Ron, they want him to be really bad, and they want me to take him out. I didn't do that.

It's fascinating to see how nine-year-old Rachel, the object of Ron's obsession, deals with her captivity. ▶

> " I wanted Ron to have a moral dilemma.... If a character has already fallen, there's no dilemma. "

An Interview with Barbara Gowdy (*continued*)

She doesn't understand why she's there, so she creates her own narrative to make sense of her situation. When you see footage of little kids in war-torn places, and they're smiling and waving for the camera, you think, How can they be smiling? Their town has just been blown up, their parents may be dead. But children are so remarkably resilient, and I think they invent narratives to bring sense to a senseless adult world.

You make much of Rachel's beauty and how she accepts her effect on people.

Rachel is a mixed child, Caucasian and black. She's exactly like a stunningly beautiful girl I saw in a park in Toronto. She was playing Frisbee with her father, who was black. She had pale, mocha skin, chromium-yellow hair with tight little curls, blue eyes, black lashes.... I felt the gratitude you feel when you see an exotic bird. People were staring at her, but she seemed completely indifferent, as I think at some point you would. There's a line in the book where someone compliments Rachel, and she says, "Thank you," and I have her mother think how she accepts compliments politely, but a little gravely, as another child might accept a gift she already has. It's her reality to be beautiful; she knows that it gives her power.

In your novel, each of the characters experiences helplessness, including the abductor, but what sources of power come into play?

> It's Rachel's reality to be beautiful; she knows that it gives her power.

The power of beauty. The terrible power of too much desire. And how power shifts. In any normal relationship, the beloved holds power over the lover. Ron obviously holds the physical power. But the emotional power very quickly shifts to Rachel. She eventually senses the shift and exploits it.

What can fiction such as *Helpless* accomplish that other types of writing cannot?

Fiction can give order and meaning to chaos. It can impart a view of life that encourages readers to reflect upon their own views. It can be a moral guide in that way. Good fiction isn't simply faked reality. Hemingway has something interesting to say about this. In an old *Paris Review* piece that I recently came across, he said, "From things that have happened and from things as they exist and from all things that you know and all those you cannot know, you make something through your invention that is not a representation but a whole new thing, truer than anything true and alive."

Selected edited excerpts are reprinted with the permission of Ramona Koval, from an interview broadcast on The Book Show, *ABC Radio National, Australia (May 21, 2007) and published in* Brick *literary journal (Winter 2007).*

&.

" Good fiction isn't simply faked reality. "

Works by
Barbara Gowdy

Through the Green Valley (1988)
In eighteenth-century Ireland, the son of a
peasant farmer struggles to find his place in
the world.

Falling Angels (1989)
This black-humoured story features three
sisters growing up during the 1950s in the
shadow of their mother's heartbreak.

We So Seldom Look on Love (1992)
Tender and empathetic, these short stories
feature people whose interests, and sometimes their very anatomy, make them complete outsiders.

Mister Sandman (1995)
In this hilarious and disturbing novel, one
family's immoderate passions and potentially
explosive secrets are exposed.

The White Bone (1998)
This engrossing fantasy plunges the reader
into the world of African elephants as they
fight to survive drought and slaughter.

The Romantic (2003)
When a mother disappears, her daughter
develops a devotion to her neighbour's pre-
cocious son.

To receive updates
on author events and
new books by Barbara
Gowdy, sign up today at
www.authortracker.ca.

Web Detective

www.prosecast.com
Listen to the HarperCollins Canada Prosecast interview with Barbara Gowdy. On the main page, scroll down to "Search this Site," and key in "Gowdy".

www.youtube.com
On the YouTube website, search for "Barbara Gowdy". View "Barbara Gowdy Talks about *Helpless*," an interview featuring Gowdy and senior editor of *The Walrus*, Marni Jackson.

www.torontolife.com/features/barbara-gowdy
Read *Toronto Life*'s interview with Barbara Gowdy.

www.eyeweekly.com/arts/features/article/804
Eye Weekly takes a look at the stage adaptation of *The White Bone*.

www.ourmissingchildren.gc.ca
This Government of Canada website provides a wealth of information, including a list of child-find organizations, a missing-children database, an explanation of AMBER Alert and safety tips for parents.

www.weeklywire.com/ww/10-12-98/austin_arts_feature1.html
Weekly Wire's article "The Man Who Loved Little Girls" (October 12, 1998) provides background on author Lewis Carroll, whose obsession with little girls Barbara Gowdy ▶

Web Detective (*continued*)

has compared to that of Ron, the abductor in *Helpless*.

www.historicaltextarchive.com/sections. php?op=viewarticle&artid=769
For anyone interested in vintage vacuums, History Text Archive offers "Vacuum Cleaners Before Electricity—and a Little-Known Inventor," which traces the history of vacuums, and includes a bibliography and list of websites with photos.

❧

An Excerpt from
The White Bone

It is the matriarchs who keep track of the days—how many since the last rainfall, how many until the black plums ripen, how many since a bull was in musth or a cow in oestrus, and so on. Their method is mysterious, even to them. Anyone can come up with the exact number eventually, by counting backwards or forwards day by day. For the matriarch, the calculation is immediate. It is not a skill she learns. She assumes the family's leadership and several hours later if somebody mentions, for instance, the evening a certain calf died, she finds herself thinking, "Four years and forty-seven days ago."

Of all the gifts that aren't Date Bed's, this precise, instantaneous measuring of the passage of time is the one she used to envy the most. As a young calf she tried to train herself to count days at matriarchal speed and when she finally accepted that it couldn't be done she devised a short-cut ("grouping," she calls it) for arriving at a close approximation. Instead of tallying the days, grouping tallies the full moons, which occur every thirty days, give or take a day. Two full moons, or two groups of thirty days, add up to sixty days. Three groups are ninety days. You only have to do the addition once to know forever afterwards how many days or years are in five groups, or thirty-five, or in seventy-three and a half.

Every morning when she chisels another scratch into her left tusk she wonders if ▶

> **❝ It is the matriarchs who keep track of the days. ❞**

An Excerpt from *The White Bone* (*continued*)

her life's remaining days will add up to the
three and a half groups that would bring her
age to exactly thirteen years. She is not very
hopeful. The wound above her right eye has
scabbed over, but behind the scab is a buzzing sensation that is only slightly relieved by
eating cycad bark. Coming to her feet she
reels through a dizzy spell, and several times
a day she falls into hallucinations—ravish-
ingly strange, and as sharply visible as if
she were looking through Mud's eyes, but
disturbing. She is walking in an immense
cavern where it is somehow as bright as
midday, and on each side of her, in phe-
nomenally straight rows, stacks of strange
fruits—sweet-scented and vividly coloured
(red, orange, yellow)—glide by; she is on a
rise of land and, all around her, tiny white
blossoms drift from a frigid sky and sting
her skin and settle on the earth like sand.

> She prays,
> despite the fact
> that she has little
> faith in prayer and
> no comprehen-
> sion of it.

None of these complaints are necessarily
deadly and they do not frighten her. What
does is that her memory is leaking. Six morn-
ings ago, a blue lizard scrambled past her
face. She could not identify it, although she
knew she had studied that breed and added
it to her lizard inventory. Since then, half of
her memories have been shadow memories:
impeccable in parts, in other parts faded or
gone altogether.

She prays, despite the fact that she has little
faith in prayer and no comprehension of it.
How can the circumstances of a preordained
life be altered by begging? Her prayers, conse-
quently, are modest. When she prays that the

remnants of her family are safe, she is thinking especially of Mud and her mother but does not presume to single anybody out. For herself she asks that she suffer no more than she can bear and that if her fate is to survive she not thwart that fate through foolishness or inattentiveness. She may add that she hopes the leaking of her memory will spontaneously stop, as haemorrhaging sometimes does, or that she comes upon a family whose nurse cow knows a remedy. "I would love to see my own family again," she throws in. Instead of pleading to find the white bone, she describes to herself, in prayer-like phrasing, various aspects of The Safe Place: "... for in that blessed realm are swamps, where grasses sweet and new...."

It is at dawn, just after she has come to her feet, that she prays. Such is her ambivalence that she can bring herself to petition the She only when she is reeling with dizziness and not quite herself and therefore the She may pardon her impertinence. When the dizziness stops she finds a sharp stone and chisels another scratch in her tusk. One scratch for every day since the slaughter. This is not yet a necessity, it is a precaution. She has no idea how quickly her memory is leaking, but she has met old cows who couldn't tell whether it had been an hour or a year since they'd last spoken with her, and she must prepare herself for becoming that addled. She thinks of the scratches as a kind of net. The apprehension of time going by may fall from her body, but here it will be, caught on her tusk.

> She finds a sharp stone and chisels another scratch in her tusk. One scratch for every day since the slaughter.